THE CHURCH AT THIRD AND MAIN

REG QUIST

The Church at Third and Main
Reg Quist

CKN Christian Publishing
An Imprint of Wolfpack Publishing
6032 Wheat Penny Avenue
Las Vegas, NV 89122

Paperback Edition

ISBN: 978-1-64119-012-1

THE CHURCH AT THIRD AND MAIN

THE ENTREATY WAS UNEXPECTED. IT WAS STARTLING IN ITS simplicity but challenging to the point of terrifying in its greatness.

It began with a phone call from Orvis Tanner.

Long known in the city and around the denominational office as 'Mr. Baptist', Orvis Tanner's reputation was supported by a long life of service and godliness. His manner and approach to issues facing the church had been named 'forceful humble-ness' by a pastor many years before. When Orvis invited you for lunch, you could be sure he had something important on his mind and that the matter had been the object of his prayers for weeks before. He was a difficult man to refuse.

"I'm calling about lunch, Mr. McCann." He named the time and place. "Did I mention that I'm buying?"

Jonathon McCann well knew that lunch with Orvis Tanner was never about the food. He was a powerhouse, a driving force behind a large part of denominational happenings in the city for the past half century. He always had a more important motive than food or fellowship, although he was careful to include those two things in his lunch meetings. There was usually a challenge involved. The old man of God had retired from the denominational office twice but the decision didn't stick either time. He was no longer drawing a salary and the word 'emeritus' had been added to his job description. But that in no way reduced the love and respect accorded him. When Orvis Tanner spoke, people listened.

A few days later, Jonathon sat quietly at the appointed time and place across the table from Mr. Tanner, waiting for the old man to open the conversation. The waitress placed a glass of ice water before each man and asked about coffee.

"I trust you are well, Mr. McCann."

"I am, Mr. Tanner. And I must say you look fit and healthy. I haven't seen you for a while. Did you spend our cold winter months under the Caribbean sun?"

Mr. Tanner tipped his head back and laughed. "I wouldn't know what to do under the Caribbean sun or at any other tropical paradise. No, I think what you might have taken for a winter tan is actually rust. At my age, I can hardly expect anything else. But the Lord has blessed me with great, good health and for that I am truly thankful. Perhaps he still has work for me to do." He paused as if to allow that thought to sink in. Piercing Jonathon with a steadfast look, he continued, "Perhaps he also has work for you to do, Jonathon." Without allowing time for a response, he asked, "May I call you Jonathon?"

Jonathon smiled at the old man. That last statement, slipped almost slyly into the conversation, was giving him pause. He left it for later, sure the meaning would become clear before the lunch was finished. "Mr. Tanner, you were calling me Jonathon when I was a young boy sitting under your teaching in the junior boys Sunday school class thirty-five years ago. The 'Mr.' thing doesn't sit well between us or sound natural."

The older man nodded and spoke softly as if reminiscing, "That was a good class. I often think of you boys and I pray for each of you still. Out of a class of twelve, three went to the mission field. Two became pastors. The rest of you hold responsible secular positions. All are married with families to be proud of, if that isn't abusing the use of the word." He paused and took a deep breath, looking directly at Jonathon. "My heart is exceedingly heavy for the two boys who walked away from the Lord. I continue to pray that God will open their hearts. And, of course, our lives were all impacted when cancer took Gary at such a young age."

Both men fell silent.

Jonathon studied his old teacher for several seconds. "You taught those classes for years. There must have been hundreds of boys. I'm amazed that you've kept track of so many."

"You are all my boys. I covenanted with the Lord to teach you and uphold you. That wasn't a temporary commitment. A promise made to the Lord holds firm until He releases you from it. He has never released me from my boys. I keep my journals as up to date as possible but, no doubt, there are many events in the lives of my boys that I am unaware of. I'm confident the Lord hears our prayers, even through our ignorance."

As the conversation went through another short lull, Mr. Tanner turned to look out the window, seeming to focus on the old heritage building directly across the street. Jonathon followed Mr. Tanner's eyes. With a flash of insight, he started to understand. This meeting had to do with the church of his youth.

Mr. Tanner had chosen the lunch location with care. Across the busy thoroughfare, on one of the highest profile and most commercially valuable corners in the city, stood First Baptist Church now renamed the Downtown Fellowship Center.

At more than a century in age, the building was a city landmark. Where once it stood almost alone in a pioneer city, the closest other building a full block away, it was now crowded in and surrounded by high-rise residential buildings plus a selection of upscale offices. Very few of the older structures had escaped the rush to redevelop the city center but the old church still stood firmly in its place. Graciously styled by 1880 standards, the church was built of brick above a concrete foundation that was faced with hand-shaped granite hauled in by horse and wagon from a road construction blasting site. The upper structure was set off with sandstone door and window pillaring. The leaded windows, created so painstakingly by a team of gifted artists, had somehow managed to survive intact since the original construction. The wide, brass-studded, oak entry doors opened into an enclosed vestibule designed and suited to keep out the extreme winter weather that occasionally thundered down from the Rocky Mountains.

Above the entryway, the brickwork continued upward becoming a tower housing a small series of bells. A city noise bylaw had kept the bells silent for many years.

The entirety of the building was protected from the weather by a lead roof as old as the building itself. On the west end of the structure, on Third Street, was an attached, single story office area. This space housed the church administration office as well as two pastors' offices, the deacon's meeting room and several other meeting spaces. In an alcove set back from the city sidewalk were two steps that led to a windowed entry door that opened to the offices. A further four steps from a door at the rear of the office rose to a short hallway and then to a side door into the sanctuary.

It was in the basement of this old building that a young Jonathon had received his early Christian training in Mr. Tanner's Sunday school class. Now, thirty-five years later, he was having lunch with his old teacher.

Mr. Tanner nodded towards the brick and stone structure. "It's not at all like it was when we were sitting in that class so many years ago, Jonathon. The old church's congregation is down to fewer than one hundred tired, aging, stubborn, sometimes quarreling souls. Just a few dozen folks hanging on to the past, hiding from the present, and fearfully denying the future."

He paused and then started again. "Fortunately, mixed among the discontented are a solid number of stable, God-loving men and women. People that provide a base to work from as the church contemplates its next steps."

The old man's eyes glistened as if he might be fighting back a tear, remembering better times. After another short pause, he continued, "The cornerstone you see beside those big oak doors says, 'To the Glory of God'. As much as that sentiment was appropriate in the past, in recent years it has become questionable. God doesn't get much glory from a mostly empty building and certainly would get none at all from a hole in the ground where the building used to stand.

"For over a century, the gospel has been faithfully put forth in that old building, free to all who would receive. From the pulpit, the choir loft, the Sunday school rooms in the basement and from the big old kitchen, the faithful served up food and fellowship for both body and soul." Mr. Tanner paused as if to let that all sink in. "But very little of that is happening anymore."

Jonathon sat in uncomfortable silence, knowing there was more to come. He finally picked up his menu. The waitress returned and the men ordered. After the waitress turned away, Orvis Tanner broke the silence.

"What little bit that is left of the work of First Baptist comes to a halt in the near future if something isn't done."

The old man spoke slowly with long pauses as if for emphasis, "Something must be done. Something big. Something incredibly difficult. Something sacrificial. Something creative. Something wonderful. Something of faith that will push everyone's comfortable boundaries. Something of repentance and submission before the Lord. In short, something of God; something greater than any human effort can accomplish. Something greater than anything done in a church in this city ever before."

Orvis Tanner turned away from the window and looked directly into Jonathon's eyes. "We must bring the old girl back to life, Jonathon. She has a ministry to lost and hurting souls that is not yet completed. And God has placed those hurting souls right at her doorstep. We have but to set the banquet table and invite the folks in for a feast of soul-nourishment that will change their lives for eternity."

Another pause was uncomfortably long for Jonathon. Not sure where the conversation was going and not wishing to interrupt, knowing his old friend had more to say, he waited.

"The work will require a very special man."

Orvis Tanner then held his opened hands towards Jonathon as if in pleading or supplication. Again looking directly into Jonathon's eyes, he said, "I believe you are that man."

After lunch, his mind reeling and overwhelmed with conflicting thoughts, Jonathon called Terry - his business partner - to say he would be away for the afternoon. The explanation could wait for another time. The noon hour conversation had been the most troubling and challenging Jonathon had experienced in all his forty-six years. He knew he had to sort out his feelings to the challenge and do it quickly. He had a successful construction business to run; he and his wife had three children just growing into their teen years. The demands on his life already seemed to be at a maximum. He wasn't a trained pastor. Why would Mr. Tanner finger him, out of all the choices available?

A big part of him screamed 'No!' without seeking further into the challenge. But had that scream come from his heart or from his fearful mind?

He walked across the street in a troubled haze. Standing in front of the church building, Jonathon looked up at the high-rise residential buildings across Third Street, close by the church property.

"Look at them all, Jonathon," Mr. Tanner had challenged over lunch. "Thousands of people living within walking distance of that wonderful old building. Troubled people. Lost people, even if they may not acknowledge their lostness. Hurting people. Many of them hating their lives and desperately wishing for someone, or something, to guide them to a better life; a life with meaning."

Jonathon walked around the corner onto Main Street where he could see a whole new set of high-rises. He counted the residential buildings even without intending to. Everywhere he looked were balconies used for storage. Barbecues, boat paddles, kayaks and a host of other adult toys gave evidence of an attempt for a life beyond the confines of the small condos and the elevators that connected them. The many bicycles attested to the fact that children were being raised to adulthood with no yard to run and play in. A tree house or a lemonade stand was out of the question; to pitch a tent and sleep in the back yard was a concept as distant as Mars.

There were two or three higher-end buildings offering executive suites but Jonathon knew the folks living there could be lost and lonely just as easily as the less wealthy.

The majority of the buildings housed families or young couples plus a goodly number of empty nesters. Whereas thirty or forty years before most people abandoned their old downtown homes and flocked to the suburbs, for many that trend had recently reversed. They couldn't return to the old homes. Those were either razed for new construction or converted to trendy offices and retail outlets. But the high-rise buildings held out a welcoming hand. They were close to work for those who had jobs in the city center and the small condos were less costly than a home in the suburbs.

Jonathon was still staring at the apartment buildings when a pedestrian who was fixated on his phone bumped into him. The man took a quick sidestep and continued on his way, oblivious to everything around him. Jonathon watched him walk away.

In silent prayer, he asked, "Is that what you're trying to show me Lord? Is that what Mr. Tanner has seen? A world obsessed with the trivial and missing the eternal? I can understand that Lord. But why me? I'm just a carpenter. I've no training except my own reading. I'm certainly not a pastor nor have I ever desired to be. The thought has never entered my mind. Why me,

Lord, when there are so many able men graduating from our seminaries?"

Jonathon climbed the stone stairs leading to the big oak, brass-studded doors. Again, he looked around at the high-rises surrounding the church building. After several minutes, he again prayed, "Lord, does Mr. Tanner really have Your heart in this? Is he really Your messenger to me? I want to be available and faithful but this seems like too much Lord. I'm not at all sure I could do this. I'm not even sure how I would start. And I have a business to run and a family to raise."

Finding the church office door unlocked, Jonathon entered. Sal, the long-serving church secretary, looked up from her work. With a smile and her crackly voice, she said, "Why, I believe it just might be Jonathon McCann come visiting. What a pleasure to see you. It's been years. What brings you this way, Jonathon?"

Sal knew everything that happened in the church and she had to have a pretty good idea why Jonathon was there. She typed and filed the confidential minutes from each deacon meeting. She knew about the board's consultation with Orvis Tanner. But she kept this knowledge to herself, giving Jonathon the option of talking about it or not.

Jonathon was nowhere near ready to discuss the challenge with Sal or anyone else until he got home and had some quiet time with his wife and then with his business partner. He simply said, "It's good to see you too, Sal, and good to see you're still keeping the boat afloat and holding it all together. Would you mind if I took a walk around?"

Sal gave him a puzzled look. "I don't expect you'll see anything much changed but you're welcome to stroll around. Take as long as you wish."

Sal, an easy-going woman who usually had a quip or a bit of banter to share, understood that this was not the time for small talk. She reached into a desk drawer and withdrew a master key. "You'll find a few doors locked."

Jonathon accepted the key and stepped towards the stairs and hallway leading to the rest of the building.

Sal, of course, was correct; Jonathon had been familiar with the building since his youth. But he hadn't come just to see the building. He had come to inquire of God.

Deeply troubled by Mr. Tanner's challenge, Jonathon walked slowly into the sanctuary. The early afternoon sunlight was filtered through the high, arched, stained-glass windows, casting a diffused but colorful glow to the interior of the old meeting place. The reds and yellows and blues were like moving reflections as one puffy cloud after another moved across the sky, first blocking the sun and then freeing it to shine on the brick structure, the leaded roof, and the multi-colored windows. He paused and glanced up at the ornate artistry. The plastic shields attached to the outside, protecting the original leaded glass, blocked and filtered a portion of the sunlight. The shields had been added just a few years before. That such stained-glass treasures needed protection was a sign of the times. In the current culture of the city, there was little left of respect for others or for beauty. But for those who cared to look, the colored glass told some of the wonderful old stories of the Bible; the creation, Moses and the tablets, the incarnation, the horror of Golgotha, the place of the skull, the resurrection, the ascension, and Jesus standing at the door, waiting.

Jonathon thought of the hundreds of souls who walked past those windows every day without ever glancing up. Even those with little to do seemed to be rushing from place to place most of the time. Few people hurrying past knew anything about the Bible, the church or the gospel stories. Very few noticed the stained-glass or admired the workmanship that went into the panes.

Jonathan climbed the four steps to the platform. He walked across the stage like he had seen great men of God do when his family attended here many years before. He stopped for a while, studying the console of the pipe organ. Broken and silent for over twenty years, the keys and the finely-carved wooden cabinet gathered dust.

He stopped at the Grand piano, an addition from his time here as a youth. Lifting the key cover, he gently struck a C-chord and followed that with a short series of scales. A near concert level pianist himself, he was pleased to hear the instrument was in tune. He closed the lid.

Jonathon stood behind the pulpit, gazing out into the sanctuary with its graciously curved oak pews. The pews - as well as the woodwork trimming, the vestibule windows, the balcony railing, and the stairway to the balcony - had all taken on a dark, attractive patina as if glorying in the century of their existence. He tried to picture those well-worn seats full of people, the way they had been years before. He delved into his memory for names and faces that had been so familiar, people he hadn't seen or thought of in years. He wondered where they were or if they were even still alive.

He allowed his mind to wander back to the time when Rev. C. T. Alden stood behind this big podium. The Rev. Alden spurned microphones and PA systems, preferring to fill the auditorium with his booming voice. Jonathon smiled a bit, remembering how that saintly man of God would pace around on the platform, thrusting his Bible at the congregation like a sword.

After slowly walking through the sanctuary, touching each pew as he passed by, he made his way up the curved stairs to the balcony and took a seat on the front pew. He let his eyes wander around the cavernous room, taking in the beauty of the place and admiring the century old workmanship. Jonathon was a carpenter and a partner in a successful construction business. His mind was never far from that trade and business, often admiring or silently wondering at the workmanship of others. As he looked at the domed ceiling that gave the building its wonderful acoustics, the finely sculpted plaster corners and cornices, and the beautifully shaped and curved balcony railing, he knew his construction crew would not be able to duplicate the work. Many of the old trades' skills were lost or had dwindled to a special few trained and skilled workmen. Then he paused and prayed, 'It's not about the beauty of the building, is it Lord? It's about the beauty of Christ; His gift of grace. Help me to always keep that foremost in my mind.'

He wasn't sure what to do next. His mind was swirling with the words that had come from Mr. Tanner. Jonathon was not trained as a pastor nor had he ever thought of becoming a pastor. But Mr. Tanner had assured him that it was Jonathon's natural gifts of imagination and organization and energy and negotiation, on top of his love for the Lord, that fitted him for the task. It was all a completely new thought to Jonathon.

He tried to remember Mr. Tanner's exact words.

"It's a new and different time, Jonathon," Mr. Tanner had said. "It calls for new and different methods. People are faced with different challenges than we or our grandparents faced. The answers are still found in the same old gospel story of forgiveness and redemption but we must cloak that story a little differently if we hope to be heard."

Mr. Tanner ended by saying, "Think of this, Jonathon. When you do this work and the Lord blesses, if you remain humble, He will receive all the glory. If you felt you were qualified and could get the job done, you would be tempted to rely on your own efforts and glory in your own accomplishments. But this is God's work. God is looking for faithful servants. He is asking that we make ourselves available, remain humble and faithful, and watch what He does."

With all these thoughts rambling through his mind, Jonathon slid forward on the bench and laid his arms on the balcony railing. With his head resting on his forearms, he prayed. He spoke to God for only a few moments. He was then silent, waiting with an open heart for God to speak.

After much time, into his mental and spiritual confusion came the old familiar thought: *'Be still and know that I am God.'*

2

THE SAME RESTAURANT JONATHON HAD MET ORVIS Tanner in was packed with the Saturday morning breakfast crowd. Jonathon sat down across from his father. He shook the older man's hand and greeted him warmly. "Morning, Dad. You must have been here for a while to lay claim to a window seat."

"I was fortunate. Got here just as the last folks were leaving. Busy in here."

Jonathon slipped off his jacket and draped it over an unused chair, then took his seat. He rested his elbows on the table top and looked at his father. "They do a good job in here. Good food and good service. And right in the middle of downtown. Can't miss."

The senior McCann dragged his eyes away from the window. "Surprising the building wasn't torn down long ago to make way for another high-rise. Hardly anything left of the old pioneer buildings anymore."

Both McCann men were silent for a moment as Wilber looked at the buildings across the road. Taking up the conversation where he had paused it, he continued, "Even that beautiful stone and brick church across the street that we called our spiritual home for so many years has been struggling to keep its grip on the land. A corner property like that is worth a fortune to a developer."

Jonathon laughed and said, "I live for the day I manage to get one step ahead of you, Dad. You've barely taken your seat and you have the purpose for our meeting figured out already. Or have you been hearing tidbits on the Baptist telegraph line?"

Before Wilber could answer, the waitress arrived with coffee and the men placed their breakfast orders.

When they were alone again, Wilber asked with a smile, "What Baptist telegraph line would that be, son?"

Both men laughed.

"News does get around," Wilber admitted. "But in this case, I promise I've heard nothing."

Neither man was given to small talk. Getting serious, Jonathon quickly outlined Mr. Tanner's challenge. He then sat back, waiting while his father digested this news. Jonathon knew his father to be a detail-oriented, considering man, slow to come to conclusions in keeping with his mechanical engineering profession. So he waited patiently.

Both men took sips from their steaming hot coffee. Jonathon leaned forward, his elbows on the table, his big carpenter's hands wrapped around the mug as if he was warming them on a cold winter morning. He looked over the rim and waited for his father to speak.

Wilber McCann put down his mug, leaned back in his chair and studied his son; this boy who was his first born and who had become a man to be proud of. The wavy blond hair and the good looks were what the periodicals like to call 'chiseled' - that chiseled look was often the result of long, strenuous hours in a gym or weight room. In Jonathon's case, it was the product of years of hard work and physical strength gained from the swinging of hammers and the lifting of timber.

His son gained his six foot, two-inch height and his strong physique from Wilber. His good looks and gentle nature were the DNA gift from his mother.

As Wilber mulled over the challenge delivered by Orvis Tanner, the restaurant noise and the buzz of conversation from the other diners was blotted from his mind. He allowed an uncomfortable amount of time to pass in silence while he considered the matter. Finally, he leaned forward on the table and looked directly into his son's eyes.

"Orvis Tanner's arm-twisting reputation goes back for many a year. There are more than a few men and women in ministry because he took them for lunch and a talk. Good man, Orvis, but difficult to refuse when he sets his sights on you. Still, I've never known a man with more spiritual wisdom than Orvis Tanner. Seems to see right through a man or a woman, or a situation, and come to a conclusion that is eminently sensible and workable."

Wilber took another sip of coffee, then put his mug down. He smiled as he thought back to happier days.

"Do you remember when that old church was packed morning and evening every Sunday? Hanna Turnbull would have the pipe organ revved up and a thousand or more people would be singing the old familiar hymns. The preaching was challenging and inspiring. At the end of the service the folks didn't want to leave. We would visit and enjoy each other's company for an hour sometimes.

"But, my, how things change. A pastor left; a new man came, and then another new man. The old folks started dying off. Most of the young adults took jobs in other cities or moved to the suburbs. Many went away to university and never came back. The traffic got heavier and the city streets seemed to be clogged at all hours. Parking was almost impossible before we purchased that piece of land beside the church. The drive into town became too much of a challenge for some of the older ones.

"It's a shame really. We can't seem to stop change from happening, but those changes went a long way towards emptying out the old city-center churches."

Jonathon gently said, "We were a part of that transition, Dad."

Wilber paused and looked back at the old church. Jonathon wasn't sure what to read from the look on his father's face; nostalgia perhaps. Or regret. Or a wishing for something that never came to be.

Quietly Wilber said, "We were. I've wondered sometimes if our reasons were totally valid." After a further short pause, he brightened. "Well, we can't change any of that. What we see across the street is the oldest and most magnificent and ornate church building left in town. There were a few others to rival it but they're all gone, torn down over the years."

Wilber turned his attention back to his cup of coffee, trying to digest the enormity of Orvis Tanner's challenge to his son. Finally, he continued, "You've talked for years about being involved in a more effective ministry if the opportunity should arise. What Orvis is suggesting is a whopper though. It's diving right into the deep end. I doubt if you had anything quite this grand in mind. There would be just nothing at all easy about the job. Do you have thoughts on it that you wish to share?"

Jonathon nodded. "You're correct. I did talk about lay ministry. Since I started teaching the adult class I've been content with that and haven't taken my thoughts any further. Certainly, I never once thought of pastoring a church."

Wilber waited while his son gathered his thoughts. "During our meeting, Mr. Tanner delved into some First Baptist history. He explained what that building and its congregation had meant to the city for more than a century. He told me how through wars, depressions and unimaginable hardships, along with a lot of good times, the truth of God's love was taught and shown by faithful men and women. Much of that history I was aware of but he added some new information as well, things from before my time.

"He talked of lives changed by the power of God's love. He also talked of some of the struggles and failures, as well as the successes the church folks worked their way through over the years. Some of their successes are worthy of praise. Some of their human failures are heart-wrenching.

"To help me understand the challenges, he said it was important I know that the history is not all sweetness and light. He reminded me that, as a child, I probably wouldn't have picked up on most of this. There were some brutal disagreements among the members. A lot of hurt pride and no small amount of stubbornness. Many good folks left to find other worship opportunities. A couple of pastors walked away in defeat. At least one pastor was instrumental in whipping up the discontent. Whether on purpose or not, who knows? Much healing has been required over the years. I'm sure there's still room for additional healing."

Jonathon gestured towards his father. "I'm sure you witnessed some of these happenings."

Wilber simply nodded.

Jonathon's voice had become softer as he repeated these details. "So now the congregation is fewer than one hundred and the church won't exist in ten years - or perhaps less - as people die off, unless big changes are made. Without a pastor, it's doubtful if the work can survive at all."

The two men sat in silence for a short time while the waitress refilled their cups. Finally, Wilber spoke "What's the bottom line, son?"

Following the lessons learned over a lifetime of watching and listening to his father, Jonathon took his time answering.

"The bottom line is that Pastor Gilks, who's been carrying the load over there for several years, has left. That news won't have reached the entire grapevine yet. It happened very quickly. Mr. Tanner took him for lunch and the next day he resigned. The church board had tried a couple of times to ease him into retirement but their suggestions fell on deaf ears. Mr. Tanner is probably the only one who could have encouraged him to accept his pension and retire without stirring up a problem of some sort.

"Last Sunday was Pastor Gilks' final day on the job. At his advanced age, he just wasn't up to it anymore. He had given his all and could give no more."

Jonathon took a sip of coffee, giving his father the opportunity to make a comment. When nothing was said, Jonathon continued, "I never knew the man but I'm told Pastor Gilks was a trustworthy servant over the years. At the same time, he was a big part of the problem. He was a hardworking, faithful man of God but he had no bend in him at all. As life and the culture changed all around him, he settled more firmly into the safe familiarity of old times. In many ways, his head was still in the forties and fifties. He seems to have equated cultural changes with doctrinal changes. Here I'm repeating what both Mr. Tanner and the board said to me.

"The church hasn't attracted a new family in several years. Janet and I attended the past two weeks to try to get a feel for the work. We saw nothing that would attract us to worship there beyond the building itself."

Again, Wilber's silence encouraged his son to continue.

"Pastor Gilks' presentations were dry and somewhat tedious. The music remains staid and, frankly, a bit dreary. In a world dominated by TV, and every other electronic device imaginable delivering the latest offerings of professional musicians, the younger generation isn't about to sit under that type of ministry."

The elder McCann looked across the table. "That's the bottom line for the church. What's the bottom line for you?"

"The bottom line for me is that the board has asked me to take on the pastoral role at Downtown Fellowship Center for a two-year period. There's no doubt that I'm an unlikely candidate. Orvis Tanner and I discussed that at some length. His position, and the position of the deacons, is that the church would have difficulty attracting a credentialed pastor. If they did attract one, they couldn't pay him adequately with their few remaining givers.

"Everyone in leadership felt it was more important to have a pastor who could relate well to the unsaved and who had vision and energy. Somehow they've convinced themselves the finger points at me."

Wilber looked at his son. "You're obviously interested or we wouldn't be sitting here talking. How do Janet and the kids feel about this?"

"Janet and I have spent many hours talking and praying. Probably nothing except the well-being of our children has put us on our knees before God more than this matter. We have also talked extensively with the kids. Janet is good with it now and we promised the kids they could stay at our current church if they choose to. Their youth groups are important to them and they're old enough to make that decision.

"I've also spent a lot of time with Terry talking about our partnership. He's quite insistent that he can handle the business. He says he'll be very disappointed in me if I don't take up the challenge. It would be difficult to find a more positive-thinking man than Terry. He's been a great partner."

Wilber sat silently, waiting for the rest of the story.

"I've met twice with the deacons and once with the congregation. All within two weeks. There's no time to waste if we wish to preserve what's left of Downtown Fellowship. I asked them to not talk about the matter until final decisions were made."

Wilber leaned forward again. "There are several things to consider, son. First, there is no doubt in my mind that you can adequately and properly fill the pulpit. Your years of adult-class teaching as well as occasional preaching have shown that you have a gift for handling the Word of God."

He paused then and bit his bottom lip, a sure sign to Jonathon that he should wait until his father was ready to continue. As was common with Wilber, it took an uncomfortably long time.

Finally, Wilber said, "There's a lot more to this challenge than filling the pulpit. The task is to fill the church. That's no small mission. Did God prepare you for this exact moment? That's quite possible. God does seem to delight in surprising us from time to time.

"I see no obvious road blocks to you taking on this ministry. You need to listen to your heart and to the heart of God and then move forward. No matter what decision you make, you can be assured of the full support of your mother and me."

Briefly changing the subject, Wilber said, "Speaking of Terry. How is he doing? It seems to me it's been five or six years since his heart attack. Can he handle the added stress of taking on the responsibility for the entire construction business?"

Jonathon responded, "We've had a couple of serious talks about that. Terry says he's fine and I hope he is. I wouldn't want the responsibility of causing him further health problems. We've agreed that if I move ahead on this we'll hire an estimator to take over that end of my work with me giving the business two days a week for job supervision. That way Terry isn't carrying all the load. He's adamant that I take up this challenge. He's a hard man to say 'no' to."

Wilber nodded and continued with his thoughts, "Finances enter into your decision, but that's between you and Janet and Terry. Then there's the whole 'why' question. Why would you upset your life and the life of your business to take on this ministry? Is it just to house-sit until the doors are finally locked or is it to grow the congregation? And since it's certainly the latter, how would you do that?"

Without waiting for an answer that he knew Jonathon didn't have, he said, "You don't have all those answers now but you will need to find them over time." Wilber paused to allow his son to respond.

"You've asked me the same questions I've asked myself, Dad.

I've gone through them as carefully and as prayerfully as I know how."

"Have you made a decision?"

"Close, Dad, all except for one thing. Janet and I wouldn't make a decision of this depth without talking with you and Mom. And just so you won't be surprised when you get home, I must tell you that Janet is visiting with Mom right now. I don't know anyone with more wisdom than you two and you certainly have your finger on the pulse of the church scene in the city. And I've supplied you with enough facts to satisfy even your inquiring mind. I'm really here this morning to listen. And after Janet and I listen to you and Mom, we'll spend the remainder of this day sorting it all out before coming to a final decision."

3

JONATHON AND JANET DID SPEND THE DAY IN PRAYERFUL discussion. Finances, time constraints, the possible demands on Janet's time in the ministry, impact on the business; all was discussed at length.

Jonathon had spent years resisting his tendency to blue-sky some matters. At times, he was almost coldly rational; other times, he saw the positive side only, missing the warning signs. In the business, it was Terry and his secretary, Bea, who kept Jonathon's feet on the ground. At home, it was always Janet. She didn't allow her husband to paint a rosy picture. She insisted on looking deeply into facts.

Jonathon and Janet discussed and analyzed the matter of disagreements among the saints; disagreements that had caused so much dissension in years past at First Baptist Church. It was only a small part of church history but it was a sordid part and could not be ignored. People had been hurt and rifts opened that had never been healed.

"How do you see yourself dealing with that, Jonathon? Preaching, music, finances; those things will come together as we get to know the people and see what is truly needed. But gossip and backbiting and self-centeredness are in a whole different category. With the deacons telling you that those issues have caused great harm in the past, coming face to face with them gives me pause."

Jonathon nodded his head as Janet made this last statement. "It gives me pause, too. It would be so easy if we could just say 'stop doing it' but it will take more than that I'm afraid. And even if that worked, it would do nothing for the past. I have a rather bold plan outlined in my mind. Listen and let me know what you think."

And so the afternoon discussions melded into an evening agreement, and a surrender to what Jonathon and Janet finally accepted as clear direction from God.

The final piece of the puzzle seemed to be an understanding with Terry. Those discussions touched on Terry's health, the goals of the company, and the added burden that Terry would be carrying in Jonathon's absence. They briefly discussed the possibility of Terry buying Jonathon's portion of the business but it was soon evident that neither man was really interested in going in that direction.

To Jonathon, it seemed like the process had taken weeks. In reality, it was only fifteen days; days of prayerful agony, sleepless nights, and hours of talk between Jonathon and Janet. It was not in any way an easy or simple process. Finally came peace. The doubts were gone. Where such confidence came from, Jonathon could not have explained in any human sense.

Jonathon rested in this confidence and accepted the call to ministry.

The talking done and the listening finished and the prayerful answers received, Jonathon was welcomed into ministry at Downtown Fellowship Center on April 4, a rainy, blustery, early spring day.

He went right to work with energy and enthusiasm.

His first task was to set a full morning aside to talk with Sal. Sally, who preferred just Sal, had been church secretary for as long as anyone cared to remember. She was single with no close family except a brother who lived halfway across the country. Jonathon would have guessed her age at around fifty. She wouldn't be considered pretty but, in her maturity, she had developed a confident countenance that inspired trust. Most people enjoyed her company. Her easy smile and good humor made her a pleasant work-mate. And she was competent at her work. She held confidences from both the pastors and the deacon board with an iron grip. She had few interests beyond the church so she put in more hours at work than was really needed or expected. She harbored a wealth of church administrative information and had been considered the 'go-to' person in all church matters for many years.

"I've never heard your last name, Sal."

"Neither have I. Not for a long time anyway. Don't hardly remember what it is. Just Sal. Just call me Sal. Call me anything except Sal and I'll probably think you're talking to someone else."

Jonathon grinned and shrugged. "Alright, Sal. Tell me everything. I'm led to believe that you helped pick out the cornerstone and have been here ever since, and that if you don't know something, it's not worth knowing."

Sal let out a delighted, crackle-voiced chuckle. "That thing about the cornerstone is a shameful exaggeration. But I have been here for a while. I'll have to honor up to that."

After a short pause, Sal continued, "The main thing I should tell you is that everything is under control. The bills are paid and there's a reasonably healthy balance in the bank thanks to a bequest from one of the long-term members. The Sunday bulletins are repetitive and easily done, the computers are old but adequate, all the office machines are in good working order, and I'm underworked and often bored."

The mischievous grin she was noted for by others was new to Jonathon. "When I'm bored, I eat snack food and when I eat snack food, I gain weight. So these extra rolls that I can no longer hide are not my fault. I accept no blame. It's the church's fault and if you don't find more work for me, it'll be your fault. And you don't want to have to bear that responsibility."

Sal was working hard to hold back an even wider grin.

Jonathon smiled. "I'll try to bear that in mind."

On a more serious note, she said, "You've taken on a monumental task but you already know that. The past is not altogether something to be proud of. On the other hand, it's not totally negative either. There have been many years of blessings and good times in the Lord.

"Not everyone in the congregation is behind you. What the leadership agrees on and puts forward is not always what a small segment of the old-timers have in mind. There are a few contrary folks here that the church might have been better off without over the years. Ignoring them won't be easy, but winning them over won't be easy either. So, good luck on that.

"But, still, you have considerable backing among the people and I pray you can do something that will win over the rest. I'm hoping that you can breathe some life back into the old joint."

Jonathon nodded and said, "I'm well aware of the task before us, Sal, and by 'us' I mean everyone. I can't do this alone and you and I together won't get it done. The congregation - and the leadership - must follow through on their commitments. But you and I will have to help them with that. We can help by establishing clear lines of communication and keeping them open. It's important that everyone knows what's happening and the reasons for it. I'm aware that every manager says those things but, in our case, they're critical. We do this together or it won't happen at all."

After that bit of bantering and encouragement, talk that was useful in breaking the ice for their new relationship, the two church employees got down to business discussing costs, bookkeeping programs, filing systems, and the rest of the administrative matters. Sal quickly came to understand that Jonathon knew what questions to ask and where to probe. The morning seemed to fly past and Sal never once reached into the drawer of snack foods. Sal's input ended with her showing Jonathon what programs were on the computer and which ones she most often used.

Jonathon indicated a notepad lying on the desk. "Alright, let's move forward. The first thing, Sal, is that you are no longer church secretary. You are now church administrator. That includes secretarial duties, at least for now. I'm sorry to say that this promotion is honorary in nature with no additional income attached. Everything will eventually end up on my desk but I will expect you to handle most things without my input. You'll find that I love delegating."

The new pastor referred to a list he held in his hand. "Here are the things I want you to work on first."

Sal picked up a pen and put her hand to the notepaper. Nothing like this had happened for years and she eagerly anticipated a new beginning to her work and for the church.

"We need some kind of entry control and security system on the office door including a camera so you can see who you're letting in. It's not an altogether friendly world out there and we might just as well admit it. You'll want to make some calls on that, see what kind of security system would suit. I'm not comfortable with you being in here alone, in the center of the city, with hundreds of people walking past the door every day.

"Next, we need a paging system of some sort. We need a master unit that will sit on your desk, and something that the custodian and I can hang from our belts. We'll want several units because we're going to have some more bodies around here pretty soon. I don't want to waste all day looking for them. We might be able to accomplish this through our cell phones. Please check into that.

"Then I want you to find us two interns. The colleges have just completed their final exams and the streets will soon be awash with young people looking for work experience. I want one who has the skills to gather the demographic information on the residential buildings around here and make a computer program of some sort to track our contacts with them. I want the other person to be skilled at research on government and charitable programs and to know something of scripture and enjoy writing.

"We're also going to examine the homeless lunch program the church has done for years and compare it to what others are doing. Both of these jobs will require computer skills but I suspect that's a given with today's youth. If one intern had the knowledge required to build a simple web page, that would be a great help."

Sal asked, "Are these to be Christian interns?"

"For the one, for sure. For the one working on the demographics, not necessarily. In some respects, it would be good to have the insight of non-Christians. But see who you can find and hire the very best available. This will be work experience and the wage will be minimal so the applications may be largely self-weeding.

"Next I want you to find someone who knows about repairing pipe organs. Get them to call me ASAP.

"As soon as you have an intern on staff, I want you to work with him or her to gather information from the post office on delivering bulk, unaddressed, localized mail drops; what the parameters are and the costs. I'm thinking light card stock about the size of a number ten envelope. Get the same information from a couple of courier or mail drop companies. See how they operate and how they would compare to the post office."

Jonathon waited until Sal finished taking notes.

"I believe the custodian comes in tomorrow. Is that accurate?"

When Sal confirmed that information, Jonathon said, "Call him please and ask him to meet me in my office at nine tomorrow morning. And to be prepared to give me a full guided tour of the property, every nook and cranny.

"And, Sal - as a signal between the two of us - when my office door is open, I'm available. When it's closed, I'm studying or in prayer or on a confidential call. I may be available anyway but I'd appreciate if we could keep interruptions to a minimum."

After another pause, Jonathon said, "This is totally confidential, Sal, although I'm sure it showed up in the deacon's minutes so you already know. I will be working without a salary. I've agreed to a two-year term on that basis. The offset is that the amount previously paid the pastor will go into a budget line for outreach. I would appreciate if you could keep a running total on that budget item and have it readily available."

Sal just nodded at this request and made a note.

Jonathon smiled as Sal said, "Alright, I'll get on this. Don't know when I'm going to get time for a snack though." She looked up at Jonathon and grinned like a kid who had just been given a new bike.

Jonathon then went to the century-old pastor's office and closed the door. His introductory sermon had been ready for a week. What he needed now was quiet time. The pastor's office had, for decades, included an ornate oak prayer bench in one corner. Jonathon saw no reason to move it. He reverently stepped towards the old bench, the kneeling shelf worn from years of use. He laid his open Bible on the top and knelt. He was still there when he heard a light tap on the door. Sal spoke just loudly enough to be heard through the wooden panel, "Your wife is on the phone."

"Thank you."

As he rose from the prayer bench and reached for the phone, he noticed the digital clock on his desk. 3:45 PM. That couldn't be accurate. He had gone to the prayer bench at 11:30 AM. A glance at his wristwatch confirmed the time and he was amazed.

4

LIKE SAL WAS JUST Sal and wished for no other name, Watson was just Watson. A short wiry man carrying not an ounce of extra flesh, Watson was a bundle of energy. He had been custodian for many years. Studying him, Jonathon estimated the man would never see sixty again. He took Jonathon on the building tour as if he had received a royal proclamation; he led, a ring of keys dangling from his hand, and Jonathon followed.

By the time the two men had completed the tour of the property, both were dusty and somewhat bewildered. Jonathon thought he knew the building well from his early days attending First Baptist. But the old building had spaces with odd-shaped corners and rooms tucked within rooms; rooms Jonathon had no idea existed. Some rooms were easily usable while others would require considerable imagination to turn them into practical quarters. Jonathon suspected he and Watson had opened doors that were shut years before and forgotten about. He saw accumulations of files, books, and junk in closet after closet. Sorting and cleaning the mess would be a monumental job that could lead to conflict between the 'keep it' group and the 'get rid of it' folks.

Nostalgia from his youth was kindled when he opened a closet packed tight with old choir anthem music. Looking through a couple of the old pieces he recalled how he had loved listening to the big choir even though he often couldn't make out all the words. Although the modern culture had little time for choirs, he remembered them fondly and missed them.

Despite the multiple small rooms, some accessible only through doorways from other spaces, he couldn't help but appreciate the overall functional mindset of the original designers and builders. The modern concept of open spaces was nowhere to be seen. But there was something comforting about rooms that could be closed off for privacy and sound control. Many of the rooms held valuable, ornate, antique furnishings. One meeting room had seating for fifty people on oak pews with fold-up kneelers.

Jonathon found himself wishing he had time to study the many enlarged and framed photos of the pioneer city and church that were hung in several rooms and along hallways.

Along one wall close to the kitchen, the cavernous basement now housed a row of tables and chairs for the soup and sandwich lunch program. For several years, the church had fed the homeless and destitute; men and women who made their homes in the alleys and doorways of the city's core. The lunch program was the church's only real attempt to reach into and serve the community.

The kitchen was large and functional but much of the equipment was well past its prime.

Years ago, the basement had been the children's center, hosting the Sunday school as well as the mid-week programs and making use of the dozen small rooms that circled the main hall. But there had been no children's programs for at least the previous ten years.

In times past, with the tables set up, the main hall was often turned into a dining room. Many church family dinners and celebrations had been held in the big basement. Looking around the hall, Jonathon paused for a moment as he remembered the great Christmas celebrations, the Easter parade gatherings, and the wonderful church dinners when he was a child. For just a moment, Jonathon was captured by the odor; it was as if the many spices used in the lunches were fighting against the soap and disinfectant used to wash the floors and restrooms. It was not at all an unpleasant combination.

A full-sized gymnasium had been built over a portion of the parking lot years before in the hopes of promoting a youth program. It had seen very little use and none at all for a decade.

Although the original building was old, the scope of possibilities in the multitude of rooms had Jonathon's mind going in several directions at the same time.

Jonathon shook Watson's hand and thanked him. 'It's pretty mind-boggling, Watson. It will take a while to digest all you've shown me. Thank you. I hope I haven't put you too far behind on your other work."

Watson shook his head. "I'm not too overworked so I'll get it all done. I enjoyed our explorations."

Jonathon started to walk away, then stopped and turned around. "I should have asked before, Watson. Who's been laying out your work for you in the past?"

"No one. I just do what's needed."

Jonathon nodded. "Alright. But Sal will be the church administrator from now on. Everything that needs doing will be fed through her office. I'd like the two of you to get together and make up a written schedule of tasks and when they're normally attended to. I know you're already on top of that but I'm not, so the information would be helpful to me."

Watson smiled and nodded mischievously. "If I pick my time right, she might share something out of her snack drawer. She does keep a fine assortment."

Jonathon forced a small smile. "Forget it. Snack time ended yesterday."

With a questioning look on his face, Watson watched the new pastor walk away.

Back in his office, Jonathon picked up the phone and called the construction company number. When Terry answered, Jonathon asked, "Terry, how goes your day?"

"Well, we were just discussing that we don't really miss you so we're wondering what you did around here." The two men shared a laugh together.

"Terry, earlier this morning I sent you a materials list by e-mail. I need a small platform built. About three hours work for two men. Do you suppose you can put that together for me? And you'll be invoicing the church so keep track of costs as usual. No rush, as long as it's completed by Friday."

Terry responded. "I'll send a couple of boys over. Glad there's no rush on that." Jonathon could sense the smile on his partner's face.

The business partners had learned years before to keep their calls short and to the point so nothing more was said.

Jonathon leaned back in his chair. "And so it starts, Lord. I'm repeating myself for perhaps the hundredth time. But I can't possibly do this alone. It's my desire to make Your thoughts my thoughts and Your ways my ways. I've had to learn to move fast in business, making quick decisions. But we're dealing with people here Lord, and all the feelings and emotions that entails. We're not pounding nails. Help me to think carefully in all that I start out to do. Slow me down when that's necessary. Put in me a humble spirit; a spirit of obedience. I'm very aware that I can't do this with my own strength or wisdom. Open my heart - and the hearts of the church deacons and members - that we might continually seek wisdom from on high. Do these things I pray, Father. Not for my benefit or even for the benefit of this church but for the benefit of those whom we hope to minister to, and to Your glory."

5

SAL HADN'T KNOWN THIS MUCH EXCITEMENT EVER BEFORE in her job. Solid and plodding might have more accurately described the former ministry and her part in it. Looking at the tasks Jonathon had set out for her, she drew a line under each separate item and then numbered them in terms of priority. She penciled in a big number '1' beside the organ repair. It took a while but she finally found the phone number for a company the church had talked with years earlier. She could make the call and put that task behind her quickly, then move on to other things.

The message she left on the organ company's answering machine was rewarded with a return call on Thursday morning. Jonathon was drinking coffee at his desk when the intercom squawked. "Jonathon. I have the pipe organ man on line one. Do you want to talk with him now or should I have him call back later?"

Jonathon answered, "Thanks, Sal," and picked up the phone. "Jonathon McCann here. Who am I talking with please?"

"Murphy McGuire, Classic Organs," came the somewhat lilting voice. "McCann, is it? How pleasant to be greeted by a son of the old sod. So, I've made a note of the name Mr. McCann, or as the Gaelic would have it, *'Mac Cana, son of Cana, the wolf cub'*. As I recall the history my dear sainted gram blessed me with at the kitchen table after the day's work was done, there was a McCann who lived up to his name by pirating and pillaging along the coasts, and among the helpless villages of the poor old Isle of Mists. But that was a while ago, perhaps in the time of our grandfather's grandfather. So tell me, 'son of wolfs', do you hold to the old ways of pillaging for your daily bread or has at least one McCann found an honorable path through this life?"

Jonathon was a little taken aback, not being a student of Irish historical names - his own or any other - and having no knowledge at all of the Gaelic or knowing if the caller was joking or serious. "Why do I feel like I should study some history before getting into that conversation with you?"

McGuire laughed and said, "Ah, Mr. McCann, I can tell already that you are a wise man. I'm sure the Scripture advises us somewhere to think before we speak and, if it doesn't, it should. It is pleasing to meet a man who takes good advice to heart. What can I do for you, sir?"

Jonathon thanked the man for taking the time to call before saying, "We have an almost century-old pipe organ. It retired itself twenty or so years ago and hasn't been heard from since. I'd like to know what it would take to bring it back to life and have it make music again. Could I impose on you to make a trip out here to examine it and estimate the damage and the repair costs?"

McGuire sighed and answered, "How very much I would relish another trip to your lovely city with its wide-open spaces and the glacier-topped mountains as a backdrop. But, alas, that is not necessary and so is not to be. I am familiar with your instrument. Your lovely organ is, wonder of wonders in this young country of ours, well past the century mark. In fact, I have your file right in front of me, saved from the one time I was in your city. It is dusty with time and dried with age and my penmanship was always the despair of my many long-suffering teachers. But I am still able to read my scribbles albeit with the assistance of strong eyeglasses. In short, Son of Wolf Cubs, your organ is old and its workings are worn out. I say that with no criticism at all in mind for many have said the same about me. In fact, I have it in my will that when my time comes to seek my reward, however humble, that I should be buried in a simple box made of worn-out organ parts nailed together."

Jonathon chuckled and tried to picture the box before saying, "Let's pray there is no need of that for a few days yet." Giving the other man no opportunity to respond, he continued, "I play a little myself and have looked at the surface parts of the machine. I know nothing at all about the workings themselves. The stop knobs and pedal board seem to move freely and the main console appears to be in good shape. I'm sure the pipes could stand a thorough cleaning but the brass still looks good. I doubt if there is any life left in the bellows but I still seem to feel there is hope for the old girl if we could apply just the right touch of kindness."

McGuire was quick to answer. "There is indeed life in the old girl, but she needs some encouragement and a truckload of new parts. I detailed all of that to the church twenty years ago. The cost of repair was more than the church felt it could absorb at that time. But since then, events have conspired and things have happily changed even more than my suggestions of yore would have acknowledged. Technology has increased and costs have decreased. In short, my friend, although there are many organ purists who cringe at the thought, the present and the future are digital. We could make that beautiful creation live again by replacing all the hundreds of tracker rods and pivot points with a large bundle of wires, a simple computer and a host of little solenoid valves. You would still need a new bellows but that is not a major cost. The physical appearance would not change in the least. Nor would the sound. The touch on the keyboard would require slightly less force so the instrument would be a bit easier to play. Let me put some cost numbers together and get them out to you. Give me your e-mail and you'll hear from me later this afternoon."

6

BY FRIDAY AFTERNOON OF THE FIRST WEEK, A NEW LOW platform was built in front of the main stage. Jonathon felt that the big pulpit and the high main stage would separate him from the small number of worshipers. He wanted to feel their presence and join them in worship. A piano moving company came and lifted the grand piano onto the new platform and tuned the instrument. Jonathon brought his own keyboard and guitar from home and set them up on the platform. He was a very competent keyboard and piano player but just an average guitarist.

He sent Sal out to purchase a large roll of light, gold-colored rope. With Watson's help, he roped off the two side rows of oak pews plus the rear half of the center portion. The goal was to get everyone seated together, close to the platform.

Watson looked at the roped-off restrictions and shook his head. "Old Isakson and his wife are going to bristle when they see this. They and a few others that have sat at the back all their lives."

Jonathon shrugged with a small smile. "They'll get used to it."

He called the deacons to meet at 2:00 PM Saturday in the sanctuary. Hanna Turnbull arrived at mid-morning the same day to work on some music with Jonathon. They would then share a sandwich lunch that Janet had packed for them.

"Hanna, you know the church leadership has authorized us to make whatever changes are needed to bring Downtown Fellowship to the place where it will be attractive to a new generation. We intend to do just that while also keeping some important traditions. And certainly, everything we do must match with Scripture and bring God glory. With all those things in mind, you and I are going to work on some new music as well as the old, if that's alright with you."

Hanna nodded and said, "My husband and I attend another church for their evening services so, even though we're no longer young, we have some feel for the new ways. There are some great worshipful new songs being written but also a lot of light, almost flippant stuff. I hope we can discern the difference."

"Between you and me, we'll try to sort them out. As a start though, let's stay with the tried and true. Play 'A Mighty Fortress is our God' the way you've always played it."

Hanna opened the hymn book and played one verse before Jonathon stopped her. "Your playing is excellent Hanna but let's try it this way. He stepped over to his keyboard and, picking up the tempo just a bit and introducing a more joyful lilt, he played. Before he finished the first verse, Hanna joined him, easily keeping up with his lead and adding some enhancements that came just from her head. Or maybe they were from her heart.

By the third verse, Jonathon nodded to Hanna to take the lead while he played a series of supporting chords and complementary harmonies. The result was astonishing.

Hanna lifted her hands from the keyboard and smiled at Jonathon. "That would pull the birds right out of the trees, it's so joyful."

Hanna addressed Jonathon in a serious vein. "You do know that Tom Bradshaw has led music for years, don't you? He might be seriously hurt if he's pushed aside."

Jonathon nodded in agreement. "He isn't being pushed aside.

I had a coffee meeting with him a couple of days ago. I like him. He has a solid knowledge of music and a good attitude. He's prepared to sit back for a while and take a rest from leading."

They went back to playing and the two of them played song after song; some new, many old and familiar. They combined their knowledge of music and their playing skills to make the slight adaptations required to bring more life to the old favorites, and laughing together when their experiments were less than wonderful. The time flew past, the lunch forgotten.

By 2:00 PM the deacons were all sitting in the front couple of rows listening to the two musicians. The pew backs were preventing Jonathon from seeing the men's feet but he was sure he heard some toe-tapping.

Jonathon stopped playing and welcomed them. "Come on up, men. We're going to do some singing." The men looked a little startled and no one moved for a few moments.

Jonathon had given Sal a list of hymns and page numbers. She typed the list and made a copy for each deacon. Jonathon held out one sheet for each man and said, "Grab a hymn book and gather around. You can't sing from way back there. You and Hanna and I make up most of the church leadership. So, what we have to do is lead. These are the songs I've picked for our first Sunday service together. Let the newness of the music soak into your souls and see if you can't worship the Lord in a new way as we sing together." He nodded at Hanna and she played.

A couple of the men held back, standing silently, but by the third song they were all joining in. Not all the voices were completely in tune and a couple of the men probably should refrain from singing in public at all. Jonathon reminded himself that the scripture invites us to make a joyful noise unto the Lord. The heart always sings in tune regardless of what the vocal chords were doing and the Lord listens to the hearts of His people.

And so they sang. They sang for half an hour and then they all knelt in prayer. Jonathon had found a stash of small cushions in a storage room. With creaking knees and complaining backs, Hanna and the men settled onto the cushions. The music had moved them all into the spirit of worship. For a half hour, the group poured out their hearts before God, seeking His presence in individual lives as well as in the singing and preaching, and in the fellowship. Specifically, they prayed that God would do His miraculous work in the hearts of the people living near the old brick and stone church on Third and Main.

Jonathon interrupted the prayers for a moment. "It's important that we have clean hearts and hands before God, and peace among the Christian family. God clearly wants our old things to be allowed to pass away so the new can come. Known sin must be confessed and our hearts opened to God's revelation of unconfessed sin. This truth is going to be our main preaching emphasis over the summer months."

After another short time of prayer, Hanna spoke to the group, "My body can take no more. I have to get up."

With laughter that was in no way un-worshipful, the men rose. One of them took Hanna by the hand and helped her rise. Jonathon looked over the group. "May God help us to keep this spirit of worship and humility with us always. And may our hearts be prepared to lead this good work. Thank you for coming on this beautiful spring day. We'll gather again tomorrow for the morning worship service."

7

SUNDAY MORNING CAME AND ON JONATHON'S instructions, the ushers opened the front doors wide, blocking them open. A weather system had moved in overnight; the day was drizzly and chilly. The inner windowed doors separating the vestibule from the foyer were kept closed to protect the gathering worshipers from the worst of the weather. An usher stationed himself there to welcome people.

For many years, the outer oak doors had been allowed to close automatically after each person entered. The big, brass-studded entry doors with their ornate brass handles, as beautiful as they were, presented a formal, intimidating, and almost unfriendly face to the public passing by. Standing on the side-walk making plans for the Sunday service, Jonathon saw the doors as a barrier. He felt the easiest way to change that was simply to open them. That decision met with some protest. Thinking of heating bills and being of a practical nature, Noble Pearson liked it the old way. Or at least he had convinced himself that this was true. He had served as usher in the church for nearly half a century and had his way of doing things. Open doors that allowed the heat to escape or the cold and rain to enter were not within his acceptable and practical parameters.

As a deacon, Noble had clearly seen that something must be done to rejuvenate his beloved spiritual home. Seeing no better option, he voted in favor of the new pastor. He had found no reason to regret that decision in the short time Jonathon had been with them. Still, he harbored some doubts and reservations about this young man who had no formal pastoral training. As he often did, he kept his thoughts to himself.

Still thinking about the blocked-open doors, Noble watched as Rudy Goetz climbed down the old, worn granite stairs carrying a new, brightly-colored A-frame sign announcing that the church welcomed anyone who might wish to enter. Noble came close to trembling in despair. He was a jumble of emotions. He well knew that the invitation of scripture was to *'whosever will may come'* but also recognized that a secret part of him hoped those who came would be much like he and his friends. In a rapidly changing city that hope would probably not be fulfilled.

Yet he had made the decision to give the new start an opportunity to succeed so he pushed his doubts out of the way. For the time being anyway. He would await further evidence before speaking out.

Rudy smiled at Noble as he climbed back up the stairs. "Get used to it, brother. New ways are upon us and sunshiny days are just around the corner."

Noble didn't bother responding to Rudy with his bright optimism. He kept adding to his secret thoughts.

As Noble walked back into the sanctuary from the foyer, he was confronted by Rolf and Frieda Isakson. His two old friends looked lost as they contemplated the gold rope blocking out the access to their long-used, familiar pew.

The Isakson family had stationed themselves in the same pew since the old days when the children were young and the sanctuary was packed for every service. As the congregation thinned out over the years, the adult Isakson offspring joined the exodus to the suburbs. Rolf and his wife remained in their places as if the departed ones would soon return and they would again be surrounded by family and friends. A sprinkling of other folks made up this small vigil, an ode to old times, in that section of the seating.

Like many of the old-timers, Rolf often thought of the many treasured friends who had passed into Glory and who would not be joining them again. Their chosen pews would remain empty. Looking at those empty pews week by week deepened his already profound loneliness for both friends and family.

No words were needed to see Rolf's despair. Noble shook his hand and said, "Good morning, brother. Some new things this morning. We voted for this so let's give it a try."

"I didn't vote for it," responded Rolf. His wife Frieda stood beside him shaking her head in silence.

Even Noble, a lover of fine clothing himself, thought Frieda might be overdressed with her several layers of finery covered over with a flowing topcoat - almost a cape - and topped off with a brown hat with a peacock feather hanging down the back. A finely-woven black lace veil rolled and pinned to the hat brim was ready for unrolling if the need should present itself. She had worn the same hat for as long as Noble could remember.

"Come on, friends. I'll walk you down to a good seat. Give it a try. What's the worst that could happen?"

He hoped his voice didn't reflect his own doubts that were welling up after so many decades of unchanging stability. But looking at his distressed friends who were greatly troubled about such a simple matter as changing seats, Noble started to see the foolishness of struggling over such a little thing. But he was a long way from admitting that openly.

Noble took a couple of steps down the aisle but when Rolf didn't follow, he turned back. Taking in the lost look on Rolf's face, Noble was startled into another realization: 'Why, he's old. Old in his thinking. Old and lost with this simple change. Him and Frieda both.'

Noble's mind flitted back some years to when Rolf was young and sharp; a chartered accountant and church treasurer. Frieda was a tall statuesque beauty, happy with her nearly six feet of height and approaching the world with confidence and grace, her tall sons and beautiful daughter beside her. Osteoporosis had reduced her height and changed her posture. The passing of time had eroded her self-confidence. Her daughter had married and moved to another city, and her sons worshiped at a suburban church. The elderly couple had maintained their chosen family pew on their own the past several years.

Noble stepped back and quietly said to his old friends, "Walk with me. I'll seat you beside Kyle Adams."

By eleven o'clock there were eighty-three people populating the twelve-hundred seat auditorium. Most of them had never sat this close to the platform before or so close together. There was some uncomfortable chatter and many a questioning look as they noticed the new platform with the grand piano on it along with Jonathon's keyboard and guitar; there was no pulpit and no microphone.

Just as the service was ready to start, the foyer doors opened and Rudy ushered three homeless men down the aisle, the men looking warily around as if they were ready to bolt for the exit at the least threat and pulling their tattered coats tightly around themselves. They had seen the sidewalk sign and their initial thoughts were that the church might be acceptable shelter from the cool spring drizzle. Despite his serious reservations, Rudy was trying to hide his grin as he led the three into a pew, seating them beside Hank Grissom who he felt would welcome the men. As they hesitantly shuffled into the space shown them and looked around, Hank, who along with his wife gave leadership to the noon soup kitchen, shook hands with the man who sat beside him. He had seen the weary man at the lunches but didn't know his name.

The last of the three men glanced anxiously around as if he had identified a threat that no one else saw. He was the youngest of the three, perhaps in his mid-thirties, frail and tragic-looking with his face shrouded behind a week of accumulated street dirt and whiskers. He had a lost and lonely look as he glanced at the people around him. He was, as were the other two, clearly in need of a shower. He wore a torn and filthy army tunic and a khaki-colored knit hat. Finally, hesitantly, he moved into the row of seating. The older man beside him reached out with a hand covered by a fingerless wool glove and urged him to sit. "It will be alright, Carl," he gently whispered to the young man.

Jonathon turned and watched this by-play from his seat on the far right side of the front pew. Among the thoughts running through his mind was a gentle pride in both Rudy and Hank.

Jonathon was aware of the steep learning curve he was leading his people into. He hadn't anticipated the additional emotional and spiritual challenge these men from the streets had brought with them but the very conservative gathering had responded well enough. For now, at least.

Hanna had been softly playing the grand as people filed in and found their seats. Jonathon waited while she finished the last song. He stood and stepped onto the low platform and took his place, standing behind the keyboard. He started playing very softly. After a long gaze over the congregation where he spotted his wife and three children sitting beside his parents, he smiled and spoke, "Good morning. Welcome. This is a new day. This is the first of what we believe will be many new days. We will be doing a few things differently but those will only be surface things. God is still God and Jesus Christ is still Lord. That is not about to change. Our expression and our manner of doing some things may change but it is all towards the worship of God, the growth of God's kingdom, and the spiritual blessing of our community.

"You will notice that there is no microphone. That's because I've got a pretty powerful voice, plus we worship more effectively when we're in fellowship and that requires that we not have too much space between us." He continued fingering some quiet chords as he spoke, "Let's start out with a song you all know. 'What a Friend We Have in Jesus' is number three hundred eighty-six. Stand or sit, just as you please and as your body dictates to you."

He nodded to Hanna and she played a bright few bars of introduction and then headed right into the song, playing the way she and the new pastor had practiced it. Jonathon added accompaniment on the keyboard and led the vocals with a strong baritone voice.

Most of the people stood, many leaning on canes or on the pew backs in front of them. The ones with failing bodies remained in their seats. Most sang the old familiar song from memory. Cracked and faltering voices spoke of the accumulation of years. Many hesitated or got lost as they sang with the habits of decades, stumbling over the new tempo and rhythm that Hanna and Jonathon were forcing them into. By the third verse, they were pulling together even if somewhat reluctantly. The younger voices among the gathered worshipers provided the foundation for the others to follow. Two of the homeless men stood. The young man in the army jacket remained seated. Jonathon noticed he was quietly weeping with his face buried in his hands.

At the end of the song, Hanna swung directly into the next hymn. It too, was familiar, but Jonathon smiled at 'his' people and said loudly, "Two fifty-seven."

They sang six hymns; two more than they usually sang. Jonathon and Hanna had carefully picked them for their joyfulness and their uplifting messages. They would leave the new, unfamiliar songs for a later time. For one of the songs, Jonathon picked up his guitar and strummed complimentary chords as he let Hanna take the lead.

One of the things Jonathon had always loved about the old timers singing the old songs was the addition of harmony parts.

He heard a smattering of alto and base as they sang and knew that, twenty years before, these voices would have been strong and lovely to listen to. The older parishioners gradually started to take their seats as they became weary. With the singing of the last chords of the song, Jonathon invited all of them to sit.

Hanna moved to take Jonathon's place at the keyboard. She had seldom tried to play while standing, and she and Jonathon had several good laughs as she practiced for this moment. Jonathon invited the ushers to take up the offering and then stepped to the piano. He and Hanna played a simple classical duet they had practiced on Saturday morning. It was both moving and joyful. One of the homeless men quietly began clapping along with the music. He stopped when no one joined him.

Hanna then took a seat in the front pew and Jonathon picked up his Bible, stepping to the edge of the little platform. He was so close to the front that he noticed a few people leaned back as if trying to put distance between themselves and the preacher. Jonathon carried his open Bible in his left hand as he slowly paced across the platform, sharing what God had put in his heart for this first day of his new life and the hoped-for new life of Downtown Fellowship Center.

At the close of the service, Jonathon invited the people to stay and visit and advised that he and a couple of the deacons would be available at the front if anyone wished to gather for prayer. No one came for prayer but a few stepped forward to shake Jonathon's hand and to introduce themselves. Several others directed questioning looks towards Jonathon; many still held serious doubts about the direction the leadership had chosen.

Jonathon had assigned the ushers to be at the door, thanking people for coming and helping them down the stairs as need demanded. This also was new. Never in the long history of First Baptist had the pastor not been at the door at the close of service. The deacons and ushers had seriously questioned this

departure from habit but Jonathon insisted it was more important to be available for prayer than to shake a lot of hands.

As the three homeless men walked slowly towards the exit,
the gathered people shunted out of the way, not friendly but not
particularly unfriendly either. Jonathon was deeply troubled by
the lost and haunted expression of despair on the face of the
young man in the army jacket.

8

MONDAY WAS THE NORMAL STAFF DAY OFF. JONATHON'S intention had been to spend those days at the construction company but his partner assured him that he could handle the load himself, for a few weeks at least, to give Jonathon the freedom to think only about the ministry he had undertaken.

The church office was closed. Jonathon spent most of the morning prowling around the neighborhood, taking note of the residential buildings and guessing at the number of suites in each one. A couple of blocks from the church, he discovered a small but pleasant coffee shop with a few discrete booths along the back wall. It was ideal for out-of-the-office coffee meetings.

Not far from the coffee shop, half hidden behind a sunken doorway of a disreputable and unmaintained old building, he found a sign announcing a drop-in church. The door was open so he went in. A weary-looking young man wearing a much-washed T-shirt and torn blue jeans rose from behind a desk that must have come from the cast-off pile at a thrift shop. "Good morning, sir. I'm Kyle. What can I do for you?"

The two men shook hands.

Jonathon hesitated, looking around the space. It was small,

perhaps the size of a triple garage. It was dark and bleak and smelled a bit like there might be a dead mouse or two inside some wall. It had been a long time since this had been a commercial office. At the side opposite the doorway there were a few rows of folding chairs and a metal music stand placed like a pulpit. Beside that was a guitar nestled on its stand.

"Good morning, Kyle. I'm Jonathon. I just happened to be strolling the neighborhood and was intrigued by your sign. I'd love to hear your story. It's nearly noon. Can you close up long enough for lunch?"

Kyle pointed around the small space. "Not much happening as you can see. I don't usually go for lunch. I like sitting in the park down by the corner if the weather is alright. Might visit with someone if opportunity provides. I brought an apple from home."

Jonathon took in the form of the rail-thin young man. "I enjoy sitting in the park too, Kyle, but I'm a bit hungry today. How about we stroll along to that coffee shop I just passed and get ourselves some lunch. My treat today."

The two men took one of the back booths. The menu was printed on a colorful board above the front counter. Both men looked at it. Kyle hesitated, waiting for the older man's lead. Jonathon figured the young pastor might have missed a few meals recently. He said, "I haven't had my quota of calories lately. That Mid-Town burger sounds like it could be a plateful." Jonathon often skipped lunch or settled for a bowl of soup. The burger was meant as an enticement for Kyle to follow. They both ordered the Mid-Town platter and a cup of coffee.

Kyle stirred cream into his coffee and put his spoon down. He looked a bit intimidated by the occasion as well as by the man sitting across from him.

Jonathon said, "So tell me about yourself and your work."

Kyle took a moment to answer. "Not much to tell about me. It's the work that matters. At least I tell myself that it does. I received my theology degree last year and felt led to minister to the down and out. The men and women who are damaged by this world need Christ as much as the rest of us. But perhaps that's foreign to you, Jonathon. Are you a Christian?"

Jonathon smiled. "That's the correct question, Kyle. And indeed, I am. I don't have a theology degree but the good folks over at the Downtown Fellowship Center have asked me to be their pastor. You've caught me just fresh on my new job. I started last week and yesterday was my first Sunday. I decided to go for a walk to orient myself to the neighborhood today. We can talk more about that later if you wish but I truly want to hear your story."

Kyle absently picked up his spoon and stirred his coffee again. "I've had the work open for about nine months now. We haven't set the world on fire but each Sunday sees twenty to twenty-five folks coming to worship. Not all of them have professed Christ but I've had the privilege of praying for salvation with eight of them. There are no executives among the congregation, and a few would benefit from a bath and a change of clothing. But their souls are precious to the Lord.

"Few of them really have anything to give so we depend on the love gifts of some faithful, personal friends. To say our budget is tight would be nothing but the truth. We get by. The old building we're in has been sold for development and the space is un-rentable so we have the free use of it until they tear the junk heap down. I have no idea what will happen after that."

Jonathon asked, "You say 'we'. Is that a figure of speech or are there others beside yourself depending on the ministry?"

"I'm married, Jonathon. Married with a three-month-old son. Natalie and I were married during my last year of college. She was also a student. Music. That's her guitar you saw in the hall."

The two men talked through lunch and then returned to the church hall where they talked for another hour. As he was preparing to leave the meeting, Jonathon opened his wallet and laid five twenties on the old desk. "I'm not wealthy Kyle. But I want you to have that today. Take some flowers home to Natalie and then take her shopping for some little thing that might brighten her day."

When Jonathon left, both men had much on their minds.

9

NOBLE PEARSON HAD SUFFERED THROUGH SEVERAL troubling days. He sat for some hours in his small study, his back to the door, the bright spring day gracing the window before him. A book lay open on his lap; there hadn't been a page turned in over an hour.

When his wife Trudy came to ask him about lunch, he didn't hear her first call. She spoke again a bit more urgently, "Noble, come back to earth. I asked you about lunch. I was going to scramble some eggs. Will that do it for you?"

Noble absently waved his hand and said, "Anything. Or nothing. I'm not all that hungry."

Trudy was now troubled. Noble had been in the study all morning. She couldn't remember him ever not taking the dog for a walk or warming up a cup of coffee mid-morning. She decided to try a light-hearted approach.

"What's on your mind, Noble? You've been cooped up in this room all morning. And you've said hardly a word since the weekend. You're not scheming another adventure, are you? We don't need the stress and our bodies are no longer receptive to big ideas. And before you ask, I have no interest at all in learning how to scuba dive or ride a mountain bike."

Noble slowly got to his feet. "The biggest idea I've had lately is to successfully bend over to tie my shoes. No, my love, no adventures. We'll have to settle for staying indoors and looking at the old photo albums." He walked away before there was time for questions that he wasn't quite ready to answer.

After lunch, Noble took the dog for a long walk, ending at a bench in the city park. It was a beautiful spring day. Kids played and moms visited all around him enjoying the warmth after the long winter months. He enjoyed watching the activity but slowly his mind blocked it all out, reverting to his morning's thoughts.

Since Sunday he had played the mental tape of the weekend over and over in his mind. Then his memory flashed over the half-century or more that his family had been involved with Downtown Fellow Center and First Baptist before that. He had served on more committees and boards than he could fully remember. He had intimate knowledge of both the good and the not so good.

Sitting quietly on the park bench, he pictured the full sanctuary of times past and he felt a dampness in his eyes as he contrasted that memory with the small remnant of seniors that currently made up the fellowship. And he knew discouragement. Deep in his soul he wept for his own blindness. A blindness that had allowed the church family to shrink - step by slow, unthinking step - to its current condition. As a deacon, he had been forced to bring these old memories back as the men worked towards a solution to their dying church. It was the struggle with this matter that had kept him in his study all morning. His thoughts over the past weeks had troubled him greatly. Silently, but reverently, he asked God to forgive him as he confessed his part in the sad affair.

And then, as if a new light shone on his mind, he prayed, "Lord, it's not just the numbers, is it? It's the pride over the years. It's the spiritual arrogance. It's the spiritual self-satisfaction. It's the stubbornness. It's the hurt people that suffered under our arrogance. People who we let disappear as if they had never existed. It's the pastors who came to serve and who walked away in defeat. But it's also the couple of pastors who came and caused division among us, and who left us the poorer for their coming. It's the lack of love between Your children when the scriptures so clearly insist that we are to love one another."

Noble sat with head bowed as people walked past and as other dogs came to sniff around his own animal. He was unaware of any of it. He was only aware that the Lord seemed to be doing a housecleaning in his heart and mind. Things that had been either unseen or unheeded over the years had a light shone on them and he could no longer pretend.

Haltingly, and with many silent pauses, he again prayed, "Lord, I remember a lot of good things that happened in our fellowship. I well remember the souls that gave their hearts to You. I well remember the ones who went on to serve in a wide range of ministries over the years. I well remember the great times of worship and fellowship. I remember those as good times.

"But I also remember the tears and the fights and the foolishness. And I remember that we tried so hard to keep the world out of the fellowship that we became unaware of how the culture was changing all around us and we were unprepared when our own children wanted something different. We lost hundreds, some to other places of worship but also a distressing number were lost to the world, their faith shaken or gone altogether. It's as if we made a fetish of an era that never really existed but that we hung onto with grim determination, demanding that our children conform.

"You blessed Trudy and me with four wonderful children. But our hearts break to acknowledge that only two of them walk with You. We are paying a terrible price Lord for our pride and stubbornness. Trudy and I are, and the church is, and the kids are. The price our lost loved ones will pay in eternity is incalculable. We can only pray that it is not too late to call some of those precious souls back to You."

He lifted his head and reached in his pocket for his handkerchief. He hadn't been aware that tears were running down his cheeks and dripping off his chin. Nor was he aware that several people had looked strangely at him as they walked past.

Slowly he expelled a long-held breath and rose to his feet. He gave a slight tug on the leash and spoke to the dog, "C'mon pooch. Let's walk some more. I've got more thinking to do."

10

BY TUESDAY OF THE NEW WEEK SAL WAS INTERVIEWING students. Only five had come forward with an interest in the internships. Sal figured the rest of the students were either needing to make money for their next year's schooling costs or were touring Europe on their parents' Visa cards.

She had no problem short-listing the few applicants. One twenty-year-old girl from a local secular college and one twenty-two-year-old young man from a Christian school showed promise. In answer to her question, Darla, the young lady, told Sal she had never attended church nor had any interest. Her studies were in business management and statistics. Robert was from a solid Christian home. His studies were in music and apologetics and were for his general interest only. He had no intentions of pursuing a Christian career such as missions or a pastorate. Both students were living at home with their parents; their need for work experience credit at college was greater than their need to earn money.

Sal explained the work to be done and then added, "But you never know, almost anything else could come up."

Robert had just one question. "Can we depend on getting a letter at the end of the summer to show the work experience?

My school demands that we have work experience and the credits apply to our final marks."

Darla nodded her assent to Robert's remarks.

Sal said, "Of course. We will expect quality work from you but we will do whatever is necessary to promote your education."

She then took them in to meet Jonathon.

The pastor shook their hands but remained standing, indicating that this would be short meeting. "Has Sal outlined the scope of the work we have planned?"

They both nodded. "Yes," was Robert's response. "Uh-huh," said Darla.

He turned to Sal. "This is your call, Sal. They'll be reporting to you and under your leadership. If you say they're the right ones, then it's fine with me."

Without further discussion, the three left Jonathon's office. Sal pulled the door closed behind her.

On Monday morning of the following week, the two interns arrived for work and Sal met with them. After a brief icebreaking session over cups of coffee in one of the meeting rooms, Sal started right in.

"Darla, your first task will be to research all of the residential buildings within reasonable walking distance of the church property. We will want building addresses as well as the number of suites in each building. If there was some way to get a handle on the average age of the residents, that would be good, too. But don't make a nuisance of yourself and don't bother with individual names. Perhaps City Hall can provide you a map of the downtown core with the properties shown. That would be helpful.

"Robert, I want you to write up several short pieces that can become the invitations that we'll send out by mail to the folks living in those buildings. Your studies in apologetics should help with that. Plan on filling a card about the size of a #10 envelope. Think post card and go from there. Be upbeat, smart and attractive. Don't offer advice and don't criticize anyone's lifestyle. Perhaps ask a question and invite people to seek the answer at the Fellowship Center. We want them to come to think of DFC as their own, a place of safety where the answers to some of their life questions can be found.

"I've got one of our men taking a new photo of the building. He's a gifted photographer so I'm expecting a quality photo that we can print on the back of the cards."

Neither intern had any questions. Sal pointed around the room. "This will be your office. Watson, our custodian, will be along shortly to help you move things around and fix up the workspace. You can do that, Robert, while Darla takes advantage of this sunny day to start her research. We'll want Darla's maps to be pinned to the walls so don't clutter it with photos or posters."

Knowing she had already assigned the young people enough work to keep them busy for a couple of weeks, Sal smiled and said, "That should keep you both busy until at least noon so off with you. Work, work, work."

Darla, surprisingly mischievous, grinned at Sal. "And what will we be doing this afternoon, boss?"

Sal was mostly hiding her smile. "I'll think of something."

11

IT WAS THURSDAY MORNING OF JONATHON'S SECOND WEEK of ministry when there was a light tap on the pastor's study door.

"Come in."

The door swung open and Jonathon saw a gray-haired man standing there; painfully thin and slightly stooped but smiling through a bristly, salt-and-pepper mustache. Jonathon guessed his age to be around sixty. The two men had met after the Sunday service but Jonathon couldn't pull the visitor's name from his memory. He stood and held out his hand. "Come in, have a seat. Sorry, I need you to help me with your name. I'm afraid I have a major failing in that area. Too many names to learn all at once."

"William Preston," the man said as he shook the outthrust hand. "Sorry to barge in. Sal isn't at her desk so I took a chance on disturbing you."

"Glad to have you visit, William. What can I do for you?"

William sat and looked around the room. As if to avoid the topic he had come to discuss, he said, "You haven't changed much in here. Obviously, Pastor Gilks took his books and wall hangings with him but otherwise it looks pretty much the same."

That short speech was followed by William taking a deep breath and letting it out with a sigh. "Anyway, that's not why I'm here.

"Actually, I wouldn't be here at all if my wife hadn't threatened me with a week of cold dinners if I didn't come." He shifted in his chair and flashed a small, sheepish grin. "She's a difficult woman to refuse when she sets her foot to a path."

Jonathon laughed. "Well, I have no problem with a cold dinner from time to time but a whole week sounds like cruel and unusual punishment. I wouldn't want that on my conscience so I'm glad you made the trip." His look encouraged the visitor to continue.

"I never talk much about this, Jonathon. Is it alright to call you Jonathon or would you prefer Pastor?"

"Jonathon is just fine."

"Well, the thing is, I'm a fair to middling guitar player. Learned it as a kid but have never played in public. Well, never in recent years. Played with a teen rock band about a hundred years ago. But I'd appreciate you keeping that between the two of us. Anyway, most of my friends have no idea. Just play for myself. I've kept up over the years and I kind of enjoy it. Don't really read music beyond just following the melody line. I kind of play what's in my head. I thought I'd offer to sit in with you during worship time if you ever feel the need."

The visitor paused and glanced at the floor. Jonathon suspected he had more to say so he waited.

Finally, William slid to the front of his chair, slapped his hands onto his knees as if signaling that he was finished, and looked up. "There. Now I've said it and I can go home and not lie to Patricia. Thanks for your time and for not laughing at me." He stood as if to leave.

Jonathon also stood. "Hold on there, partner," he said with a smile. "You can't just lay that on me and then walk out. Come with me."

Sal was back at her desk. Jonathon spoke as he walked by, "Just going into the sanctuary for a bit."

Sal said, "Morning, William," and then watched as Jonathon held the door for him.

The two men disappeared through the door and up the four steps to the sanctuary level. The sanctuary was only partially but adequately lit by the morning sun. Mixed with the brightness of the sun through the clear portions of the large leaded windows were flashes of the multitude of colors that always caught Jonathon's admiration, all reflecting the Bible stories told in the window artwork. As the windblown clouds scuttled across the sky, the reflected light alternated from dazzling spring sunshine to a dull half-light causing the room to almost glow in the multi-colored reflections one moment and then to dull down to a more subdued but still glorious display of color. Jonathon remembered following the colors across the floor as a child, trying to step on each one before the sun and clouds moved it on.

Jonathon stepped onto the low platform and flipped the 'on' switch on his keyboard. He motioned to William and nodded towards the guitar resting in its stand. William hesitantly picked up the instrument and swung the strap over his head. He found a pick woven into the strings and cautiously hit a C-chord just to check the tuning and the touch.

Jonathon played a few chords and then moved into 'What a Friend We Have in Jesus', playing by ear. William quietly chorded along until Jonathon had completed one stanza. As Jonathon swung into a second stanza, William started playing a little more boldly, picking out the melody and adding some complimentary chords. By the end of the verse, Jonathon was smiling and nodding in pleased acceptance.

Jonathon spoke over the instruments, "Take one, William."

The pastor watched William as the guitarist's fingers made the six-string Gibson sing the song. Jonathon enhanced the sound with a series of quiet chords and filler notes. Jonathon sensed an underlying rhythm much like fifties' rock and roll in

William's playing, as if the player was holding back his true musical feelings.

William played one more verse and then swung into 'Blessed Assurance'. Jonathon picked right up on the change and the two men made music, playing song after song. What started out as an impromptu audition had turned into impromptu worship.

Jonathon had been totally wrapped up in the music. He opened his eyes and, glancing sideways, saw Sal and the two interns standing just inside the doorway listening.

When the playing stopped, the three listeners broke into eager applause. "Wonderful," said Sal. "You've been holding out on us all these years, William. I had no idea."

Robert stepped forward. "May I join you for a number?" Without waiting for an answer, he moved to the grand piano and took a seat. He folded the keyboard cover back and ran his fingers up and down the keys, getting the feel of the instrument. He then chorded his way into 'To God be the Glory'.

William and Jonathon stood silent for half a verse and then started picking up the rhythm, enhancing it with accompaniment. After playing the melody twice, Robert broke into the words with a strong baritone voice.

They played and sang two more hymns together and then Jonathon shut off his keyboard. The silence was loud in their ears. Finally, Jonathon smiled at the two men and said, "You're hired."

Robert laughed and said, "I already have a job. This was just for fun."

Sal spoke up, "I could rewrite your job description, Robert." That brought more laughter.

Jonathon said, "It really was fun, Robert, but it was more than that. It was wonderful and worshipful. But we all have work to do so back into the dungeon you three."

Darla patted Robert on the back as he passed. "Well done, Fingers."

When Sal and the interns were gone, Jonathon turned to

William who was just setting the guitar back into the stand. "William, I want you to thank your wife for me. She's right. And so is Sal. You've been holding out."

"Not really holding out, Jonathon. It's more just what I play and the way I play it has never fit with pipe organs and formal services. There was really no place for my picking."

"Well, there is now and I very much want you on the platform. Do you play anything else?"

William nodded. "Actually, I prefer the electric guitar to the acoustic but I don't play anything else. Well, the banjo a little bit and the bass if forced into it."

"Who else is holding out, William? You must know all the secrets here."

William smiled at Jonathon. "You might want to talk with Madison Palmer. He plays the sweetest clarinet. The sounds he gets out of that little pipe will make you want to laugh and cry all at the same time. Run chills up your back. Used to play in a dance band before he was saved."

After a short pause, William continued, "I hesitate to mention it for fear of being read out of the church for breaking a confidence but one of the best kept secrets around here is that Madison's wife, Tilly, is one of the most competent drummers I've ever heard. She and Madison met when they were playing in that dance band. She doesn't really want that known around so you need to walk easy on that."

The pastor nodded and smiled. "Sure glad you came in, William. But I also have work to do so I'd better get back to it. How would it be if I have Hanna give you a call and arrange for a practice? She's in charge of music."

"Any time," answered William. "It's not as if I need a Day Timer to keep track of my appointments anymore. There's a lot of free time in this retirement thing."

The two men shook hands and Jonathon went back to work.

THE PHONE CALL CAME AT 8:00 AM TUESDAY, THE THIRD week of Jonathon's ministry just as Sal was putting her purse in the desk drawer. She picked up the receiver and listened for a moment before saying, "Hold a minute, Lewis. I'll see if he's available."

Choosing discretion over the more public intercom button on her phone, Sal tapped on Jonathon's door and, at his invitation, stepped inside. "I have Lewis Jamison on the phone. He sounds upset and he insists on talking with you. Do you want to take it or call him back?"

"I'll take it. Any idea what his issue is?"

Sal said, "Probably music but he didn't tell me. He's very traditional and determined, not much bend in him. So I suspect he'll tell you quickly enough."

Jonathon picked up the phone. "Morning, Mr. Jamison. Good to hear from you. What can I do for you?"

An unnecessarily loud voice said, "You can quit playing those confounded instruments and ruining our wonderful old hymns. That's what you can do. And the quicker, the better. I don't know why you young fellows think you need to throw away all the good things your forefathers worked so hard for and cared so much about. What's wrong with the old, trusted and well-known hymns, young fella? And where do you get off coming in here and changing everything?"

It sounded like the caller was going to say more but Jonathon grabbed the opportunity to speak.

"Well, first, Mr. Jamison, thanks for calling me young. That lightens my day. I'm not really young anymore but some days I try to delude myself on the topic. And thanks for calling. Everyone's concerns and opinions matter.

"But Mr. Jamison, we had very open and honest discussions on this before I took on the job. The leadership and the congregation were in agreement that we had to appeal to the unchurched and unsaved if we are to build up the Kingdom of God in our city center. And we decided among us that Downtown Fellowship had little reason to continue existing if we couldn't attract the unsaved and introduce them to the Lord."

Mr. Jamison interjected, "That's all well and good but I don't remember anything about you changing all our music around."

Jonathon continued, "We're actually singing the same songs that you and I have always sung. I'm going to start introducing some great new music but so far, we've stuck with the familiar hymns. We're just rearranging them a bit to make them more joyful and uplifting. Do you not believe the Christian message should be joyful and uplifting, Mr. Jamison?"

The man ignored the question. "And what's with that electric whatever it is you play? We have a perfectly good piano that we paid a lot of money for. We don't need anything more than that. And if that's not bad enough, now you have William and Madison playing those foolish dance band instruments. I didn't even know they could play them. Kept it a secret all these years. Ashamed of it I would guess. It has to stop, Pastor, or my wife and I will find another place to worship."

Jonathon took a deep breath. He knew this was going to happen. Anyone could have predicted it. But Jonathon had told

Sal he would be delegating some tasks to others and now was the time.

"Mr. Jamison, may I suggest that you give Roland Trembley a call? He's the deacon assigned to watch over the adjustment period in our transition to a more modern approach to Kingdom building. He led the board discussions on these matters and I know he would welcome your call."

Lewis Jamison continued to fill the phone with a much too loud voice. "I'll call him. But I meant what I said. I will see the end to these radical changes or you've seen the last of me."

Jonathon paused to see if the caller had more to say. Finally, into the silence he said as gently as he knew how, "I'd be sorry to see you go Mr. Jamison but my mandate from the leadership is clear. Do give Roland a call."

The man was gone without saying goodbye.

JONATHON WAS STANDING IN THE IMPRESSIVE FOYER OF
the Crown Construction Company office. Crown Construction
was as old as the city itself. The walls were burdened with the
photos of the many structures completed by the company over
the years; highway bridges, water treatment facilities, manufac-
turing plants, several small petroleum refineries, downtown
high-rise towers. As a small contractor himself, Jonathon could
only shake his head at the amazing display of the work accomplished.

A deep bass voice spoke from behind, "Jonathon. I've known
your name for some years but, somehow, we've never met.
Welcome. Millard Crown."

Jonathon turned to see a big, trim, well-built man holding
out his hand. Jonathon's own hand was considered large by most
standards but it was swallowed up in the hand of the greeter.
The broad shoulders and trim waist belied the age of the smiling
Millard Crown. Jonathon knew him to be in his mid-sixties. He
suspected that Millard spent considerable time at the gym, or
more likely in his personal studio. Wealth has its privileges.

The carefully trimmed head of silver hair, the capped teeth,
and the finely-cut suit all spoke of care and wealth.

"Thank you for meeting with me, Mr. Crown. I've seen you across the room at Construction Association meetings."

Millard led Jonathon into a small conference room where there was coffee and a silver tray of pastries available. Millard stepped to the side table and reached for a cup. "I'm having a coffee. Will you join me?"

Coffee cups in hand, the two men sat across from one another at the oval teakwood conference table.

The unsmiling Millard said, "You've taken a couple of jobs that we were bidding on."

Jonathon caught his breath, not at all sure how to respond. Finally, he decided a bold, direct approach was the way to go. "Proctor-McCann is a small contracting company, Mr. Crown. We needed those jobs. I suspect you had bigger fish to fry." His returned smile was a bit tentative and he sat there wondering what was next.

Finally, Millard laughed out loud. "Well done, Jonathon. Don't let anyone bamboozle you. I don't remember the details on those jobs but we probably did have bigger fish to fry. I hope you made a few dollars on them. I guess you did since you're still in business. What can I do for you?"

Jonathon opened a small leather binder he had carried with him. "First, Mr. Crown, I need to update you. We are still in business but I have taken a two-year leave from the construction company to pastor the Downtown Fellowship Center." Millard nodded but said nothing. Jonathon wondered if he already knew this. Successful people tend to be well-informed.

Jonathon pulled a fresh reprint of an old eight-by-ten-inch photo from the leather binder and wordlessly slid it across the table. He lifted his coffee cup to allow the other man time to study the photo. The owner of Crown Construction picked up the photo and leaned back in his chair, studying the print carefully. Within a few seconds, he was smiling and shaking his head. He sat forward and leaned his elbows on the table, still studying the photo. Without looking up he said, "I never met the man but that's my great-grandfather, Isaac, standing there with the roll of blueprints tucked under his arm. He was already an old man when this picture was taken. I've seen some family photos of him and Grandmother Mattie. The partial building in the background is the beginnings of First Baptist." It seemed he couldn't take his eyes from the photo.

"We still have that roll of blueprints," said Jonathon.

He slid another photo across the desk. Again, Millard picked it up and studied it. It took only a few moments for Millard to place one finger on the photo. "This man I knew as a boy. That's Grandpa James. Who is this group of men?"

Jonathon settled back in his chair, cradling the coffee cup in his two hands. "That group of men, Mr. Crown, is the board of deacons of First Baptist. The photo was taken around 1920 as far as we can figure out. Your great-grandfather was not just the contractor on the church building; he and your great-grandmother, Mattie, were two of the sixteen founding members years before this photo was taken. Your grandparents carried on the family tradition and then your parents. Your father was a deacon for many years. But, of course, you know that."

The two men sat looking at each other for a few moments. Finally, Millard said, "I do know that history. What I don't know is why that issue is on the table now."

Jonathon put down his coffee cup. "I confess I wasn't aware of that history. There would be no reason for me to know. I've had no involvement with First Baptist since I was a child. And, of course, many things change over time and history isn't particularly important to a child."

After a short pause, Jonathon said, "I suspect you know Orvis Tanner."

Millard laughed. "Everyone in town who has ever had any church involvement at all knows Orvis Tanner. He's been on the denomination office staff for years. Great guy. We had lunch a couple of weeks ago."

Jonathon tried not to show his surprise as he thought, 'now, that's interesting'.

The silence seemed to suggest that Millard was not going to expand on his lunch with Orvis Tanner so Jonathon said, "It was Mr. Tanner who suggested that I consider serving Downtown Fellowship. As he was giving me a brief outline of the history, your family name came up. Although we had never met I was certainly aware of your family and your business. I am also aware that you, along with a small group of influential business men and women, are great patrons of the arts."

This appeared to be a rather stark change of topic. The two men silently studied each other for just the briefest moment.

While Jonathon was reaching into the leather binder again, he said, "When I came on staff at the church, I discovered that the grand old pipe organ had retired itself some twenty years ago. I would like to reverse that."

Jonathon slid a sheet of paper across the desk.

"That's a quotation for the repair of the organ. It's much less than I originally feared it would be but it's still more than our small congregation can handle at this time."

Millard scanned the document and then looked up. "So, jumping ahead, if I can anticipate where this is going, you're suggesting that our Arts Support Board come on side and pick up this tab for you."

"Not for me, Mr. Crown, for Downtown Fellowship and, ultimately, for the community.

"There's a further purpose in the proposal. As I'm sure you're aware, governments at all levels are taking a hard look at their taxation policies. Taxing church properties is high on their list. Many are saying that churches don't really add any social benefit to the community and so should be taxed like any other private holding."

Millard nodded. Again, the thought rushed through Jonathon's mind that successful people know what's going on in their communities.

Jonathon continued, "Downtown Fellowship has done a lunch program for many years. An AA group meets in one of the small rooms. A community choir practices in the back hall. Many weddings take place in the sanctuary or one of the smaller chapel areas every year and we're open to serving in other ways, all without charging any rental fees. On occasion, the user group will make a donation but none is ever asked for. We're hoping the city council will keep those things in mind during their taxation study. But very little of that is known by the community at large.

"Having the organ repaired and available for concerts would greatly enhance the arts community and add to the public services the taxation study is looking for. So, while repairing the organ is primarily for the benefit of our worship services, we would also make it available for concerts and special functions. This would be very much a benefit to the community.

"I'm also going to ask you for something else so I might just as well put it on the table right now."

Millard Crown was looking intently at Jonathon. There was a time, many years before, when that look would have frozen Jonathon into an unthinking, non-speaking lump. But he had gotten past that in the rough and tumble of the construction world. So, after just the briefest pause, he continued, "One of the nation's greatest organ virtuoso's, Mr. Gladius Strung - who happens to also be a Christian - has just a few days ago announced that he's coming out of his one-year sabbatical and is planning a tour. Your Arts Support Board has some very influential people on it including yourself, of course. I was thinking of a package deal."

Watching Millard, Jonathon saw very clearly that the man was already ahead of him.

"So, putting the package together, here is what I'm asking for. I'm requesting that your Arts Board work with us to repair the organ while at the same time approaching Mr. Strung to add our city to his tour. The earlier, the better. Of course, Downtown

Fellowship will make the building and the organ available for the concert without charge.

"Our building seats twelve-hundred people. No other local venue seats that many except the Smithson Arts Center and they don't have an organ. In fact, unless I've missed something, we have the only pipe organ left in the city.

"We would make this further commitment: Although the primary purpose and use of the building will always remain worship and preaching of the Word of God, we see no difficulty in sharing the building with those who will respect it, abide by our guidelines and not abuse the privilege. And again, the organ adds immeasurably to those possibilities."

His pitch made, Jonathon thought it was time to be quiet. Any further words from him might just clutter the air with useless noise.

Millard leaned back in his chair, studying the younger man intently. Slowly he picked up the quotation for the organ repair and looked at it again. He then stood, indicating that the meeting was over. "Leave this with me. I'm sensing some urgency on this, not so much for the organ repair but more to get a bid in to Mr. Strung before he's booked solid. I make no promises except to take it to our Board and give it a fair hearing. You'll hear from me shortly. It's been a pleasure to meet you. I wish you every success in your work at First Baptist."

He held out his hand and Jonathon shook it, thankful that Millard felt no need to demonstrate his strength.

14

DARLA HAD THE OFFICE WALLS PLASTERED WITH MAPS AND aerial photos of the city, some showing the overall area and some showing close-up details. With a felt marker she had written the street address and number of suites on the roof outlines of each building; the number of residences within walking distance was far larger than any of them had originally thought.

Robert had a stack of computer-generated draft outlines for the mailouts complete with borders, a variety of fonts and colors, and other visual enhancements. Sal looked at them and was amazed, as she had often been, at the computer skills that seemed to come naturally to young people. At the beginning, the cards were cluttered with too much text but Robert soon worked his way through that. Like any good editor, he carefully removed every unnecessary or ineffective word. He then pushed the stack of cards across the layout table to Darla. "Look at these and give me your honest opinion."

She pushed the cards back towards Robert. "You know I've never gone to church, Robert. I know nothing at all about it. I doubt I'm the one to ask on this."

Robert pushed the cards back to her, holding his hand on top of the stack to prevent her from returning them. "But you're perfect. Most of the people who receive these invitations also know exactly nothing about church except what Hollywood and the popular media have told them. So you're a one-person focus group. Try to imagine going to your mailbox at home and finding this invitation. You read it. You get a reaction. What is that reaction? That's what I want to know.

"We're not expecting miracles from the first mailout. But if the mailout makes a few people wonder or ask themselves a question and call us, we'll consider that a success. On the other hand, if the mailouts anger people or worse - elicit no response at all - we need to know that as well."

Darla asked, "What kind of return are you hoping for?"

Robert answered, "From what I've read, the bulk mailing people say a 5% positive return is amazing and signifies an exceptionally successful campaign. A 1% return is more typical. So, based on those small numbers, it's critical that we identify problems in the cards before they're sent out. And as we continue advertising, perhaps the Lord will bless the effort."

Darla reluctantly picked up the cards. Before heading back to her own desk, she said, "I don't even know what you mean when you say things like 'the Lord will bless.'"

Robert smiled a bit and silently thought 'You will before this summer is over'.

With Darla's help, he then got creative on the word processor and came up with some truly inspiring mailout possibilities. He had more copy than they would ever use but he figured that was better than having too little.

The new photo of the church building was a stroke of genius. Gary Garcia, the church member Sal had tagged to do the photo, had wormed his way into a second-floor office of the building across the street to take the picture. The elevation and the angle were nearly perfect. It was a sunny day with just a thin layer of cloud cover to dampen the harshness of the sun. No outdoor photographer could ask for more.

Robert researched the cost of delivery, comparing the post office to various other such services. A small company with the uninspiring name 'Downtown Delivery' clearly wanted the business and showed it with their costs and their services. But, in the end, he and Sal agreed to use the post office.

Next, he sorted out the cost of printing and discovered that the church could lease a new top-of-the-line printer that would do everything that needed doing with less overall cost than commercial printing. "And we can do it on demand," he explained to Jonathon to further justify the cost.

The two interns advised Sal that they were ready to present their findings. It was just one more thing for Sal to sort out in what was developing into a very busy week.

Before there was time for the interns to meet with Jonathon, Sal's phone rang. She listened for a time and then said, "Hold a minute please. I'll see if I can interrupt the pastor."

Sal tapped on the office door and entered at Jonathon's invitation. Talking quietly and confidentially she said, "Well, this is interesting. I have the booking organizer from the Classical School of Music on the phone."

Jonathon looked puzzled. "Never heard of them."

Sal said, "They're a very large Christian school from the East Coast. They mainly teach music, although they have some bachelor-level programs in Bible and theology. She wants to talk about putting on a concert. Do you want to talk to her?"

With a puzzled look on his face, Jonathon picked up the phone. "Jonathon McCann here, how may I help you?"

A youthful, vibrant female voice spoke, "Mr. McCann, Virginia Weathersby here. I'm calling for the Classical School of Music. We take our senior choir on an extended tour each spring. This year there are eighty-two vocalists and musicians in the group. We're always booked solid at least a year in advance. Yesterday, for the first time ever, I received a call with a last-minute cancellation from a church just a few miles from you. I have no experience with cancellations so I wasn't sure what to do. We're already on the road and heading your way.

"But then I remembered that I met a young man from your city at a music fest last year. Fortunately, we exchanged phone numbers at that time and I managed to catch him with a text this morning. Since he's familiar with your area, I wanted to see if he had any suggestions. He thought a call to you might be worthwhile. He says he's interning with you folks for the summer."

Jonathon said, "You're talking about Robert, of course."

"Robert, yes. Well anyway, he described your church facilities and gave me your name and phone number. So here I am. Asking for help and offering a free concert by a rather accomplished choir. Do you think this might merit further discussion?"

A short while later Jonathon pressed Robert's number on the paging system Sal had purchased and installed. "Robert here."

Jonathon answered, "Robert, bring Darla and Sal with you and come here please."

When everyone was gathered, Jonathon gestured to Robert and Darla. "What are each of you working on right now?"

The two interns looked at each other, waiting for the other to speak. Finally, Robert took the lead. "We're up to speed on the mailouts and the web page is progressing. Sal has sent us off on other research."

Jonathon looked at Sal. "If we pushed all of you into a different direction for two or three days, would anything important suffer?"

Sal glanced at the two interns and then back to Jonathon. "I think the work is at a place where we can take some time away from it. What do you have in mind?"

Jonathon told them about the call from the Classical School of Music. "A young lady named Virginia tells me that you are to be either thanked, or blamed, for her calling me, Robert. But in any case, I've accepted her offer of a short-notice almost impromptu concert. So here's what I want you to do. We only have a little less than two weeks so this will have to move right along."

He then outlined the work necessary to get the word out to the community. The first challenge was the creation of a concert invitation mailout to all the high-rise residences in the area. "This can be our initial experience with direct mail. We'll pay close attention to the responses and learn from the effort."

Jonathon continued to outline the work ahead of them. "The next big challenge will be finding billets for the accommodation of the choir members. We'll go to our own people, of course, but we'll also try leaning on other churches. Hopefully, those churches will get the word out to their own people and to as broad a group as possible. There's no time to lose."

15

AS THE NEXT SUNDAY SERVICE BEGAN, JONATHON WAS BOTH surprised and pleased to see Lewis Jamison and his wife in attendance. His admiration for the deacon board and their wisdom in appointing Roland Trembley as transition director rose considerably. He wondered exactly what Roland had said that convinced the complaining couple to continue their attendance.

Jonathon was not aware of the close friendship between Lewis and Noble Pearson. Nor did he know that when Lewis had taken his complaints to Noble expecting a sympathetic ear, he instead was met with a well-reasoned and gentle narrating of how the Lord had worked in Noble's heart while sitting on that park bench.

Jonathon was equally pleased to see the three homeless men sitting with Hank Grissom again. The men had been there for all four Sundays that Jonathon had led the services. The youngest of the three carried the same lost, care-worn look Jonathon had noticed before. Jonathon silently prayed, 'Lord, if my eyes are seeing true, that young man is hurting worse than any man I've ever met. Please touch his heart and mind and give us compassion and wisdom in our fellowship with him.'

Near the back, he saw Millard Crown sitting with a handsome, carefully-attired lady and another well-dressed couple. He had discovered as he was researching the organ renewal proposal that the Crowns only occasionally attended a large church on the outskirts of the city. The devout example of the three previous generations of Crowns appeared to have been set aside by Millard and his wife. He didn't know the other couple.

Robert was also in attendance but there was no sign of Darla.

As the music portion of the service ended, Jonathon stepped to the front of the platform. The congregation sat silently while Jonathon took considerable time looking over the small gathering and then even longer as he intently looked over every corner of the sanctuary and up at the high, vaulted ceiling. He turned in a slow circle as he took in the pipe organ and platform behind him, then the choir loft, before finally turning back to the people. He could sense some fidgeting and unease as the silent time went past.

Finally, he spoke, "I am going to ask you to stand once more."

When those who were able were standing, he said, "I want you to take a careful look at this room. Go ahead, look around; turn until you have taken in every corner. Take your time."

After a lengthy pause, he said, "You're thinking that you've seen it a thousand times but look again. Open new eyes. Look up at the ceiling. Look at the graceful arches that make up that high dome and think of the skill and workmanship that went into creating it. And know that it is this design and workmanship that give the room its wonderful acoustics." He paused to give them time.

"Look at the stained-glass windows and think of the Bible-story messages they have displayed all these years. Think of the craftsmanship and the skill it took to put them there."

Again, Jonathon gave the people time to consider.

"Look at the organ that has been silent for over twenty years." With a tender voice, he continued, "Look at the choir loft that hasn't heard an anthem in over a decade."

This pause was even longer.

"Look at the pulpit where faithful men of God have preached Scriptural truth for a century and longer. Think of where your life and your eternal destiny, along with the lives and eternal destinies of thousands of others over the decades, would be without that preached truth, either from this pulpit or another like it."

He stood for a long time intently studying their faces as the people visually took in the organ, the choir loft, and the pulpit.

"And then look at the workmanship and care that went into putting all this together. Look at the carvings and the scroll work on the door panels. Look at how the woodwork is so carefully fitted. Look, and realize that what you are seeing is over a century old.

"The Scriptures promise that God will bless the work of our hands. While not every hand that God used to put this beautiful space together was a Christian hand, they were all blessed with skills that God alone can give. Together they fulfilled the promise that is chiseled into the cornerstone out front; 'To the Glory of God.'"

He gave them lots of time.

Then he swept his hand from side to side, pointing to the sanctuary.

"Look at all the empty seats."

Slowly he lifted his hand to the balcony. "Look at the balcony. There's not a soul sitting there. Nor has there been for many years."

Jonathon invited the people to sit.

When everyone was seated, he continued, "To the Glory of God does not primarily refer to the workmanship that went into putting up this magnificent structure. Far more, it refers to the preaching, the teaching, the singing, the giving, the worship and the changed lives of those who have passed through those doors in the past century and to those yet to come. Generations before us have, each in their own way, glorified God in and through this place. Can we possibly do less?"

He let a few moments go by as he gathered his thoughts.

"It is obvious that the sight of these empty pews struck a responsive chord in your leadership. The decision was made months ago to attempt to again glorify God by filling those pews and the hearts of those who will fill them. Following many meetings - more discussions than I can fully bring to mind, hours of soul-searching prayer by all concerned, as well as counseling from trusted elders of the church - I stand here before you with a fresh mandate from your leaders.

"You need to fully understand that this was not my idea. If I had been asked to plot my future, being here at this time and in this role would never have entered my mind. The first mention of this idea set me right back onto my heels."

Jonathon had an emotional moment when he couldn't speak. A long look at the folks gathered before him convinced him that he had their attention. When he had collected himself, he continued, "We want to bring glory to God. Your leadership does. I do. I am convinced that you do. A dying church brings no one glory. God receives glory in many ways but, from people, it is primarily in two ways: first from the human heart that responds to the blood-purchased offer of salvation in Jesus Christ. The second is in the worship of those same responsive hearts."

Jonathon was silent as he carefully opened his Bible. When he had the passage he was seeking, he held the book up high and spoke from memory, "Hear the Word of God as it is written in Rev. 22:17: *The Spirit and the bride say, 'Come!' And let the one who hears say, 'Come!' Let the one who is thirsty come; and let the one who wishes to take the free gift of the water of life come.*

"It is this message that has changed the hearts of all the millions of people throughout history who have called themselves Christian. Or, more importantly, that God has called Christian.

"There are a lot of empty seats to fill in this sanctuary and a lot of empty hearts in the residential and office buildings around us. We intend to make every effort to put the two together."

Jonathon continued to outline the plan the leadership had devised to reach out to the people living within walking distance of the church. He used carefully selected Scripture to clearly confirm God's will that none should be lost for eternity. He showed clearly from Scripture what was required in those seeking to know God.

He talked about the wisdom they, as mature Christians and elder citizens, had absorbed over their long lives and outlined how that wisdom could be a blessing to any folks who responded to the invitation to seek God. He emphasized the need for love and discretion, and boldly advised against being judgmental.

"We will find that few of today's younger folks think the way we do. We will find that the world view held by most of the people living around us will be at odds with our world view. If we start out being condemning or judgmental, we will lose the battle before it has properly begun.

"Our task is to love people and let the Lord deal with their hearts and their lives. There may come a time when we can speak into their lives. But that will not likely be on the first contact or perhaps not even after many contacts. We can speak into their lives only when they allow us to. In the meantime, I repeat, our job is to love people and pray for them."

Changing the topic for a few minutes, Jonathan said, "You know that we have hired two interns for the summer months. Robert is with us this morning." Gesturing in Robert's direction he said, "Since this is your first opportunity to be welcomed, please stand for a moment, Robert."

Robert stood and there was a light smattering of welcoming applause. Robert sat down and Jonathon said, "Darla, the young lady who works with Robert, is not with us this morning. I'm sure she would be pleased if a few of you were to drop in to the office and greet her.

"Robert and Darla have mapped out the entire downtown core of the city and prepared a series of printed invitations ready for delivery. A sample of the first invitation is in your bulletin."

The pastor then went on to briefly tell what the work of the interns entailed and what the overall plan of outreach was.

Jonathon held up his Bible again. "Now let's see if we can't find a heaping helping of God's love and encouragement for ourselves this morning.

"Please turn to John 14. 27: *'Peace I leave with you; my peace I give you. I do not give to you as the world gives. Do not let your hearts be troubled and do not be afraid.'*"

16

ON WEDNESDAY MORNING, Millard Crown phoned. Sal put the call through to Jonathon. The pastor picked up the phone and said, "Good morning. It's good to hear from you, Mr. Crown. And it was good to see you at the service on Sunday morning."

Millard chuckled a bit and said, "I'm afraid our attendance at any church has lagged over the years and it has been too long since we were at First Baptist. It brought back a flood of memories, not all of them good." His silence following this statement seemed to invite a comment.

Jonathon hesitated and then said, "If you would allow me to buy you lunch one day, I'd love to hear those remembrances."

"You might not enjoy that story as much as you think. But perhaps we'll do lunch anyway. I'll call you on that. In the meantime, here's where we're at. I talked with Gladius Strung. He's already starting to get booked up but he has a date open five weeks from now. When I told him of your proposal, his interest rose considerably. I think what he said was, 'Anything to advance the work of the Lord.'

"So, our board is prepared to fund the organ repair, plus the travel costs for Gladius, provided you can have the organ ready for that date. We'll leave the repair details to you and your group. The board wants nothing financial in return. If a small note of appreciation could be added to the advertising posters, that would make the contributors very content."

Jonathon silently pumped his fist and tried to keep his voice calm as he replied, "I'll get on the phone to Classic Organs right now and get back to you by e-mail as soon I have their answer. And thank you very much. You and your board. We look forward to working with you. Having Mr. Strung in our community will mean a lot to the church as well as for the city itself."

In business, both men had learned the art of concise phone calls so they said no more. Jonathon was soon on the phone to Classic Organs. The secretary put him through to Murphy McGuire. "Good morning, Son of Wolves. I hope all is well in your world."

"Good morning, Mr. McGuire. All is indeed well and getting better. Getting better, that is, provided you and I can make a timely deal." Jonathon described the visit from Gladius Strung and the timeframe involved. He could hear the listener taking in a deep breath of excitement.

"Young man, I am too old for this kind of excitement. You need to work slowly into these things for the elderly or you will find yourself responsible for my demise. However, I will do my very best to continue breathing until I get the unspeakable privilege of listening to the rapturous sounds that only Gladius Strung is capable of coaxing from your magnificent instrument."

Jonathon laughed and said, "Mr. McGuire, I believe I should take elocution lessons from you before I do much more preaching. Or perhaps I am too far removed, generationally, from that beautiful green land to ever have your gift of tongues.

"But in the meantime, here is the plain question. Is it possible for your people to have our instrument repaired and available for Mr. Strung by the date in question?"

"It is not only possible but I guarantee it. The parts needed are common and easily accessed. In fact, we have most of them in stock. I will have them assembled and on their way to you tomorrow. Our work crew will be there next Monday morning. I will e-mail you their travel plans and ask that you have someone pick them up at the airport. There will be four men. If you could book rooms and transport for them for a three-week stay, that would be a great help. Now, while I have said we can meet your timeframe, please understand that we would prefer to have twice that time to work. The men will be working long hours and will need access to the building on their own schedule. I'm sure you can arrange that. Oh, this is wonderful. What a golden opportunity you have been given. We'll talk again but I must go now and get this started."

The phone went dead without a goodbye.

THE PLANNING FOR THE CHOIR VISIT HAD PUSHED THE interns' work back by three days. By the end of that time, they had mailout cards designed and printed. In a flight of enthusiasm, Jonathon had instructed that enough cards be printed for distribution to all the apartments within one half-mile of the church building. The whole operation would stretch their budget but if the first step in reaching the target group was through music, it would be worth it.

The young people found it a more challenging task to get the news out to the local churches. There was no clearinghouse of contact information. They looked up the phone numbers one church at a time, created a list for future use, and made the calls. Not all their calls were welcomed. Robert was disappointed by some of the responses and Darla was puzzled.

During a coffee break, Darla asked, "Aren't you all on the same team? In some of my calls, I detected a distinct coolness."

Unable to think of a logical, simple answer and not wishing to get into a more complicated discussion, Robert replied, "There's no accounting for the attitudes of some folks. Protecting their own turf, I guess."

The invitation cards would be sent out one week before the concert.

Robert and Darla were soon back to their original tasks. With the work on the concert invitation cards wrapped up, the two young people worked together to create a simple website. The front page was the new photo of the brick building. Along the top were the typical drop-down menus.

The team decided to delay the original mailout program until after the visit by Gladius Strung. Still, they wanted to be ready. So, with the final touches put to the design and wording, the cards were printed and bundled in packs of fifty. When the program was initiated, the cards would be delivered to the post office on a Thursday morning for delivery on Friday. Jonathon wanted them in the recipient's hands as close to the weekend as possible. Darla developed a computer program for keeping track of the mailings and responses.

When this work was completed, the interns gathered with Sal and Jonathon to pray for the hoped-for results from the mailing. Darla was distinctly uncomfortable but she remained quietly in her chair while the others prayed.

As they prayed, a portion of Jonathon's mind was wondering about Darla. Did she ever think about God or any kind of a 'greater being'? What did she think as she listened to each of them pray? Were they being a positive influence on her as they worked together? Were they properly representing God in their interactions with her? Would she be a small test sample for the work they were trying to accomplish?

They rose from prayer and Jonathon congratulated the two interns and Sal on their work. He smiled at the three of them. "You've done a great job. Thank you. It's just coming to lunch time. Why don't you all take the afternoon off and do something outside of the church? Enjoy yourselves. We'll start again in the morning."

The next morning, Sal had new tasks for the interns. They picked up pens and notepads.

"Robert, I want you to get a handle on the situation with the homeless and others who use the free lunch programs. There are several groups duplicating what we do. We'd like to have an overall picture. Gather as much detailed information as you can including where the food comes from. Is it purchased or donated by the stores?

"Perhaps the most important thing is finding out if there are excess services available or is there a shortage? Try to get a handle on what might be missing from the various programs."

She turned to Darla. "Young lady, I want you to take a master key and go back to the gymnasium. That space hasn't been used for years. Ask Watson to go with you. He knows where all the building plans are kept. You will need a set of gymnasium plans. Don't put any marks on the originals. Find a copy service that can duplicate a page that large.

"Watson will either give you a tape measure or he might even work with you, depending on his workload. Measure the entire area and see if the plans are accurate. Then make a careful note of all the side rooms and what's in them. Take a close look for problems that might have to be addressed before the space is opened for public use again. Building and fire codes change over time so we need to be sure where we stand. You might have to make a trip to city hall.

"Call a kitchen supply company and have someone look at the facility. We want to know if it's possible to install a small, commercial-style kitchen somewhere close to the gym.

"The gym already has toilets and showers available for both men and women. Call a plumber and have someone give us advice on installing additional facilities. I want both of you to write up your findings in a report for the board."

She looked at the two interns, "Any questions?"

Darla asked, "What's the reason for moving the lunches to the gym?"

Sal answered, "It's a more modern structure, easily accessed from the street, and it has better washroom facilities. The overall reason though is that the board would like to have the basement available to be used for other purposes."

Darla, ever mischievous and knowing this was the work of many days, grinned at her. "OK, makes sense. But again, I ask. So, what will we be doing this afternoon?"

Sal returned her grin. "Get out of here. I have work to do."

18

JONATHON WAS OFTEN OVERWHELMED, KNOWING THAT much had to be done if the church was to be transformed and made functional and successful. It wasn't so much the work that overwhelmed him but the timeframe and the shaky ground from which they were building. The past seemed to rise up and mock him at every turn. During his prayer times, the enemy whispered doubts into his mind. He had surrendered his thoughts to God but the enemy was relentless.

Troubles such as the church had gone through were never kept secret for very long. Was the knowledge of these events known just within evangelical circles or had the news gotten out to the larger community? Was this to be an added burden, something else to overcome in reaching out with the message of salvation in Christ? It was common for people to blame God for the actions of His people. Over the centuries, many people had turned away from the message of redemption, equating the foolishness of men and women as being somehow the actions of God Himself. And, of course, the enemy took full advantage of that errant thinking.

In the case of Downtown Fellowship Center, Jonathon wasn't sure what to do about it. He had a fairly well-developed plan in mind but he still needed a lot of confirmation before moving forward.

He felt that there would be no second chance. If the work muddled into mediocrity and became 'normal' or plodding, they would have failed. He, and the leaders and the people, had to get it right the first time, and quickly. And he had to identify the people who would take on responsibilities and follow through to their completion. There was no chance of one man doing all that had to be done. Even on his sunniest, most blue-sky days he understood that bringing Downtown Fellowship Center back to life was going to take the work of many hands.

He had spent hours in prayer seeking God's wisdom and boldly asking questions of the Lord. He became convinced that everything started so far, although important, paled in significance to what he believed had to be done next.

He and the board had a very solemn and troubling meeting. The subject of the meeting had the potential to backfire or even explode, ending his ministry before it really got going. Great wisdom and care would be required.

After an hour of soul-searching discussion with the men - where the old painful history was brought up and laid bare, where there was much silence, and not a few tears - the men bent to prayer.

Jonathon wrapped the meeting up with a final comment. "Men, I have great respect for you. You have demonstrated your love for the Lord and your willingness to adapt in order that the work assigned by God to the church can go forward in an age and a culture that none of us are really comfortable with.

"You have shed considerable light on a troubled past that I was only dimly aware of. But as troubling as it is, and as much as we wish it would just go away, that portion of the history of First Baptist remains with us. We deny history at our peril. That God calls His children to love one another is so ubiquitous in scripture that we don't even really have to look up particular verses. We all know the verses and the context. We simply can't get around them. There is no room for unresolved conflicts within the family of God. Nor can we hope that unresolved conflicts will heal themselves or just somehow go away over time or that God will overlook them. We cannot rely on the old adage that 'time heals all wounds'. That has never been true and it's not true today."

Jonathon paused to allow others to comment. The men remained silent so the pastor continued, "Psalm 51 gives clear guidance on this matter. David, a man of great heart but also a man of great appetites, had momentarily allowed his appetite for sex to overrule his appetite for God. He looked on Bathsheba and was smitten. David's sin was great in God's eyes and eventually in David's own eyes. In reading the Psalm, I seem to sense grave emotion and guilt almost overwhelming David. In his repentance, he confessed his sin and then entreated, '*Create in me a clean heart, Oh God.*'"

Jonathon paused again, looking over these men whom he had come to love and respect.

"That is the key to moving forward with God. Covering up or ignoring or denying sin may make us comfortable for a while. But on that great day when we realize we can't live any longer without victory in our lives, when we want old things to pass away and new things to come, a time of confession and forgiveness will be required of us. And if we truly want God to open the floodgates of blessing to Downtown Fellowship and to the people we intend to reach for Christ, nothing less will be required of us.

"We will need to talk much more about this."

Jonathon was intending to close the meeting at that point but Noble Pearson held out his hand like a traffic cop signaling to wait. He was so quiet when he spoke that the gathered men had to lean forward to hear him.

"A short while ago, God took me for a walk in the park. I thought I was taking the dog for a walk but the outing turned out to be about me, not the dog. It was the week after Jonathon's first Sunday with us and I was trying desperately to hang on to the old comfortable things, all the time knowing I wouldn't be able to." He went on to tell about his day of discovery in the park.

"Reflecting on that day, I was ashamed of myself. Is that really what my beliefs had come down to? I sat on that park bench and asked God for forgiveness, hoping that would be the end of the matter."

Noble reached in his pocket for a handkerchief. He blew his nose and wiped his eyes. The men waited patiently. The troubled man continued, "But God had a much larger issue that had to be sorted out. And I must admit He spared me no pain in the process. As kids played all around me and dogs barked, all manner of things were rattling around in my head including the unhappy past of First Baptist.

"It was right at that time that God used another scripture to break my heart. This one was also about David and Bathsheba, when Nathan confronted David and said, *'you are the man'*. You all know the story. I knew immediately what I had to do but so far I haven't done it. Let me correct that now."

He looked across the table at his fellow deacon. "Roland, some years ago, you and I had a rather strong disagreement. The details are forgotten and no longer important. But I said some unkind things to you at the time that in my heart of hearts I knew might not be true. You have been more than gracious over the years but you need to know that my heart has often been troubled when the memory of that incident came up. I have done nothing about my guilt except confess it to God. But He made it clear on that park bench that there is another that needs to hear my confession."

The men sat silently, looking at the table top. There was not a sound as Noble again wiped his eyes.

"Roland, you are one of the kindest and godliest men I have ever known. My harsh words to you were unfair and uncalled for. I have been greatly burdened by that incident without doing anything to correct it."

He stood up and reached his hand across the table. "Brother, will you forgive me for that foolishness, that sin?"

Roland didn't reach for the outstretched hand. Instead, he stood and walked around the table and wrapped Noble in his arms. "My old friend, all was forgiven and pushed aside years ago. But it's good to be obedient to the Lord so I appreciate your words. All is well."

After a short wait in the silence, Jonathon stood and prayed a benediction on the meeting, especially thanking God for working in each man's heart and asking for wisdom as they moved forward.

His final words were, "Men, what happens in this room stays in this room until the time comes to make it public." He then made the rounds shaking each man's hand and looking each man in the eye.

Jonathon went directly from that meeting to his office and closed the door. He looked up the phone number he wanted and dialed. On the third ring, a deep voice answered, "Orvis Tanner here."

The next afternoon, Orvis Tanner met Jonathon at the door and ushered him directly to his private study. He closed the door and they each found a seat. Orvis was not one for wasting time on small talk.

"I take it we are meeting in my home in the interests of privacy."

He caught Jonathon a bit off-guard. Jonathon had expected to be asked a question or two about the ministry and how matters were progressing at Downtown Fellowship. But he quickly adjusted to the abrupt question.

"I thought it best. I appreciate you agreeing on short notice."

Again, Jonathon had expected a question but the old man of God sat silently, studying the pastor.

Jonathon had resolved to be forthright in this discussion so he started right in. "Over the years, I've heard some rumblings of discontent regarding the downtown church. This is a large city with many churches. There's always something happening but since my family and I weren't involved, I put it down to either gossip or into the category of none of my business. Now, being on staff there, everything has become my business. Of course, you gave me clear warning in our initial discussion. I'm not forgetting that.

"I didn't go searching into the past or purposely dig up old issues but after a short time there, a couple of things came to my ears. I tried to dismiss them as gossip.

"Then I had a visit from a former member. We sometimes overwork the expression 'in love', but I found myself believing this man really did come in love to tell his story. As I listened to him, I heard nothing but sadness in his voice. His closing comments to me were, 'I don't see how you can hope to enjoy the full blessings of God to re-establish this ministry until the past is admitted and dealt with.'"

Jonathon continued, "Of course, with you giving me some insight into the issue plus my own small research and a few things the deacons have said, I already knew in my heart that the topic couldn't be avoided for long."

Again, Orvis's studied look gave Jonathon silent permission to continue.

"I've had to resolve some very uncomfortable issues in the secular, business world. It's amazing what businessmen, unions and workmen can find to fight over. And I've never had a Pollyanna approach to the church."

Jonathon was studying Mr. Tanner as he spoke, trying to sense his response to what had been said. Mr. Tanner was listening intently but was giving away no silent messages.

Finally, Jonathon said, "So I met with the deacons and we had a frank and open discussion. Some of the things that came out in that meeting are well beyond what I might have imagined or would have thought possible; things done by both laymen as well as pastors. Most of the issues in and of themselves were really quite petty. But when they were mixed with the egos of strong-minded men and women, they became much bigger.

"I've come to where I agree with my visitor. These things must be addressed in some way. As I said, I've taken up the matter with the board. That was a tense and tearful meeting that actually ended rather well, although we didn't find a ready solution.

"To help each of us in our thinking and praying, I purchased a number of copies of Rev. Mort Jenner's book. You will remember that he's had a successful reconciliation ministry in his own church. Each deacon was given a copy. I asked them to read it carefully so we could discuss the issues arising from it. There might be some helpful insights picked up from Rev. Jenner's experience. I have some thoughts but, before I express them, I would listen to your wisdom."

Orvis Tanner silently, intently, studied Jonathon for so long that Jonathon started to feel uncomfortable and wondered if the meeting was a mistake.

Finally, the old man of God took a deep breath and started to talk.

19

THE ORGAN REPAIR CREW ARRIVED ON SCHEDULE AND went right to work. Their first task was to remove the large old-fashioned bellows to give them space to work. Next, they unbolted and removed several choir pews and lifted the old carpet to get access to the floor board. Removing these boards exposed a large framed-in duct where a multitude of wooden rods lay. As Jonathon watched the crew, one of the workers explained that these wooden rods were known as trackers. The trackers were what transferred the organist's finger movements to the mechanical valves that allowed air into the pipes. There was a veritable multitude of rods and links.

In the small space behind the wall of large visible pipes were hundreds of smaller pipes, each responsible for generating one tone. These were connected to the keyboard through an eye-watering maze of trackers, air pipes and control linkages.

Each key on the keyboard controlled the action of one tracker rod. This control was further broken down through the use of the keyboard stops, each of which also connected to a tracker rod. Taken all together, the machine was a wonderful and very complex piece of nineteenth-century engineering and workmanship.

A few trackers were broken and more than a few were warped with age. Some of the metal corner linkages were seized up with rust. There were signs of old mouse nests and some sawdust where the mice had chewed on the wooden trackers. Jonathon thought to himself that there was not much to eat in there; that perhaps that was where the saying 'poor as a church mouse' came from.

Jonathon had never known how a pipe organ worked. He had never really questioned it and now he wondered why he hadn't been more curious. He was fascinated watching the men work. He didn't want to get in the way but he thought one question might not delay the work for too long.

"Could I ask you to give me a brief outline of your work and the timeframe? Then I promise to keep out of your way."

A large man who had introduced himself as Andy Coghill stepped over to Jonathon and pointed at the keyboard console and the floor ducting.

"After we strip all of this out and clean out the ducting we'll lay a cable in the duct and close it all up again so you can have your choir concert. Then we'll install a small computer in the back of the console. That computer gets connected to the keyboard through a series of switches after we refurbish the key workings. Then we'll connect the cable to the computer. The other end of the cable will be connected to a matching computer in the back room where the main body of pipes is located. We'll install an electronically-controlled switch and a new air valve on each pipe and connect them to the computer.

"The organ will look and sound exactly as it did before and no one needs to know there's a computer involved. The key action will require slightly less finger force because the organist doesn't have to overcome air pressure any more. The player will soon get used to that. So, working longer than usual hours, we should wrap it up within three weeks."

Jonathon looked again at the maze of workings and smiled at the foreman.

"I suspect you've given me the layman's version and that the real work is much more complicated. But I also suspect that what you've told me is about all I could understand. I would say, though, that even my unskilled eyes tell me that with all those warped wooden trackers and the rust, it's no wonder the instrument didn't play. Thanks again for being here. If there's anything at all that you need just let Sal know, down in the office."

With that, both men went back to their respective tasks.

As he had promised, Jonathon stayed away from the crew working on the organ. Andy Coghill made a couple of trips into the office to talk with Sal and the two of them worked through whatever issues had come up.

After supervising many construction projects, it required all of Jonathon's willpower to stay in his office while the men repaired the organ. But time was moving along and the great organ concert with Gladius Strung was drawing close; the choir date was even closer. Jonathon couldn't help being just a bit anxious about the timing.

As promised by Millard Crown, the Arts Support Board had plastered every bulletin board in town with concert notices.

One of the Arts Support board members had connections in the media. He had managed to arrange for free publicity on radio, in the newspaper, and a short blurb on local TV. At the start, these were restricted to the arts or public affairs programs. Finally, the newsrooms picked up the concert when someone realized who it was that was coming and understood that this visit from the great organ maestro was newsworthy. From that point on there was no stopping the promotional effort.

Sal put a call from Millard Crown through to Jonathon. "Mr. Crown, it's good to have you call. How are things going?"

Millard, never one for small talk, said, "I've just gotten off the phone with Gladius. We've had so much publicity I thought we should think about expanding the weekend. So, with the approval of the church, Gladius has agreed to do three concerts.

We'll have one Friday evening, a Saturday matinee, and a Saturday evening wind-up. Except it won't really be a wind-up. Gladius would also like to play for your Sunday morning service but that's not to be announced to the public. I told him I'd confirm after talking to you. What do you think? Will that work for the church? Do you need some time to think about it?"

Jonathon was having trouble taking it all in. He responded with a short, nervous laugh. "What's to think about? Of course, that will work for us. He can play every night of the week if he wants to."

Millard chuckled at hearing this. "I couldn't imagine you saying anything different. I'll confirm with Gladius. Then I'll see about getting the publicity amended to include the new times."

After only a brief pause he asked, "How's the organ rebuild coming along? I hear the crew found a bit of a mess under the floor."

Jonathon, wondering how this man seemed to know things that few others knew, said, "Well, that's true but they had the old mess cleaned up in less than a day. I've never seen such a tangle of wood and metal joints but it's all gone now. They promise they're on schedule and that Mr. Strung will have an organ to play. The floor is back in place and the choir pews installed so we're ready for the school choir visit."

Just at that time the church sanctuary was filled with a blast of organ sounds that spilled over into the office, the first sounds out of that instrument in twenty years. Sal raised her arms in the air and let out a whoop that Jonathon was sure his caller could hear. As the blast from the organ continued, he held the phone towards the open office door for a moment and then brought it back to his mouth. "Can you hear that? It sounds like the old girl is coming back to life."

"I can hear it. I'm sure Gladius will make sweeter sounds but that will do for a start. And, Jonathon, I'm a little ill at ease saying this given my own track record in recent years, but there are a lot of people praying for this concert and for a new beginning for First Baptist."

Jonathon didn't have a ready comment but finally he said, "Thank you for that encouragement. It's our prayer that God will glorify Himself and be glorified by the service of His people. We are also praying that lives will be changed for the better by everything His people do. Thank you again for your efforts on this matter."

Knowing the call was over, without further words, Jonathon gently laid down the phone.

In addition to the hard work of the Arts Support board, the church was doing its own promotions. The interns put a mailer together that was to be sent to all the high-rise buildings a week in advance of the organ concerts.

20

IT HAD BEEN A BUSY FEW WEEKS AND MUCH HAD BEEN accomplished. The interns had worked out better than anyone could have hoped for. The two students seemed to rise to each challenge, producing excellent work.

On Friday at noon, Jonathon called Sal on the intercom. "Sal, how would you like to order in some pizza for lunch? Find out what the young people like and order enough for the four of us. I'll pay for it when it arrives."

There was silence on the other end until a laughing, crackling voice asked, "Who is this? You must have a wrong number."

Jonathon chuckled before saying, "Just order the pizza."

When the four staff members were seated around the work table in the interns' office, Jonathon said, "Robert, how would you like to give thanks?"

Robert prayed and everyone reached for a piece of pizza. Jonathon said, "Don't start thinking that this will become standard practice. It's just a small way of saying that the three of you have done a good deal of quality work in the past few weeks. I'm pleased with your progress."

Sal swallowed her first bite before crackling out, "It has been a busy time. But kind of fun, too. Lots of new things and a few learning curves. Good stuff."

The two interns, their mouths full, just nodded.

As they were cleaning up the debris from the pizza lunch, the filtered but still audible blare of air horns sounded from the rear parking lot. Jonathon said, "I'll bet that's the choir. I understand they travel in two Greyhound buses. And I'm told they have a lot of work to do setting up for tomorrow's concert. Robert, Darla, why don't you go and welcome them. Take the afternoon and see if you can help in some way. After they're settled, I'd like to meet Virginia, the lady who organized all this so I can thank her personally."

As predicted, the work of setting up for the choir took several hours. The organ crew kept out of the way by concentrating their work in the back room.

The Classical School of Music Choir Concert was a huge success. Every available seat in the building was filled. Most of the visitors seemed to be from the area churches but, judging from the numbers of folks Jonathon saw walking from the high-rise buildings, he figured the mailouts had found an audience who were prepared to take advantage of a free concert. A number of young couples brought their children along. Watching this, Jonathon visualized the same thing happening for worship services and Sunday school.

The thought crossed his mind that perhaps the concert mailouts - together with the Gladius Strung mailouts - would ease the acceptance of the invitations that would be going out the following weeks.

Even in the few hours the choir was there, Robert and Virginia seemed to find several opportunities to spend time together.

Early on the morning following the concert, the equipment was loaded on the buses and the choir members were assembled, ready to climb aboard.

Jonathon called Robert over and quietly said, "I'd like it if you would inquire if Virginia could put Downtown Fellowship Center on the school's tour for next year."

He grinned a bit at Robert. "That will give you one more opportunity to talk with her."

Robert started walking away, smiling to himself.

Within a few minutes, accompanied again by the blast of air horns and the smiling, waving faces in the windows, the school was off to their next venue.

WITH THE INTERNS WORKING ON THEIR NEW ASSIGNMENTS, Sal had some additional free time. Jonathon called her into his office and closed the door. She took a seat and laid a yellow notepad on her knee, holding her pen expectantly. Jonathon smiled at her. "Good anticipation. And here, just a few weeks ago, you were concerned about not having enough to do."

"I don't remember anything of the sort. You must have made that up." Sal's crackling voice was even more distorted, talking through her grin.

Jonathon leaned forward in his swivel chair and looked intently at Sal. "This is a bit awkward, Sal, and what we are going to talk about is not for public consumption. I will also say that this issue could backfire on us so we need to be exceptionally careful and certainly private. At least for now.

"Most of the congregation is aware of our past difficulties. The leadership is convinced that we must address those difficulties. But the last thing we want to do is bring hurtful issues forward and renew them. We must move most carefully.

"What I would like you to do is choose two couples from the congregation. People whom you trust totally and who have the respect of the congregation; people who have been here for some years. It's important that they be sensitive and graceful, able to keep a confidence until it's time to share with the wider audience.

"I want them to go over all the old attendance and membership records and make a list. I think we should go back far enough to identify anyone who might still be alive. Do the same for the pastors who have served here. You work with these couples as your time allows. And don't let the interns anywhere near this.

"If one of the people you choose has good typing skills and some computer savvy, that would be a bonus. You can set them up with that unused laptop.

"Have Watson clean out a nice room for them. They'll need a good table and comfortable chairs. A little distance from this office would be good. Make sure there's a lock on the door. Nothing is to be taken from that room. They are to do all the work in that room and speak to absolutely no one until the time is right.

"We'll need names and addresses only. I don't anticipate making phone calls. There are several Internet programs for tracking people. The researchers may want to use these to get current information. You could help on that part if they get bogged down on the Net.

"I expect this will take some time but, when it's complete, I would like you to make a Word document with the information. Do it in such a way that we can do mail merge for both letters and envelopes. We'll develop the letter a bit later. Save the document and all the research behind a solid password."

Sal looked up from her notepad. There were tears in her eyes. Her voice crackled more that it usually did. "May I assume that it's your hope to address some old issues?"

"Not some, Sal. All of them. Not by trying to sort them out; no one could possibly do that. But by confession, forgiveness and grace. Some of the hurts will be very deep and memories are long. Probably not everyone will be open to our overture but at least we will have tried."

Sal dug a tissue out of her sleeve. Speaking haltingly, she said, "This should have been done years ago. When the issues were still small and manageable. What's interesting, Jonathon, is that First Baptist has never faced any great challenges to doctrine, our position on Scripture, arguments about who Jesus was - or is - or any of the big things that have so plagued other ministries. Here, it was all little things. Wagging tongues mostly. Gossip, opinions, likes and dislikes. It was all so petty and so needless but oh, so harmful. I pray God will bless this effort. So many people were hurt. There was so much pride and stubbornness. Some believed they alone had a corner on the truth. Some believed theirs was the only opinion that mattered. There were times I was ashamed to be a part of this fellowship."

Sal found another dry tissue and gave her nose a most unlady-like blow. "You know what the really sad thing is, Jonathon? Most of what went on was the work of just a very small handful of people. The good news is that none of those people are with us anymore. We've had peace since they moved along although the church body never really recovered."

Jonathon listened and nodded as Sal spoke. When she was finished, he said, "Doctrinally, Sal, we all know that giving our hearts to the Lord doesn't bring instant change to every part of our thinking and actions. Sanctification is a lifelong process. I expect we all have weaknesses. I certainly know that I have.

"As for the leadership, they're praying that the people we contact will receive an overture from the church graciously and that the response will allow us to turn the page; to move forward in confidence. We're praying that this matter can be closed and never mentioned again. But as I said earlier, this could backfire so let's keep it confidential until we're totally prepared."

22

IF THE CHOIR CONCERT WAS A SUCCESS, THE ORGAN concerts with Gladius Strung were nothing short of sensational. The century-old organ had never sounded better and Mr. Strung acted as if he was truly happy to be back on tour, specifically at Downtown Fellowship Center. He was not only one of the world's great organists, he was also a natural showman.

The building was packed; every seat taken for every concert. The doors were left open so those gathered on the front stairs could listen even though they couldn't get in. Every window that would open was swung wide. The organist played to one standing ovation after another.

Jonathon chuckled to himself as he viewed the Saturday evening audience. There were a goodly number of the city's 'high society' there; people from the business, political and arts communities decked out in their expensive finery including one couple in evening attire.

In the previous generation, every person attending would have worn their best. But most of the concert audience wore casual clothing. Several couples wore shorts and T-shirts.

Jonathon wondered if this mix was the true meaning of

eclectic. Looking over the audience he said to himself, 'This is our constituency. This is who we must work with. The couple in evening attire and the folks in shorts have completely different world views. How we are going to minister to them all is beyond me at this point.'

The encore ovations on Saturday night threatened to have the organist playing until dawn. Finally, he stood and stepped to the side of the great instrument and took a long bow. He then walked to the choir entry door, gave a quick wave and a smile, and disappeared. The packed house was buzzing with excited talk.

A small group of those most involved with the concert were invited to a private dinner at the end of the evening. The church was represented by Jonathon and Janet plus Sal and the two interns. Mr. Strung, of course, was the guest of honor. Mr. and Mrs. Crown acted as hosts, welcoming people and introducing their associates from the Arts Committee. Murphy McGuire was there as well.

The manager of Classic Organs had made a special trip to hear the refurbished organ being played by the maestro. He shook the organist's hand. "Ah, Gladius, I haven't had the great pleasure of your presence or your masterful playing for far too long. What a privilege it is to be in your company again. I couldn't possibly pass up this majestic opportunity. I am convinced the angels have been smiling for the past couple of hours as you use your God-given gifts to bring glory to His name."

Gladius Strung smiled modestly and said, "It's good to see you again, Mr. McGuire."

The dinner and the visiting seemed destined to go on until the early hours of the morning. Jonathon glanced at his watch and then at Janet. Rising from their seats, Jonathon spoke to the group, "Our thanks seem inadequate for all that has been accomplished by those gathered here and by those others who worked so hard to put this week together. No small thanks must go to the Classic Organs repair crew. In three weeks of long days, they completed work that would normally be scheduled for twice that time.

"Thank you all again. We must take our leave now. Good evening, everyone, and God bless."

23

ON SUNDAY MORNING AS PEOPLE STARTED ARRIVING FOR service, it became clear from the number of visitors that the word had leaked out. While a portion of the congregation was amazed when Mr. Strung arrived unannounced, most of the others seemed to have heard of his plans to play for the service. It was a glorious, sunny summer morning. The ushers blocked the doors open, then went through the sanctuary and opened every possible window. Walking past Jonathon after doing this, Rudy Goetz grinned and said, "It's time we started sharing with the world."

Rising to the platform, Jonathon laughed out loud as he looked around the packed sanctuary and addressed those in attendance. "This was perhaps the most poorly kept secret in town judging by the numbers of filled seats. I'm not at all sure how you heard about Mr. Strung being here this morning but you're all most welcome. We long for the day when this old building will be filled like this for every service."

Jonathon introduced the organist who was still seated in the front pew. "Although Mr. Strung has played three marvelous concerts over the past two days, he is not here this morning for a concert. He's here to play for the worship service and to join in worship himself."

Jonathon gestured towards the man seated beside Mr. Strung. "For many years, Mr. Tom Bradshaw has been the music leader at Downtown Fellowship. Tom, please come and lead us in worship this morning."

Tom took his place behind the big oak pulpit. Addressing the congregation, he said, "Mrs. Hanna Turnbull has been the long-time pianist and organist at First Baptist and, later, at Downtown Fellowship Center. Please welcome her to this wonderfully rebuilt instrument for the first couple of hymns."

Hanna, nearly overcome with emotion, climbed the stairs to the platform and took her seat at the organ console. She bowed her head for a brief prayer and then struck the first chords. Although this opportunity was prearranged and she had practiced on the rebuilt organ in the empty hall, none of that compared to playing before over one thousand people and in front of the great maestro. But play she did in the newer upbeat style that she and Jonathon had been working on. The voices raised in song nearly overcame her.

After the second hymn, she rose and gestured to Mr. Strung. The man stood from his seat and led the congregation in thunderous applause in a tribute to Hanna. He then took his place at the organ. Jonathon and the deacon board had agreed that, for just this one Sunday, the song service would be extended and the preaching kept to a minimum.

When the memorable worship service came to a close and the applause ended, Jonathon stood and walked to the pulpit. It seemed for a while like he would never speak as he looked over the nearly full hall.

Finally, he opened his Bible to Psalm 147. "I can do no better this morning than agree with the Psalmist when he writes: *'Praise the Lord, for it is good to sing praises to our God.'*" He read slowly from that point right to the end of Psalm 150. *'Let everything that has breath praise the Lord. Praise the Lord.'*

After a short encouragement to know, worship, and live for God through Jesus, he said, "Amen. We go into the world now, to our homes, to our jobs, or to fellowship with each other. Take this glorious music and the life-giving truths of Scripture with you. Go with God in your hearts and with His praises on your lips."

At home later that day, Jonathon and Janet were resting on their lounge chairs in the sunny back yard.

Janet looked over at him. "Quite a weekend, wouldn't you say?"

Jonathon took a moment and then smiled at her. "Quite a weekend and quite a month. I don't know as we'll ever see another quite like it. Sometimes I think everything has gone so well that it just can't continue. I know that sounds like a lack of faith but there it is anyway."

Janet said, "Nothing in this world ever runs completely smoothly. I expect the work to face some challenges. When they come, we'll all have to be strong in the Lord."

24

THE FIRST INVITATION MAILOUTS WENT TO FOUR apartment buildings. There was no response the first week. The plan was to target the same building for four weeks and then reduce the invitations to those tenants to once per month and target another group of buildings for weekly mailouts.

After the second mailout, two recipients dialed the church number. The first caller was an elderly man who had lost his wife a few months before. He was dreadfully lonely and mostly wanted to talk. Jonathon invited him to meet for coffee and a visit but was told "perhaps another time."

"Alright," responded Jonathon. "Let's just leave it with a phone conversation for now. Tell me about yourself and what happened with your wife. I have some time so let's talk."

The second caller was a young mom with two preschoolers. She, too, just wanted to talk on the phone, saying that maybe they would meet later. "That's fine," Jonathan assured her. "Tell me your situation and how we can help. And perhaps tell me just your first name to make conversation easier."

There was an uncomfortable few moments of silence before the quiet voice said, "I'm Joanie. My situation isn't really complicated, just difficult. My husband, Hal, is a good and loving husband and father. We have a good marriage even if it has more than its share of stresses. He's a policeman. I'm a nurse. We both work twelve-hour shifts. We come home so tired it's sometimes difficult to stay awake for a meal. Our kids spend far too much time being cared for by strangers who charge us a fortune. Hal and I are so often on opposite shifts it seems like we spend almost no time together. We sometimes go a week without sitting down for a family dinner.

"It's hard to keep a marriage going under those circumstances. Sometimes, when Hal is at work and after I put the kids to bed in the evening, I find myself sitting alone, so lonely I could scream. I usually settle for weeping.

"The crazy part of all this is that, even with two good jobs, we aren't getting ahead financially. The cost of living in the city seems to suck up every dollar we can bring home. Daycare for the kids eats up almost half my salary. We could never dream of buying a house in a subdivision. Of course, I keep the kids at home when I'm off work but I still have to pay the daycare or lose the spots. And then the kids seem to be sick half the time. Nothing serious, just never-ending problems with sniffles and flu. I think they bring the sniffles home from the daycare center but what can I possibly do about that? Some days I'm at my wits end."

When Jonathon inquired about their church experience, Joanie answered, "We were both raised in the church but haven't attended since our teen years."

After another uncomfortable silence that Jonathon had trouble waiting through, Joanie said, "I'm not even sure why I called. I know you can't help with our situation. But I appreciate you listening."

Jonathon knew he had to say something. He couldn't let this young mom feel that her call was wasted.

"Joanie, what one thing would help you the most?"

Joanie was silent for a while and then she said, "A better situation for the kids until Hal and I figure out our work situations.

But it's really difficult. Daycare spaces are nearly impossible to get and every facility has a waiting list. I suppose we should be grateful for what we have even with the frequent sniffles."

Jonathon sensed it was time to bring the conversation to a close. Joanie had stated her case and there really wasn't much more to say. "Joanie, I'd like you to give me a bit of time to think on this and to talk to some people. Will you either give me your phone number or promise me that you'll call back in a few days?"

Again there was a pause. "I'll call back after my next round of night shifts. That's about one week from now. Thank you for listening to me. I didn't mean to bore you with my troubles."

"I'm not the least bit bored, Joanie. But I don't have a ready answer either. I'll make some inquiries and look forward to your call. In the meantime, do you mind if we pray together right now?"

"Oh! Well, I guess that would be alright."

Jonathon kept his prayer short and totally focused on Joanie and Hal's needs, thanking God for His love and mercy. When the call ended, Jonathon leaned back in his chair. "Well, Lord, I don't think I anticipated the problems that Joanie and Hal are facing. And I don't think we're ready to open a daycare facility. Will You open my mind and give me Your wisdom? Thank You."

The continuing mailouts resulted in several phone calls. A couple of the callers were angry at God, the church, and perhaps life in general. But most expressed a wide variety of problems. Jonathon's head was spinning as he listened to the issues people were dealing with behind their closed doors.

There were no visitors at Sunday services although several former members attended, perhaps out of curiosity or to see what this new preacher was all about. Jonathon had been hoping for an attendance bounce following the two concerts but so far there was no sign of this.

THREE WEEKS AFTER THE MAILOUTS STARTED, JONATHON'S office intercom buzzed. "Line two please, Pastor. I told the caller you were busy but he's most insistent."

Jonathon answered, "Got it.

"Jonathon McCann here. Who am I speaking with please?"

"Mr. McCann, this is Buzz Grappler. We're live on the Can You Believe This? afternoon show on talk radio WKS. My radio audience has a couple of questions for you."

The well-trained professional radio voice was breathless and urgent.

Jonathon hesitated, trying to place the name but nothing came to him. "I apologize, sir. I don't recognize the name. Tell me again who you are and what I can do for you."

The voice took on even more urgency and perhaps a bit of frustration as if it was impossible that anyone with a working brain wouldn't recognize the name. The rapid-fire words jammed together in Jonathon's ears and became almost unintelligible.

"Buzz Grappler!" he said again. "We're live on the radio, Mr. McCann; the afternoon Can You Believe This Show? on WKS.

My listeners would like me to ask you a couple of questions about what's going on over at your church."

It sounded like the caller was going to charge straight ahead with his questions but when he paused to take a breath Jonathon jumped in. "Again, I'm sorry, sir. I never listen to the radio. I don't recognize your name or that of the station. Hang on a moment please."

Jonathon purposely left the line open while he punched the intercom. "Sal, I'm not sure if someone's pulling my leg here or not. Do you happen to know if there's a radio station in the city called WKS?"

"I never listen to it but, yes," came the crackly-voiced answer. "I think it's mostly a call-in station. You know, housewives still in their housecoats in the middle of the afternoon with curlers in their hair and nothing else to do, complaining about life in general and city workers in particular."

Jonathon cringed. "Thanks, Sal. That's probably a little more information than I really needed."

He punched the intercom off and spoke to the man on the phone, "I'm hoping you didn't hear all of that," knowing full well that he had.

"Well, Mr. McCann, I did hear it and so did my listeners. It was great, although I doubt if that's a truthful description of my audience. And it's the truth we're all about here on Can You Believe This? Getting at the no-holds-barred truth.

"I think I would like Sal. Everyone needs a secretary who will lay things out plainly for them. But my questions are for you, Mr. McCann. Or should I call you Pastor or Reverend or some other title?"

"Call me Jonathon. That will do just fine. But perhaps you can tell me how you managed to single me out for a call, still making the assumption that this is not a prank by someone having fun at my expense. I'm hardly what you might consider someone in the public interest category."

The announcer chuckled a bit. "You might not consider

yourself that way, Jonathon, but you and your church have become newsworthy over the past few weeks, what with all the advertising and promotion you've been doing and with the crowds filing in to your concerts."

"Well, Buzz, I have to correct you on at least one thing right away lest you and your listeners come to the wrong conclusion. It's not my church. It's not my advertising. They're not my concerts. I'm the appointed leader of a small group of Christians. Together, those men and women make up the Downtown Fellowship Center at Third and Main. In my position as interim pastor, I answer to those people.

"They have given me some leeway on my actions but it's still not my church, or theirs either if we think rightly about it. The church belongs to God. The church is people, Buzz, not buildings or organizations."

The office door burst open and Sal charged in with a small portable radio blaring out the WKS talk show, repeating Jonathon's words a couple of seconds after he first spoke them. She smiled as she held the radio closer to Jonathon. A feedback circuit was immediately set up from Sal's radio through Jonathon's phone to the radio station, out to the world again, and back to the listeners' radios with an additional slight delay. The feedback became a high-decibel screeching, squawking noise. Jonathon was forced to pull the phone from his ear.

He waved Sal away and, after a moment, said, "I apologize, Buzz. That was Sal. She found your program on the portable radio and came to show me. I hope that didn't blow any circuits at the station."

Buzz laughed for the first time. "Well, I think the circuits are alright but I don't know about my listeners' ears, or mine either for that matter. Again, I think I would like Sal. But perhaps I would like her better if she were to stay at her desk for now."

Jonathon grasped the opportunity to speak again. "Well, anyway, I guess that puts to rest my wondering if you are who you said you are. But what I was going to say before that interruption, Buzz, is that the church is made up of people who love and trust Jesus Christ. I am just one of those people. I happen to have the privilege of caring for a small part of God's church but that does not make me special. It just means that, for now, I have this job to do."

"That's all well and good, Jonathon, and perhaps we can discuss that at another time. But right now my listeners want to know by what right you're gathering the names and addresses of residents living in your area, and what your purpose is in sending them weekly mailouts. Is this not an invasion of privacy and an unwelcome intrusion into peoples' lives?"

Jonathon wasn't about to fall for a baited question. "As I'm sure you know, Buzz, names and addresses and phone numbers are public information, easily accessible in the phone book, on the Internet, or any number of other sources. So that can't possibly be an invasion of privacy. But even with that all being true, we are not gathering names and addresses. Or phone numbers either. We use the mail-drop program the post office offers on their bulk mailing service. One drop to each residence. No names or addresses involved. If your listeners would look at the mailout they received, they will see there is no name or address anywhere on the card."

Buzz seemed to talk a bit louder with every question. "But how do folks know that you're not gathering their personal information? And even if you're not, the mailouts are still an intrusion into their lives."

"Settle down, Buzz. We have no reason to gather personal information nor do we have the time or staff to do that. As to being an intrusion into folks' lives, it's no more intrusive than the advertising on the side of your cereal box. You can read the cereal box or ignore it, by your own choice. No one can force you to read it.

"You and I and every one of your listeners are bombarded all day long every day with what could be considered intrusions into our privacy. It's called advertising, Buzz. I'm sure you know a bit about that. Your station would go off the air and you would be out of a job without advertising.

"If someone is interested in what our mailouts have to say, they'll let us know one way or another. Our contact information is clearly shown. The rest of the folks simply throw the card away along with all the other mailouts they receive. An offer is made; some explore it further, some do not. No harm done. No intrusion of privacy."

Buzz spoke up, "But Jonathon. My listeners have come to the fearful conclusion that you will be phoning or knocking on their doors asking for donations or that you will be selling your mailing lists."

Jonathon answered with a loud chuckle.

"Buzz, Buzz, Buzz. I'm having trouble believing that. For what you say to be true you would have to have a lot of listeners in the high-rise residences around Third and Main downtown. That's the only place we've advertised. So, if we're going to be honest with each other and I really think that would be the best approach, you should probably go ahead and admit that it's you who has these thoughts. And with that being true we would logically have to wonder where these thoughts come from. Perhaps you live in one of the high-rises and saw an opportunity to fill some air time."

"Where I live is not the issue, Jonathon. The issue is the gathering and misuse of personal information."

"Asked and answered, Buzz. I'm busy even if you're not, so let's move on. Have you ever heard of a church calling random folks asking for donations or doing anything remotely like that? I haven't. A political party, a charity, school kids selling cookies; alright. But I've never known of a church seeking funding from the public and neither have you. As to selling mailing lists, since we have no mailing lists that would be pretty much impossible. So, what really is your point, Buzz?"

"My point would be, in this secular world with the church having become pretty much redundant, all this noise and advertising seems a desperate, almost frantic, last gasp effort to revive something that should probably be allowed to die. And, of course, there's always money involved.

"You have to get the money from somewhere to do all this advertising and to run that big church. My guess is that, if you haven't asked for money yet in your mailouts, you soon will.

"How about coming clean for the listeners, Jonathon, and telling us where the money comes from, where it goes, and what you're trying to accomplish. And how much you get out of all this."

Buzz took on an almost conspiratorial voice. "I looked you up, Jonathon. You're a wealthy man. Doesn't seem right that you should ask poor folks to give their hard-earned money to run your church while you're getting wealthier."

The announcer seemed to be able to keep talking while he took a deep breath. "And speaking of getting wealthier, Jonathon, you have recently advertised two free concerts. By all reports your building was bursting at the seams, every seat filled. The biggest concert crowds this town has seen for years except for rock concerts and country music stars. But the concerts weren't really free, were they, Jonathon? Were the concert-goers not asked for money once they were inside the building, and did you not have collection boxes placed all around the room? That's pretty deceptive, Pastor. I've heard complaints about it. So tell us, Jonathon, why the deception and how much cash did the church take in during those concerts?"

Buzz finally gave Jonathon the opportunity to answer.

"I wonder, Buzz, if you're really a cynic or is that just the practiced front you use on air to try to stir up some dust. But in any case, here's the answer to your questions, going in no particular order.

"First, I'm hardly what anyone would call wealthy. I'm a partner in a building construction company. It's true that the business has done well the past few years. That's after many years of hard work and struggle, by the way. But neither my partner nor I are anywhere close to wealthy.

"Secondly, I take not one cent from the church. I fill a volunteer position. There is no income involved nor will there ever be. My income comes from the construction business.

"Now let's talk about the concerts. There was no deception of any nature. It was clearly stated on all the advertising that there would be a free-will offering opportunity. There was not one word said about money at any of the concerts. Nor was there any pressure. No one was asked to give. People gave in support of the artists or they didn't. It was a purely private decision. There was no one watching what people gave."

Buzz jumped in. "That's not true Jonathon. There was a man stationed at every collection box. Is that not intimidation?"

Jonathon answered the challenge. "To know all those details, Buzz, you obviously had to have been there. I hope you enjoyed the evenings' musical offerings. Now, let's get down to it. You will have to admit, Buzz, that this is not a totally pure and trustworthy world. The doors were opened to the entire community with no restrictions so we felt that a note of caution would be wise. The men watching the boxes were there strictly for security. It's unfortunate that security is needed at a music concert in a church but that's the world we live in.

"As for the income to the church, that was zero. We didn't even charge for the cost of keeping the lights on. Both the choir and Gladius Strung have always covered their travel and living costs with free-will offerings. One-hundred percent of all the money received went to the touring groups.

"Finally, Buzz, God's people - Christians, in other words - are instructed in the Scriptures to give of their abundance and to give joyfully. That giving by our people here at Third and Main pays the bills, keeps the lights on, and the furnace working in our century-old building. It also pays for the advertising. No outside money is asked for or received. Never has been. We're not about money, Buzz. We will never under any circumstances ask for donations from the public, in our advertising or anywhere else.

Jonathon was pleased when Buzz allowed him to continue.

"As to what we're trying to accomplish, I'm glad you asked. Our goal is to tell a cynical, hurting and wounded world that the answers to their hurts and wounds in life are found in Jesus Christ. We offer no human solutions beyond listening ears and compassionate hearts. I can't fix anyone's hurts or forgive their sins but I can tell them about the One who can do those things. That's why we're here and that's what the Christian church has done for two thousand years now.

"The Christian mandate has never changed, Buzz. It is, and always has been, to tell the world that God loves them. That's why we advertise. That's why we meet as a group of believers on Sunday mornings. And that's why we invite folks to join us. Why would you have a problem with that, Buzz?"

The question was followed by a few moments of uncomfortable dead air. Silence is the enemy of talk radio but the announcer was silent. Finally, a defiant Buzz said, "I don't know how much of that I or my listeners will believe, Jonathon, but now I need to do one of those commercials you talked about. We'll talk again." The station went to commercial.

THE EVENTS AT DOWNTOWN FELLOWSHIP WERE MOVING along well. Perhaps too well to remain unchallenged. Nothing in this world ever seemed to move ahead without difficulty, raising its ugly head from one direction or another. Satan, that great enemy of the church and of the human soul, was unlikely to sit still while a piece of his earthly kingdom was being challenged. And when the first major challenge presented itself, it arose from an entirely unexpected direction.

Monday morning came and Jonathon was alone in the church office when his cell phone vibrated in his pocket. He answered and heard the strained voice of Terry, his business partner. There were no preliminary comments or greetings. His troubled voice simply said, "We have to meet. Can you get away now?"

The urgency of the question startled Jonathon. "Sure, I can come right over. What's up?"

"Let's leave it until you get here."

"Give me forty-five minutes."

Both men hung up without further comment.

Arriving at the construction company office, Jonathon

poured himself a cup of coffee in the small lunchroom. He took a seat in the visitor's chair at his partner's desk. "What's up, Terry, and how bad is it?"

"It couldn't be much worse. Take a quick read." He slid a multi-page document across the desk and waited while Jonathon picked it up and settled back in his chair.

Jonathon did a quick scan of the first two pages. Adjusting himself in the chair and setting his coffee cup down on the desk, he did a more detailed reading, his brow furrowing as he absorbed the document. Finally, he lifted his eyes to his partner.

"Bankrupt? Global is a big company. We've done several of their projects. How can they be bankrupt?"

Terry said, "I've managed to dig out a few details but it's all still new and vague. The lawyers aren't saying much. But the broad stroke seems to be that one of Global's biggest developments - a hotel and golf course project clear across the country from here - has folded. They guessed the market wrong. They've taken losses. The dollar numbers on those losses are shockingly large. The situation is threatening to leave a trail of misery across all the Global projects.

"The major creditor bank on the problem project filed legal documents on Friday afternoon and the whole thing became public. Global immediately filed for bankruptcy as if they were already prepared for that need. Not much news leaked out over the weekend but this morning it's all coming down. Global is trying to hold them off but it doesn't look hopeful. I'm guessing it was a busy weekend for the bankers and lawyers. The result is that fax you're holding."

Jonathon shook his head. "Crazy. It's just crazy. We've worked for Global for years, always believing they were a strong development and management corporation. I couldn't imagine they carried a debt load like this document shows. It's like they've never really been solvent, just leaping from one project to another. Like a Ponzi scheme."

The two men were silent for some time, thinking their own thoughts.

Jonathon finally asked the critical question, "Is Global current on our billings?"

Proctor-McCann was the lead contractor on a medium-sized shopping center for Global Enterprises. The monthly supplies and subcontractor billings were significant. Any stoppage of cash flow from Global would be felt immediately. The size of the project was at the top end of Proctor-McCann's comfort zone. With the project nearing completion, the tenants were installing their leasehold improvements and a projected opening date had already been announced. The timing of Global's problems could hardly be worse.

Terry passed another printout across the desk. "This is our last month's statement. Interestingly enough, Global's certified check arrived by courier on Friday. They've never used a courier or certified checks before so that raised some questions for me. But I never would have guessed the rest of it. The good news is that we're covered for everything to the end of last month. Thank God for that. Global obviously knew what was coming and was trying to salvage something out of the mess. Whether Global was salvaging the shopping center or its reputation with us, I don't know but I'm very thankful for that check.

"But you know how rumors fly. I've already had several calls this morning from sub-trades nervous about getting paid. A couple of the calls were from trades on our other projects. Projects that have nothing to do with Global.

"To hold our own business together, we have days at the most. Maybe only hours. Any delay in finding a solution and the shopping center project will collapse. That would have an immediate impact on everyone involved; us as the general contractor most of all. We're not in financial difficulty on any of our projects but that won't change anything when the dominoes fall. People will believe what they believe regardless of what we try to tell them."

Both men sat silently. Jonathon finally stood and went to the coffee room. He returned with the full pot as if he planned on staying a while.

He took a long look at Terry and sensed the tension in the other man. After a short pause, he asked, "We have three other projects under way. Involving them would lead to disaster. What are our options?"

Terry said, "We only have a couple. It's really early in the game but I made some calls while you were driving here. I talked with Global's lawyer. I wondered if the problem was temporary and if perhaps they could pull it together. He said that wasn't going to happen. Clearly, hoping for a solution from Global is not a good option."

Jonathon asked, "What do we want to happen? What's best for Proctor-McCann?"

When Terry offered no immediate answer, Jonathon said, "Here's what I think we should do. File a builder's lien immediately. Call Joe at the job site and have him shut the project down. Then, with our own funds and perhaps a bit from our bank, bring all the trades and suppliers up to date including their lean holdbacks. That protects our other projects and prevents cluttering up the Global project with dozens of liens. Eventually, we will be paid on the Global project."

Terry looked at Jonathon as if seeing him in a new light. He picked up his phone and pressed the speed dial for the company lawyer. After a short talk, he hung up and turned back to Jonathon. "He'll have the lien filed in the next few minutes." He smiled for the first time since Jonathon walked into the office. "I've never heard you thinking that aggressively before."

Jonathon nodded. "No one has ever threatened the company before."

Terry just nodded. He then said to Jonathon, "We'll leave it at that for now. I'm sure this will move along quickly so don't turn your phone off. I think I need to stick close to the office but, if you can spare some more time, may I suggest you make a tour of the other projects. Put in an appearance. Press some flesh. Assure the crews and the trades that we'll watch out for everyone. I can't think of anything you could do that would be more valuable at this time."

DARLA WRAPPED UP HER MEETINGS WITH THE CITY officials. She came away with a letter giving approval to use the gymnasium for public gatherings. The only condition was that the exit lights had to be changed to meet the current code. She still had the plumbing and kitchen people to see.

Robert gathered considerable information from the city about lunch programs for the homeless and had begun making the rounds of the other lunch providers. There was still much to learn. He hadn't even touched on the funding issues yet. The various levels of government each offered funding programs that could be accessed. The current lunch program at Downtown Fellowship Center was a low-budget affair. They received a small city grant to cover just the cost of food. All the staff were volunteers.

Going to the public for donations was the option used by most helping charities. It was clear the church would never sanction that approach in their name as that choice would require the setting up of a separate charity. Figuring it all out and keeping the church's name out of it would be a challenge.

Jonathon called the interns and Sal into his office to hear the report on their findings so far. He listened and then said,

"Robert, I'm going to ask you to change direction just a bit for one day only. You've seen the three homeless men who come to services faithfully. I've arranged for them to meet you here right after lunch tomorrow. Their names are Carl, Samuel and Peter. Carl is the youngest. I believe he has some special needs but I don't know what they are. I suspect PTSD but I know very little about that condition.

"Sal is going to give you some money from petty cash and a key to the outside gymnasium door. I want you to walk these men over to the Salvation Army store and let them pick out some fresh clothing; everything, underwear to jackets. Get a couple of outfits for each. You pay for it, get a receipt for Sal's records, and then bring the men back here. Let them enjoy a hot shower in the gym and dress in their new duds. Try to get them to discard the old clothing. Be sure to let them understand that they must clean up the shower room when they're done. Alright so far?"

When Robert nodded, Jonathon continued, "Sal went shopping. She purchased soap, shampoo, shaving gear, and towels. She also found some small carry pouches with a toothbrush, toothpaste, a comb, some Band-Aids, hand sanitizer and maybe a couple of other items. They appear to be put together for camping or hiking. The men are welcome to take one each. It's all up in the men's shower room in the gym."

Robert looked a bit out of his element but he nodded agreement again.

Jonathon went on, "When they finish with that, I'd like you to spend some time just visiting with them. Take them for coffee if you wish. See what you can find out about each one but be very sensitive to their privacy and respect their pride.

"Specifically, I'd like to know if Carl has a health or emotional need that we might find some help for. And Darla, you keep your trades people away while the men are there and stay away yourself."

Darla nodded. "Understood."

The interns left and Jonathon turned to Sal. "How are our name researchers coming along? Are we going to end up with a workable list of names?"

Sal's usual chuckling, pleasant manner was nowhere in sight. She looked as serious as Jonathon had ever seen her.

"We've given those two couples a difficult and emotional task. They've poured over all the old records and made a long list of names. It's brought back a lot of memories. Many happy memories but oh, so many sad ones. So many recollections. So many old friends passed on to glory. So many others hurting and estranged from the fellowship.

"I went to see how they were doing yesterday and found the two men with serious, sad faces and the two women weeping as they poured over old name lists. I really believe this had to be done, Pastor, and I'm confident you've grasped the mind of God on the matter. But watching these people work at it, I have so wished there had been an easier way."

Jonathon listened intently as Sal spoke, feeling the pain of hurtful things being brought back to life.

Finally, he asked, "Are they going to be able to finish or is it overwhelming them?"

"They're almost done. A couple more hours this afternoon should do it. There are still some addresses to find. I'll help them with that as much as I can, although they're doing pretty well with the Internet searches themselves. Then there'll just be the final typing of the mailing list. I'll handle that. They'll be alright but a visit from you might perk them up. Especially if you were carrying some pastries to go along with their coffee."

"Thanks for your help on this, Sal. I know it's been difficult for you, too," answered Jonathon, laying a ten-dollar bill on the desk. "If you'd pick out something gooey and unhealthy from that bakery across the street and bring it here, I'll go up later and help them eat it."

After Jonathon visited with the two couples, sharing their

coffee, tea and baked treats, he closed the door to his study and went back to sermon preparation.

In the past few weeks, there had been a slow but growing response to the mailers. Most of the responses were by telephone. Jonathon continued to be astounded at the range of life's problems expressed by the callers. Slowly, together with the help of the deacons and some trusted church members, he was able to assist some of the callers including Joanie, the nurse who was the second to call. Most of the assistance would be temporary. It was made clear to all that the goal was to give help until the folks got their feet back on the ground and found their own longer-term solutions.

Many of the issues brought forward, however, were beyond anything Jonathon was expecting or had answers for. A heartbreaking number of calls revolved around family matters; broken relationships, estranged parents and children, marriages falling apart. There were some well-hidden addiction struggles and financial problems. When Jonathon had told Buzz on the radio interview that Downtown Fellowship was there to minister to a hurting and broken world, he hadn't yet known the half of it.

Jonathon and a couple of the deacons who had been answering calls became adept at turning the conversations to spiritual matters. There had been many interesting discussions and many questions asked and answered. So far none of the calls had gone beyond the conversation stage. Still, most of the callers seemed to welcome a short time of prayer before hanging up.

Following their phone calls, two lonely bachelors had dropped into the office to chat. Sal took the time to have a coffee and a visit with them even though it put her behind on her normal work. Her casual approach and infectious, crackling laugh seemed to set a good tone for the meetings. She then introduced them to a couple of widowers from the congregation. When Sal heard the men laughing and joking in the coffee room, she figured they were probably telling old war stories.

The laughter was a pleasant sound. Perhaps the loneliness would be set aside for a short while at least.

The staff coffee room was being well used as more people started dropping in. Jonathon's prayer continued to be that some of the visitors would find their way to church on Sunday and that God would do a work in their hearts that only He could do. Sal had started purchasing coffee in larger quantities. Either she or one of the interns kept a fresh pot available throughout the day.

There had been some aggressive phone calls. Two men and one woman who held hard feelings from past, hurtful church experiences expressed themselves in a way that left no doubt about their position on the matter. Jonathon invited each to meet him face to face. None had done so.

None of the callers mentioned Buzz Grappler or his call-in radio program.

The past Sunday, one couple from an upscale condo building had come to the worship service. Although Jonathon was pleased, he was also surprised. He had been expecting the break-through, when it came, would be with a needy family.

TERRY PHONED FROM THE CONSTRUCTION OFFICE. "HOW goes it partner?" asked Jonathon.

"It's been a whole lot better in times past but I'm happy it's not worse. I now have all the trades' invoices up to date and we can just barely cover them. Do you still feel that's our best approach?"

Jonathon was longer than usual answering. Finally, he said, "It's what we talked about before and I'm still alright with it. There's some risk but it does protect our other projects. With many of the same trades working on all the projects, we can't risk losing any of them."

"I'll see to it," was Terry's response.

As usual, the two men hung up without further comment.

Almost immediately Jonathon's cell phone vibrated again. He answered and heard the voice of Millard Crown. "Have you got a moment, Jonathon?"

"There is always a minute for you, Mr. Crown."

"This truly will be just a moment. In fact, this call isn't happening."

There was a slight pause which Jonathon took as an opportunity for him to agree or object. Millard Crowd took his silence as agreement.

"The news about Global is all over town. I know you're deeply involved and probably vulnerable. If an old industry war horse can offer a private piece of advice, I would tell you to never fully trust the bank. Never trust the other guy's lawyer. Only half trust your own lawyer. Do your own thinking. Don't do anything on a verbal guarantee. Double- and triple-check all the paperwork. If you don't look after your own interests, I guarantee that no one else will. Your primary responsibility is your own company. Finally, if it comes down to it, your first loss is your best loss."

Jonathon heaved a great sigh into the phone. "Mr. Crown, I received almost the same advice from a mentor many years ago. I hope you wouldn't mind if I added accountants to the list. Not that they themselves shouldn't be trusted but I have found them prone to making errors. In any case, thank you very much for this call that never happened. I promise we will heed your advice."

Jonathon hung up the phone thinking, 'I need to remember to be thankful for friends; business or personal. People who hang in when the going gets tough. If ever I needed to delegate and trust as well as compartmentalize the business and church situations, this is the time.'

Jonathon had a meeting with the deacons scheduled for right after lunch. Since all the visitors had begun gathering in the coffee room, Jonathon had been eating at his desk. He had 'brown-bagged' his lunch all his school and working years and was still happy with that arrangement. He and Janet had had some fun at dinner a few evenings before trying to add up all the lunches Janet had put together over the years. One of the boys finally interrupted, "Stop it, you two, you're spoiling my appetite. When I get on my own, I never want to see another brown bag."

His younger brother put in his two cents worth. "When I get a job and my own house, I'm going to eat pizza every meal."

It was Jonathon's turn to raise his hands in mock horror. "Stop. Now you're spoiling my appetite."

The discussion ended with much laughter and with them still having no idea how many lunches Janet had made, the kids arguing that they had helped with lots of the lunch-making.

Jonathon and the deacons met in an upstairs room. When the men were seated, their first order of business was a lengthy prayer time. Although Jonathon had prepared and printed out an update of current matters that they would bring before the Lord, most of their time would be spent on worship.

Several times they waited while one man or another read a short scripture, usually emphasizing the Glory of God and His love for His people. Jonathon treasured these worship times. His position was that God already knew all about the needs on the list before them. The times of intercession were kept short. There was no need for each man to go over the list in detail. He saw their task as demonstrating to God that the men themselves understood these needs and were relying on God and His Holy Spirit to bring wisdom and clarity on the role each man should be playing.

Jonathon felt the board was pulling together in a new way and truly becoming as one in their determination to lead Downtown Fellowship. The board had seemed to be of one mind from the time of Jonathon's first contact with them. Still, he privately dated the new closeness among the men to the day Noble Pearson made his confession and asked forgiveness.

With the prayer time over, the men each poured themselves a cup of coffee. Janet had sent in a container of oatmeal cookies. They then went right to business.

Jonathon said, "The first item I wish to discuss today has to do with sharing the church building with another small ministry. You've heard me talk about a young man named Kyle who leads a small street ministry a few blocks away. He's been working out of an old, unmaintained building that's due for demolition. He was given free rent until the developer was ready to take the building down. Kyle found out a few days ago that the time has come. He must find a new location. He has no money so a formal rental in a newer building isn't going to happen.

"I've been thinking of the room down the hall here where the youth used to meet. It has an outside door onto the parking lot for a private entrance. There are some old stacking chairs in the room already. Seating would max out at about forty, more than adequate for Kyle at this time. We have a vague hope of a youth program sometime in the future but no real need for the space right now. How would you feel if we offer the space to Kyle and his ministry?"

Roland Trembley said, "I went down and met Kyle a couple of weeks ago. Nice young man. Thinks the sun rises and sets on you, Pastor. We talked about his beliefs and what he teaches. He was very open about it all. I found nothing to concern me. I like his humility. I see no problem with him using that room. Of course, it might be a short-term solution for him again. It's possible his work will outgrow the space but that would be his issue to solve. I say let's make him welcome."

Although no one spoke, there were nodding heads around the table.

Orville Palmer, the deacon who had managed the building functions and overseen the maintenance for many years, said, "I'm in favor. Do you mind if I break the news to him? That will give me the opportunity to talk to him about group liability, care of the facilities, insurance, access to washrooms, etc."

A quick vote showed full agreement and the board moved on to the next issue.

Jonathon brought the men up to date on the work of the interns.

They then moved to the matter of the hoped-for reconciliation with those that had left the fellowship over the years.

Jonathon assured them that a complete list of names and mailing addresses was just days from completion. How were they to proceed?

No one spoke. Jonathon looked around the table at the men. They were certainly aware of the potential downside of this initiative. He sensed their fear and concern; he had the same concerns but it had all been discussed before. Nothing had changed and no new ideas had been put forward.

Finally, Noble Pearson spoke, "Men, we've been over this more than once. Even before Jonathon joined us on staff we had talked of this. Although overall First Baptist and Downtown Fellowship have a history of preaching scriptural truth and loving one another, there is still that other truth; that failure was too frequent and too deep, touching too many lives. In my experience, the issues that caused problems always started small but were allowed to grow. I'm ashamed to realize that with a bit of backbone I - and we - could have nipped many problems while they were still budding. We failed the people, and the Lord, when we failed to do that.

"Even if we were to say that the failures were only a small part of the whole, they would still have to be acknowledged and dealt with if we're to move forward in the work of the Lord." He flipped to where his Bible held a bookmark. We're all familiar with Song of Solomon, 2:15: *Catch for us the foxes, the little foxes that ruin the vineyards, our vineyards that are in bloom.*

"We didn't do that. In my opinion, we have it to do now."

There followed a short discussion on how best to proceed.

Clive Warner, a recently-appointed deacon, said, "How would it work, Jonathon, if you were to put together the basics of a letter? Each of us could carefully go over the letter and offer opinions or changes. When all of us are satisfied, we could send it out with all our signatures. I believe Sal could scan the signatures into the document. That might be better than simply typing in our names. Perhaps you could then sign each letter as pastor."

That was agreed upon and, with a closing prayer, the meeting broke up.

Noble Pearson poured himself a half-cup of fresh coffee and said to no one in particular, "I'm not leaving until these oatmeal cookies are dealt with." Three others sat back down and reached for a cookie.

29

JONATHON WAS BARELY SEATED BACK AT HIS DESK WHEN his cell phone vibrated. He pressed the receive button but before he had a chance to even say hello, Terry started to talk.

"I did something major without running it past you, buddy. Sorry about that but it seemed so urgent that I just never thought."

"Tell me," said Jonathon.

"I was going over some of the Global documents again and the light came on. We had a sizable deposit on hand that would look very tempting to one of the rogue lawyers acting for the Global creditors. Some of those guys appear to be real bandits. But the truth is that most of that money is what's left of our own working capital, or came from the non-Global projects and is owed to those suppliers and trades. When that light flashed, I leaped out of my chair, grabbed a blank check and made a beeline to the bank. I certified a check for almost all the funds available and headed over to our accountant's office. The funds are now deposited in his trust account. He's agreed to receive all deposits from non-Global projects and pay all the bills. I'll get a letter out to the principals advising that future draws should be made payable to the accountant, in trust. Without a court order, no one can touch us on those jobs."

Jonathon laughed out loud. This was the best business news he had heard in days. "Terry, you're a genius. Picking you for a partner just shows how smart I am. Keep thinking, partner, and watch for other lights to come popping on."

Jonathon wasn't surprised when the call went dead.

As welcome as Terry's call had been, Jonathon really needed some time free of phone calls and interruptions. He had a sermon to complete and needed time to concentrate on other matters. When Sal buzzed him on the intercom, he considered telling her to refuse the call. Then he thought better of it.

He pushed line one and said, "Hello, Buzz. This isn't a real convenient time for a conversation. I don't mind talking with you but I do wish you would call Sal and arrange a time in the future. What's on your mind today?"

The announcer's always excitable voice said, "It isn't just what's on my mind, Pastor. It's what's on the minds of my listeners at WKS on the 'Can You Believe This?' show. I keep getting calls. People are still concerned and suspicious about those advertisements you're sending out. They're wondering when the other shoe is going to drop. When are you going to start asking for money for your church and how aggressive are you going to be in your pleas?"

Jonathon was tired of the whole discussion and was tempted to cut the call short. But one of the deacons had suggested that talking with Buzz could have a positive outcome. They certainly couldn't afford to purchase that much advertising time on the radio and Buzz was giving it to them for free. So what if he was aggressive? Let him rant. It was all good exposure. Jonathon finally came to see the wisdom of that approach so he waited while Buzz prattled on.

"And now a new issue has come to light. The news around town is that your contracting company is facing bankruptcy along with a company called Global who was trying to build a big shopping center without having the necessary capital. Are you going to be asking the public to bail you out of that one too, Pastor?"

Jonathon was thunderstruck. Not by the fact that the news of Global's troubles had become public, but by the fact that a media person could be so uninformed and purposely destructive.

"If you're done with your ridiculous rant, Buzz, could I say a word or two?"

"Go ahead, Pastor. We aim for the truth on this program and we certainly aim to be fair and open."

"You do no such thing, Buzz. You're deceiving your listeners. You have no intentions of being fair or seeking the truth. What you're seeking is sensationalism no matter who you hurt in the process. If you really want the truth, I'll give it to you.

"Let's start with the church advertising. We really discussed this to death on our last call. There's nothing new to say. We don't ask for money from the public and we never will. The church and its work is solvent and has no need for money from your listeners. If that settles that, Buzz, we can get on to the matter of Global's financial problems."

Buzz cut in just long enough to say, "We only have a few minutes, Pastor, but go ahead."

"Buzz, it's interesting how you call me, make wild, ridiculous accusations, and then tell me you're out of time.

"Here's the truth of the matter. Proctor-McCann, the construction company I have an ownership position in, is a solvent, well-financed company. We have four projects under-way. Three of them are proceeding normally. Global, a company we have worked for several times in the past with good success, is in trouble on a hotel project thousands of miles from here. It has absolutely nothing to do with the shopping center. It's possible that the hotel project will impact other Global business ventures but that's not Proctor-McCann's issue to deal with. The shopping center we're building for them is on time and on budget. Both Global's and Proctor-McCann's contractual obligations are up to date. Our company is in no financial trouble at all. We're watching these happenings very carefully and have taken the appropriate measures to protect ourselves and our customers.

"To spread a known falsehood about our company is unconscionable, Buzz. Now, you say you're seeking the truth. I've just given you the truth. Perhaps if you would pry yourself from behind your microphone and do some simple research like any good reporter would do, you could come a bit closer to knowing the truth and sharing that real truth with your listeners. So, is there anything else today, Buzz? If not, I have work to do."

The station went to commercial with no further word from the announcer.

Jonathon was so upset by the phone call from the radio station that he left his office and said, "Back in a few minutes," as he passed Sal's desk and went outside. He walked around several blocks while he mentally replayed the radio call. Each step seemed to drain a tiny bit of emotion from him. Jonathon was usually the steadiest person around when a problem arose but Buzz had really upset him. He found himself wondering why. And then he knew. It was not the church seeking donations from the public. That nonsense wouldn't fly. But rumors of business bankruptcy could fly like an eagle.

A rumor, once started, was almost impossible to quell. False rumors had destroyed politicians, businesses, school teachers accused of child abuse, men accused of sexual abuse and women accused of child neglect, and a host of other innocent people. The list of ruined lives, suicides, and business closures was long. He felt that no qualified, reasonable media person should be free to spout nonsense without recrimination of some sort.

Jonathon was perfectly familiar with stress. That troubling emotion seemed to be unavoidable in the fast-moving, high-stakes building construction industry. But dealing with business matters in such a public manner was a stress he had no experience with.

As he walked and mulled through these thoughts, he started to settle down. He finally thought, 'Well, that was a new experience. Not sure how well I handled it. Certainly not Mr. Cool today.'

His final solace was always in prayer. With the hum of traffic on the street, music blaring from some storefront, horns honking, kids playing in a downtown park and people walking all around him, he silently sought that solace. Slowly, as he told the Lord his fears and hopes, he was comforted with a comfort that could come from no one but God.

30

EARLY THE NEXT MORNING, JONATHON MUMBLED A distracted, "Come in," when a light rap sounded on his office door. Robert stuck his head into the partly-opened door and asked, "Got a minute?"

With his eyes still glued to the sermon spread before him on the computer screen, Jonathon lifted one hand from the keyboard and waved the intern in. After a few more keystrokes, he turned to the young man. "What's up?"

Robert took a seat beside the desk. "I'm a day late with this but I got into something that I felt justified the extra time. The new clothes and the shower were like gifts from heaven for those three men. I thought they just might stay in the shower for the rest of the day. Two of them became so talkative that I stayed with them all that day and then most of yesterday. I'm glad I did because it wasn't until yesterday afternoon that Carl began to trust me enough to share a bit. With Peter and Samuel, it's the normal story of addictions, employment failure, family break-down, and a loss of the will to find their way back. Listening to them, I felt there was still hope if they made some better choices.

"With Carl, it's different. He claims to have no addictions. Doesn't drink or smoke tobacco or anything else. He appears to be very self-disciplined. It turns out that he spent over a decade in the military. Applied for - and was posted to - Special Forces. His athletic ability and stamina, coupled with his uncanny ability with firearms, had a lot to do with the posting. He served on many covert missions. He's been tasked with difficult operations behind enemy lines where he says he was scared to death the whole time. He's served in a few too many hot spots, done things he wishes he could forget, and found himself unable to face more of the same. What he said to me was, "I didn't want to kill anyone else ever again and I certainly didn't wish to be killed myself.

"One day he found himself huddled on his bunk, alternating between weeping uncontrollably and wanting to shout in rage.

"When he refused an assignment, his CO called him a coward. Carl beat the man nearly to death. Apparently, there were extenuating circumstances which Carl didn't explain. Because of those unique circumstances, he was offered a deal. In exchange for not having charges brought against him, Carl signed off on all military liability and accepted a dishonorable discharge.

"This would appear to be a classic case of PTSD but all veteran's assistance is lost to him because of the way he left the service.

"He went home for a while. Although he says he had some good days, he had many more that were not good. He couldn't hold a job. He slept most of the time. Finally, the pressure of the whole thing was too much. His wife gave up and told him to leave. It's been street corners and a downward spiral since then. He says it's Peter and Samuel that hold him on a steady track.

"Now, understand, that's Carl's story. I have no way of checking the truth of it and I certainly would have no idea of how to help."

Jonathon was silent, staring at the ceiling for so long that Robert became uneasy. Finally, the intern stood, planning to slip out of the office. His movements seemed to bring Jonathon back to earth. "Good work, young man. Leave it with me. And thanks. I know that was a tough one. Please ask Sal to come in when she gets a moment."

Sal came in almost immediately. She stood in the doorway, one hand still holding the doorknob, waiting for instructions. Jonathon had a faraway look in his eyes, something Sal had never seen before. She waited for him to speak.

"Sal, we need a veteran. Someone who's personally been through the mill and seen action. The higher the rank, the better. Any name come to mind?"

Sal took a couple of steps and sat down. "We have several vets. We used to have dozens of them but they're dying off. There's still a couple of WW2 guys left although they're obviously no longer young. Several from Korea and a smattering of others. We don't seem to attract the younger vets from the more recent actions. Specifically, what are you looking for?"

Jonathon said, "We need someone who can talk man-to-man with a victim of PTSD and who might also know his way around the veteran's services bureaucracy."

Sal snapped her fingers as if a light had come on. "Phillip Garneau. Career, ex-army. Discharged as a full colonel. Involved in veteran's affairs all the time. Phillip and Lena are a great couple. They don't attend here anymore but I still have their phone number. Do you want me to call him for you?"

Jonathon nodded. "Thanks, Sal. Call him and ask if he could come in for a talk."

When Jonathon's cell buzzed again, he wasn't surprised to hear Terry on the other end. "Morning, partner. What we feared has happened but I think we're positioned to withstand the nonsense. One of Global's larger creditors has challenged Global - and us - on that last payment, the one that came as a certified check. They claim Global played favorites after their intention to seek bankruptcy protection was already decided on by their corporate board. They intend to go to court to demand the money back. I just got off the phone with our lawyer. He talked with Global's lawyer and the bankruptcy lawyer and called me back. They all guarantee the complainer hasn't a leg to stand on. Hopefully, they're correct. There's nothing more either of us can do at this point. I just wanted to bring a bit of sunshine into your life this morning."

"Thanks for that, partner. Please do call again if you have any other sunshine to spread around." Jonathon ended the call wondering what could possibly be next but also amazed at Terry's lighthearted attitude. Absently, he wondered if they were both losing their minds.

Sal stuck her head back in the door. "Thought you might like to know. Kyle and his wife are down at the old youth room. Orville Palmer is with them. They're looking at what has to be done before they move in. I think it's mostly dusting and cleaning. I'm sure they can handle it."

Jonathon listened and then said, "Good, ask the interns to see what they can do to help. A change of scene will do them good for a day or two. Send Watson down, too, if he's around today."

The Pastor then closed the door and moved to the prayer bench in the corner. As he knelt to pray, he found himself feeling like a juggler who had tossed one too many balls in the air. It comforted him to know that he had assistance available to him from Sal, the interns, the deacons, and other volunteers. 'Delegate, delegate, delegate', he said to himself.

His prayer time did wonders for his peace of heart and mind. After an hour, he was back staring at the computer screen preparing for Sunday morning. He worked through lunch without realizing what time is was.

Finally, he rose from the chair, stretched his arms above his head, did a few half-hearted toe touches to get the kinks out of his back, and decided to see how Kyle's move-in was coming.

He found Kyle and his wife Natalie busy with buckets of hot water, a short stepladder, and a selection of sponges and wash rags.

Kyle introduced the pastor to Natalie. The young couple

were both profuse in their show of appreciation for the use of the room.

"Are you settling in alright?" he asked. "Anything else we can do for you?"

Kyle answered, "We have enough and plenty. We can't thank you and Downtown Fellowship adequately."

Jonathon looked around. "You've still got some cleaning to do. This room hasn't been used for years. Actually, I sent you some help but I don't see them."

Natalie laughed. "Take a look in the next room. I think you'll find both of them."

Jonathon stepped out and down the hallway to what used to be the adult Sunday school room. He found Darla sitting on a couch holding the sleeping baby. Robert was looking over an old piano that had been covered with a cloth and pushed into a corner. Neither heard his approach.

"Well," he said and laughed. "That's a sight. How will we put that on your end-of-summer internship report? One of you can't stay away from musical instruments and the other is practicing being a mother. I'm not sure how that's going to do much for your grades."

Darla looked up and put her index finger over her lips. "Shush, he just finally fell asleep. Isn't he just the sweetest little guy?"

Jonathon laughed again, quietly this time.

Robert waved Jonathon over to the old piano. He, too, spoke quietly, "Do you think the board would let us move this piano to the next room? Before the baby went to sleep and took over our lives, I played it a bit. It could stand a tuning but, overall, it's not bad. Has a pretty good tone. I might be of some use to Kyle on Sunday mornings if this was available. What do you think?"

Jonathon looked over the old instrument. He gently played a few chords. "Not bad, like you said. Did you try to move it? It seems to be on wheels."

Robert nodded. "Moves easy as could be."

Jonathon gave the old instrument a bit of a push. It moved without much effort. "I'll talk with Sal, and the board if necessary. But I doubt anyone would complain."

He left them to their tasks and turned to go back to his office. As he was leaving, he said to Darla, "You do realize they don't have to be held all the time, don't you?"

Darla, at her sassy best, smiled and stuck out her tongue at the same time.

Jonathon was still grinning as he walked away, feeling better than he had for some time. He thought for a moment and then said to himself, 'Just good to be around young folks once in a while'.

When he mentioned the piano to Sal, she chuckled. "That piano is almost as old as the building. Tell the kids to move it wherever they want. It would be good to see it back in use. Do you want me to find some funding for a tuning? I could massage the petty cash a bit."

Jonathon nodded. "Good idea. Then, how about making some calls about an expanded telephone system? Our advertising isn't filling the pews but it's certainly filling our lay-counselor's schedules with phone calls. We're going to need more volunteers and more phone lines at the rate we're going."

31

THE SECOND WEEK OF JULY, THE VACATION SEASON WAS well underway. Few of the older folks from Downtown Fellowship bothered with summer vacations. The ones who vacationed at all were more likely to escape a bit of the winter, traveling to Hawaii or some other hot spot. Several church regulars showed up on Sunday mornings with visiting families in tow. Jonathon spoke to as many as he could with no real hope of remembering all the names.

Jonathon watched from across the room as two couples he judged to be in their fifties received friendly greetings from some regular attendees, giving every indication that they were known previously. After service, Jonathon made a point of meeting them. Sal was standing nearby. She made the introductions. "Pastor, I'd like you to meet Billy and May Cranston, and Howard and Betty Miller. We've known each other forever."

They shook hands all around. "It's good to have you with us today, folks. I pray the Lord met you in worship."

Betty Miller said, "Speaking for myself, I enjoyed the service very much. I had no idea William and Madison were so musically gifted. Their talents should have been put to use years ago. We've been attending the Evening View church over on the West side but this was our home church for many years. There's recently been folks talking about you and the work here, Pastor, and we decided to come and see for ourselves. We came to both the choir and organ concerts but that's not the same as a church service. It was great to hear the organ again though."

Jonathon answered, "I hope what you heard from other folks wasn't too negative. We've slowly been making a few changes. It's a great bunch of people we're working with here. They're being very patient with me."

As the two couples walked away, another visiting couple made their way to Jonathon who said, "Morning folks," holding his hand out in greeting; they ignored the gesture. The short, heavily-bearded man spoke with what sounded to Jonathon like self-appointed authority; belligerent and making no room for discussion.

"We attended here some years ago," he said officiously, "back when the truth was still being preached and we sang proper hymns. Then the liberals took over so we left to seek a place to worship in the proper, scriptural way. Heard about a new preacher taking over here so we came to see. But it's plain you're just another liberal."

With that, the couple turned and left Jonathon standing there with a puzzled look on his face and a bit of a sinking feeling in his heart. Hanna was walking past as the bearded man was speaking.

When the unhappy couple left, she said to Jonathon, "That's Mark and Greta Bannister. I hate to have to say it, Pastor, but that couple was the source of a great deal of the trouble in the past. They're never happy no matter what anyone does. I know how critical that sounds but you really don't want them here unless something dramatic has happened in their hearts. I saw no indication of that in his words. I'd leave them be if it were up to me."

Jonathon expelled a long-held breath, nodded to Hanna, and walked over to greet another couple.

The ropes isolating the side sections of the seating were still in place. The center section had been opened. The attendees were clustered in the two aisles and at the rear, all of them slowly making their way towards the big oak doors.

The pastor stepped back towards the front of the room, making himself available to any who wished to pray or simply talk.

Kyle held his first service in the old youth room that morning. He had scheduled the services for one half-hour earlier than the meeting in the sanctuary. After Jonathon spoke to as many folks as he could, he walked over to Janet. "Let's you and I go see how the morning went for Kyle."

They made their way into the back hallway and towards the room Kyle and his group were using. Before they reached the room, they could hear talking and laughter. In the background, they heard the piano playing softly as a few people sang. Jonathon didn't recognize the song. The sound from the piano told Jonathon that Sal hadn't managed to get the tuner there yet. The singers didn't seem to mind.

When they entered the room, the first person they saw was Darla. She was holding the baby again. Jonathon was startled but pleased to see her. The staff and other volunteers had been careful over the past weeks to not push the young unbeliever. Jonathon's private prayer had been that Darla would see a demonstration of grace and love among the people as she did her work and would be attracted to the gospel.

A further glance around the room showed about fifteen people visiting and drinking coffee. They all seemed to be talking at once, nearly drowning out the singers. The thought crossed his mind that the younger generation seemed to thrive on chaos. His own teenagers were somehow able to sort out conflicting sounds from their selection of devices. He had given up on understanding it all.

Kyle noticed Jonathon and Janet standing in the doorway. He shot a big grin their way and waved them in. Loud enough to be heard over the din of conversation, he said, "Quiet for a moment please, folks." It took a bit of time for the conversation and the music to glide to a stop. "I want you all to meet Pastor and Mrs. McCann. Pastor McCann is responsible for us having this fine meeting place this morning." The young pastor half-turned to the gathering and swung his arm in a semi-circular motion that enclosed the people in the room. "I won't try to give you all the names, Pastor. I'll just say that collectively, we - and those who have already left - are much in your and the church's debt for providing us this opportunity. Thank you."

The fifteen coffee drinkers and the half-dozen singers shouted out their thanks. A few pumped their fists in the air. Others raised their coffee mugs as if in salute.

Jonathon moved into the room, speaking to individuals and asking their names. Janet made her way over to Darla.

"Darla, you seem to be a natural at this baby stuff. You'll have to be careful. The next thing you know you'll be having domestic thoughts and there's no going back from that point." The two women had a quiet laugh together while Janet opened the soft blanket covering the sleeping baby. She saw Natalie smiling at them.

Within a few minutes, Orville Palmer showed up. He waited until the room was straightened up, the coffee pot washed out, and the last person gone. He then closed and locked all the doors. Jonathon and Janet waited while he completed the task.

As they walked back together, Orville said, "It's a shame, isn't it? The city has really changed. Years ago, not that we were care-less, we didn't have to worry so much about an unlocked door. We never had any problems. People seemed to respect the prop-erty of others and especially churches. What changed it for us was the insurance companies. After several break-ins at other churches, they sent a man around to look at our security program. They threatened to refuse us coverage if we didn't upgrade some things."

Jonathon and Janet thanked Orville for locking up the building, then walked to their car. As they drove away, Jonathon said, "I'm looking forward to our visit with the folks. My mother will have dinner about ready. Let's not stay too long though. I'd like an afternoon with just you and the kids. That is, if they'll stay home for more than a few minutes."

They both laughed as they chatted about the boys' preoccupation with girls and balls. Only a few special girls seemed to hold their attention but any kind of ball would do; basketball, football, baseball. As long as it was a ball, they were happy.

JONATHON HAD STARTED BEING CAREFUL ABOUT TAKING Mondays off from church work. The construction business needed him. There was a lot at stake. Global's bankruptcy problems appeared to be close to resolution, at least on the shopping center job, the only one that impacted Proctor-McCann. But until the final papers were signed, the funding guaranteed and everything approved in writing by the bankruptcy court, neither Terry nor Jonathon were prepared to take any further risk. The bank had promised resolution within the next few days but Jonathon and Terry were both feeling the extra stress brought on by the situation.

Gregory, the new estimator Terry had hired, was given three projects to work on and pull together. Bids were closing for one project within the week so he had been working on that one first, wrapping up the final details. Gregory was confident that the estimate was all but complete. Like the shopping center, the project was big enough to push Proctor-McCann's financial and administrative capacity almost to the limits. Terry and Jonathon wanted the job. They both saw it as the next step in the growth of the company. The completion of the shopping center would free up both capital and the crew for the new job. If only the lawyers would get their act together so they could resume the shopping center work.

Jonathon spent Monday morning working with Gregory double-checking everything in the quotation.

When Gregory showed a hint of frustration, Jonathon said, "Gregory, I've been doing materials take-offs and estimating labor costs for nearly twenty years. When I think I'm finished and all wrapped up, I start over again. I check and re-check and re-check again. I set my ego aside while both Terry and the office manager go over the numbers, looking for errors in my calculations. It's only after all of us are satisfied that we write up the quote."

Gregory shuffled uncomfortably in his chair while Jonathon continued, "You can see that we're dealing with very large numbers here. Those aren't just numbers on a page, Gregory, those are dollars. Enough dollars to make or break this company. There cannot be any room for mistakes. If Terry and I have any doubts after all the re-checking, whether you do the estimate or I do it, we'll pass on the job."

The two men looked at each other as Jonathon said, "None of this re-checking means you're not doing a good job. It simply means that we must eliminate any chance of error. I would add that this is so much easier with the computer programs. When I started, it was all paper and pencil. One time I misplaced a sheet of paper and quoted the job wrongly because of that. We were fortunate to not have that contract awarded to us. My mistake would have caused serious financial repercussions. With the computers, that doesn't happen anymore."

He looked the frustrated estimator in the eyes. "This is not optional, Gregory. It's how it is. Are you going to be alright with that or would you be happier working somewhere else?"

Gregory dug up a lopsided grin. "No, I like it here. Actually, I wouldn't mind if you were to keep your pastor's job and this position could become permanent. You and Terry are great people. I apologize for not getting your approach without being told. I'm a very cautious man myself. I'm not offended at your double-checking. I was thinking more of those other two files lying there. I'm kind of anxious to get into them. Anyway, let's go over this all again."

Jonathon stood and stretched. "Good idea, but it would go better if I dumped this cold coffee out and got a fresh one."

First thing Tuesday morning Jonathon called the interns into the office. Sal came with them.

He started the meeting kidding Robert about getting into something with Kyle's group he couldn't get out of. "You do realize that you have now taken on a permanent piano playing role, don't you?"

Robert laughed and shrugged his shoulders. "If it's permanent it will only be until the end of summer. After that, we'll have to see how busy my next school semester is."

Jonathon then turned to Darla. "So, bring us up to date on your work in the gymnasium."

Darla had a file of information with her but didn't bother referring to it. She knew all the details by heart. "The washroom expansions are possible in the existing spaces. It wouldn't give us all we hoped for but it would probably do for a start. We could get two more toilet stalls and one additional shower stall in each washroom. I know that's minimum for what we have planned but anything further than that would mean breaking out walls and a major renovation. The cost would be considerable. I could get those costs if you really want them."

Jonathon was pleased to hear Darla refer to the project using 'us' and 'we'. He took it as a sign that the intern was taking some ownership on the planned homeless ministry and the church work in general.

Darla continued, "The kitchen is another matter altogether. The only space available would be the coat rooms. One coat room wouldn't be anywhere close to adequate. The two rooms made into one would still be tight but the kitchen designer says it could be done. If we wished to prepare full-on banquets for large groups, it wouldn't be adequate. But for what he called 'short order' which he confirmed would include a normal lunch or breakfast menu, it would work. Taking out the dividing wall is not a big job. Getting wiring and natural gas to the space will push up the costs though. I have the cost sheet here." She handed Jonathon and Sal each a typed page of estimates. She had already discussed the job with Robert so he had the estimates in his file. Passing out a second sheet, she said, "Here are the costs for the stove and the other fixtures required."

After waiting for the others to look over the estimate sheets, she said, "Of course, we would no longer have coat rooms. Perhaps we could settle for a series of wooden pegs along the walls."

Jonathon glanced over the numbers and nodded. "Thank you, young lady. You've done a good job on this. There's much for the board to think about." Turning to Robert, he asked, "Are we ready for this week's mailout?"

Robert nodded. "The mailouts keep getting bigger as we add new high-rise buildings to the list. Everything is ready though. The cards are printed, bundled, and labeled for delivery."

Jonathon thanked the young man and then said, "Alright. That's good information and good work, too. Now, tell me where we stand on the homeless lunch inquiry. I know I've distracted you from that a time or two but bring us up to date anyway."

Robert referred to the file resting on his knees although, like Darla, he had all the information memorized. He passed a sheet of paper to Jonathon and another to Sal. Darla already had one. "This is a list of all the agencies offering lunch programs. At the bottom is an estimate of the number of clients. It's an estimate only because this can be a transient group but it's pretty close." He paused to give them time to look at the information.

"The bottom line, in my opinion, is that the available lunch programs exceed the need. Many times the tables remain less than full and the prepared food is going to waste. Because the providers never know how many will show up for a meal, they often prepare more than is needed. The unused portion goes to waste if it can't be used for soup the next day. If our program here was to cease, the others would soon fill the gap and everyone would be better off for the change. There would be less food wasted, planning would be easier, and the volunteers would be better utilized.

"Now, you asked me to look into food sources and funding. The funding is the same for all involved. It's a mix of government funding and donations from the public. That probably will never change.

"As to food sources, many of the big food stores make their unsold stock available to volunteers who come to pick it up. That's good of them but for the agencies it has always proven unreliable. There is no consistency of supply and much of the supply is stale-dated, and of somewhat questionable quality. A lot of it goes into the dumpster. Most of the funding the agencies receive is spent on food that's purchased fresh from various wholesalers. A small portion of funding goes to staff but very little. Most agencies of this sort are local only and are run with volunteers.

"I talked with a number of homeless folks including our own Carl, Samuel and Peter. I also had discussions with the other providers. They all confirmed that what would be most helpful to the men and women involved - the clients, that is - would be a breakfast.

"The upside of us providing a morning meal, especially if it included an opportunity for a shower, is that both morning food and personal hygiene are almost impossible for the clients in the current situation. We would be providing a much-needed service."

Jonathon and Sal were listening closely, each scribbling a few notes.

"One downside would be that the volunteers would be starting their days in the early morning. That may weed out a few of them. Probably the bigger downside is that it would be the only breakfast and shower available in town. We'd have every homeless person for miles around arriving. Of course, that's fine too if we can accommodate them. But I see some real challenges with the possible numbers involved."

Jonathon again thanked the two interns and gave them a new assignment. "Your research has confirmed some thoughts I've had for a while. What I want you two to do now is go back to your office and dream a bit. I want you to visualize a breakfast program and all that could entail. You know the dimensions of the gymnasium. Sketch out the floor layout for tables and chairs. Think about how the bathroom facilities and showers could be used, estimating from the total number of clients you found. Estimate how many volunteers would be needed. Think about the shuffling in and out as the people come and go. Think about stacking and storage of tables and chairs so the gym can still become a basketball or volleyball court when that need arises.

"Let your minds go as wild as you want as long as what you come up with at the end is workable. And don't forget about the winter months and the added complications from the weather during that time. Stretch yourselves, and the program. That will cause both me and the board, and the present volunteers, to take a broader look. Take several days. Then put it all on a datasheet of some kind so you can present it to Sal and me, then to the board.

"Finally, remember at all times that we are a church. While we are certainly interested in compassionate help for those in need, we see the client's greatest need as having a personal relationship with Jesus Christ. We have no intention of preaching while the clients eat but we are also not going to hide who we are."

The two interns sat there staring at the pastor as if he'd just asked them to learn Greek in one day. Darla, ever impudent, said, "Perhaps we could do birthday cakes for the clients, too, and pass out balloons." Her expressive face got her out of a lot of tight spots.

Jonathon grinned at the kids. "Get out of here. I have work to do."

JONATHON ARRIVED A FEW MINUTES EARLY FOR HIS morning appointment at Orvis Tanner's home where he was ushered into the old man's private study. With coffee cups in hand, they settled into comfortable chairs. Wasting no time, Mr. Tanner said, "So bring me up to date."

Jonathon placed his cup on the low table beside his chair and looked carefully at his mentor. He suspected that most of what had been happening was already well-known. The church grapevine was ever present and efficient. Although Jonathon's mandate, thrust upon him by Orvis Tanner, was to build up and re-establish the Downtown Fellowship Center, both men were troubled by the stumbling block of the church's past reputation. The two men had previously touched on their hopes of dealing with that unhappy past. Jonathon came prepared to discuss the matter but wished to hold the topic off to the end of the meeting.

He started their discussion with an outline of the events that had transpired since he took on the role of pastor. Briefly, he went over the hiring of the interns, the small changes in the music, the repair of the organ, the two concerts, the beginning of the mailout program and the responses to that project. He touched on the delegation of responsibilities to individual deacons and other volunteers from the congregation.

He paused for a sip of coffee and then continued, "Of course, you already know all of that but I felt it was good to put it back on the table to help us work towards the bigger picture."

Jonathon then moved into the discussion of the homeless project. Orvis Tanner asked for details. He took notes while Jonathon talked. When Jonathon was finished with the program outline, Mr. Tanner asked, "Just to help me understand, why would you wish to expand in that direction?"

Jonathon had expected the question.

"The repair of the organ and opening up the building to concerts is a service to one segment of society. I suppose we could leave it at that but, in Scripture, we see both Jesus and the disciples doing good works and assisting the down-and-out of society. While the preaching of the gospel and the salvation of souls will always be the main focus of the church, we feel that we must interact with the whole society around us whenever that's possible. We can't do everything that needs to be done in this broken world but we can probably do this one thing, at least. A note in our future dream list is the desire to find some way to assist the working poor, those who live on the fringes of family life, struggling with low income and lost expectations. We don't have the people or the funding to do two programs at once so that one will remain a wish for now. A couple of other thoughts are in the idea incubator but we'll leave those until they hatch a bit.

"The lunch program has been in place for several years and has been well-received. But we felt the organization, while well-meaning, was perhaps a bit loose with no real connection to what others are doing. The interns were put to work researching the situation in some depth. Their conclusion was that the lunch at Downtown Fellowship isn't really needed in the city. Others are providing lunches and doing a good job of it. The gap for the clients is breakfast and personal hygiene. Along with the good we believe moving in that direction would bring, there are some glaring risks and significant costs. They are all outlined on that sheet of paper I gave you."

Both men rose and refilled their coffee cups from the carafe that Mrs. Tanner had placed on the side table.

Jonathon continued, "One of the risks of an expanded program is that it will become too popular. If that happened, it could overwhelm our ability to provide. We would need to have some control mechanism in place that weeded out the truly needy from those who were simply taking advantage. We haven't thought that all out yet.

"And then there is the issue of costs. Both start-up costs and operating costs could prove to be a challenge. We feel the optics of the church going to the public for support - even for a clearly-defined, standalone social program like this - would be negative. We are determined not to go there in fear of damaging the main purpose of the church. Like the control system, we haven't fully found an answer to the financing issue. We're working on it."

The two men discussed the matter for another while, with Orvis Tanner showing considerable wisdom in the questions he asked. After a brief pause, he said, "I'm sure you appreciate that there will be failures and discouragements while working with these people. Most of them will resist change. Some are addicts with problems beyond what you or I can understand, or help. There are also many on our streets with mental problems; men and women who should be in care facilities of some sort. Our foolish governments have somehow managed to convince themselves that to place these poor souls in care facilities is to take away their human rights. Our governments are very short-sighted on this matter.

"There are, happily, some clients who will gratefully receive assistance. Perhaps it's not too much to hope that some will get their dignity and their families back. We can pray to that end.

"As long as the front-line workers in the program are aware of the challenges, and are emotionally and spiritually prepared for failures, I believe this is a commendable program. I applaud the church for being willing to venture in this direction. With your permission, I will bring the denomination board up to speed on this."

Jonathon felt that last comment needed no response.

They then moved on to the final and most important topic: the planned putting away of old troublesome things.

Jonathon laid another document on the desk and gave Orvis time to read it. Jonathon sipped coffee and watched nervously for a reaction as the other man was reading. He was sure there would be a response but all he saw was a furrowed brow as Mr. Tanner read the document at least three times. Finally, the old man sat back in his chair and held the page before him, while studying Jonathon intently.

Downtown Fellowship Center

To all pastors, members, adherents, and those involved in Downtown Fellowship Center or First Baptist Church now or ever in the past:

Your participation in a time of worship, praise, forgiveness, reconciliation and healing is eagerly sought for the evening of Saturday, Sept 23, at 6:00 PM.

As the elected or appointed leaders of Downtown Fellowship Center, we are eternally grateful for the many years of God's blessing on His church. At the same time, we are aware of and deeply concerned about the times of troubles and difficulties. It seems clear that many people still carry hurts and scars directly related to those times. Wishing to move forward in God's service, it is our prayerful intention to hold those hurtful things up before the Lord and to beg Him, and each other, for forgiveness and healing.

There will be no attempt made at this meeting to "sort out" the past or to re-discuss old issues. There will be no open mic. Your confession or forgiveness is between you and God, and perhaps between you and the offended individual. We are mindful that harboring old hurts leads to bitterness and ineffectiveness in God's service and in our personal lives. Forgiveness is the path to ending bitterness.

The intension is to gather together as God's people, confess our own failures before Him, simply forgive one another no matter what took place in the past, and humbly seek God's forgiveness for our own actions, depending on Him for healing.

We recognize that a broken and damaged human spirit must be healed if a life of victory in Christ is to be achieved. Only God, through His Holy Spirit, can bring that healing to His people.

Spiritual healing and forgiveness is a miracle of God. He is more than pleased to hold that miracle out to His church as a free gift of His grace. You are invited to come and partake of that miracle in full measure.

Please join us for a time of worshipful singing, an encouraging message delivered by guest speaker Rev. Mort Jenner, and a time of soul refreshment as we pour our hurts and heartaches out before Him, and our hearts of love and forgiveness to God and to each other.

It is clear in Scripture that God would have His people live victorious lives. Holding nothing between each other, or between ourselves and God, is essential for that victorious life.

Please join us for this special evening.

There will be a time of fellowship following the meeting.

AFTER AN UNCOMFORTABLY LONG TIME, Orvis Tanner laid the letter on his desk and raised his eyes to Jonathon. Speaking slowly and carefully, he said, "This is a bold move, young man. Is it a wise one? Humanly speaking, time will provide an answer to that question. Scripturally speaking, I can find no fault. How will people respond? That's an unknown. I know a couple of the old pastors have moved across the country. Will they choose to take on the cost of travel to be at the meeting? Is the issue seen as important to them? Again, an unknown. One man was so broken during his time here that he dropped from the ministry and never really recovered. It would be so good to see him again and to have him be set free. I would cover his travel costs myself if he would come."

Jonathon said, "That would be Rev. Heffner. Isaiah Heffner."

Mr. Tanner nodded. "Yes. He's had all the loving counseling his fellow pastors can give him but he's somehow never been able to find freedom. Tilly, his wife, finally found it in her heart to forgive and move on. She did what she could to encourage Isaiah, all to no avail. He took a secular job and put the ministry behind him. The couple of times I've seen him since, I saw a broken man. Even worse, I saw a man who refused healing."

The two men were silent for a few moments as if in contemplation.

"We talk a lot about the need for prayer. If ever there was an issue that demanded humble, pleading prayer, it would be this one.

"The modern-day church is facing unprecedented opposition. It is as if the entire culture stands against the things of God. There is no doubt in my mind that Satan, the enemy of our souls and of the church of God, is pouring out his most determined opposition on the church. If First Baptist is to survive and thrive, being used of God to complete the work assigned to her, these old animosities, these sins, must be healed and laid aside. If that isn't done, there is every chance that the Lord will take away His light and allow the church to die while He finds others to fill the gap.

"God Bless you and the board, Jonathon, as you move forward with this initiative. Would you give me permission after the letter is sent out to contact a couple of the old pastors and encourage them to come? And would you further give me permission to contact area pastors to encourage them and their flock to pray?"

Jonathon sensed a great weight lifted from him. The approval and support of Orvis Tanner meant much to Jonathon and to the leadership team. "I hadn't thought of having you contact the former pastors but that's a great idea. Your name and approval will mean a lot. Including those men and their families would close a great gap in the healing we're striving for. I wish we could afford to offer them their travel expenses but that's beyond our means."

Mr. Tanner nodded. "I'm more than happy to help in any way I can. I'm hoping you will be opening the meeting to a few of the local pastors. And I would very much like to be there myself."

Jonathon spread his hands in a welcoming gesture. "Of course, you and the pastors will be welcome. To fill the church with local visitors might defeat the purpose but the leaders are always welcome."

Orvis Tanner rendered one of his rare smiles. "Now, tell me how you managed to convince Mort Jenner to travel here on a weekend. He's seldom away from his own pulpit."

"It wasn't easy. I've lost track of how many e-mails and phone calls we exchanged. You're right, traveling isn't his favorite thing. But he's had an astoundingly successful forgiveness and healing ministry within his own congregation. It isn't his sole focus, of course; he still pastors the church with the whole counsel of God.

"He reaches out to the larger church by consulting and giving guidance when asked. His book on healing through forgiveness was a commercial failure he tells me but I believe it should be compulsory reading for every Christian.

"At first, he simply said no, he didn't wish to travel on the weekend. But I sensed him softening when I managed to get him to listen long enough to understand our history and our goals. I think it was the ministry to the city center that finally got to him. And then, when I e-mailed that proposed letter to him, he called back and said that if we were really this serious he would come. He made one condition on his participation; he also wants the pulpit on Sunday morning after the Saturday evening meeting. We were more than happy to comply."

The meeting had covered everything and Jonathon stood to leave. Mr. Tanner said, "Just one more thing before you go. Does your own congregation know about this yet?"

Jonathon said, "They will on Sunday morning. I intend to take a good portion of the service time to explain what's planned and to ask them to pray."

WHILE THE NUMBER OF PHONE CALLS FROM THE MAILOUT program wasn't overwhelming, they were soon beyond Jonathon's ability to deal with on his own. The few volunteers who had been assisting in the task were now stretched. More volunteers were being recruited and trained. Sal had the new phone system in place with two extra lines. It turned out that the change was simple and inexpensive. The new phones were purchased and the telephone company came and ran some wires. The installer warned Sal that adding further lines would entail considerably more work and cost.

Mason Gentry, a long-term deacon, had taken on the task of finding volunteers to staff the phones. He and Jonathon developed a short list of things to do and say during the calls and a longer list of things to avoid. Mason gave initial training to each volunteer after he and Jonathon had massaged the plan until they believed they had a workable format.

The phone calls led to many interesting conversations as people poured out their difficulties and their loneliness to the volunteers. For the young families, the matter of daycare was by far the most pressing. For the retirees, loneliness was the major issue. There were a few stay-at-home moms. For these women, the matter of loneliness and the need to have meaningful, adult interaction with other women was almost overwhelming.

The loneliness seemed to be increased by the confines of the high-rise buildings. No one knew their neighbors and going for a walk entailed an elevator ride that simply placed people onto a busy downtown street. There was nothing that could be called a neighborhood and certainly no neighborhood feelings.

An inquiry by Darla came up with the information that all the buildings had community rooms built into them. Why these meeting spaces were not used more by the tenants was a mystery.

The calls were kept on a first name basis. No attempt was made at follow-up unless the caller specifically requested one. The goal of the mailout program and the resultant phone ministry was to bring Downtown Fellowship to people's attention and to put a human face to what many saw as an unfamiliar, mysterious organization. For too much of the current generation, the organized church was irrelevant. Choosing his words with care, Jonathon had tried to explain this to the congregation. The message was not well-received by many of the older members, people who had trouble believing that their world had changed so much. Fortunately, the deacon board had come to see the truth of the situation.

"We want to see those oak pews filled to capacity," Jonathon told the board. "But it seems to me that we have to introduce ourselves, and the church, to our neighbors before they'll start to listen to our message. If we come to believe that this will be accomplished easily or quickly, we'll be setting ourselves up for disappointment. But we've made a start and folks are beginning to respond. I take each phone call as a small victory that can lead to a bigger victory."

Unexpected and unplanned for, the calls had led to a thriving coffee and visiting ministry within the church building. An easily accessed room close to the office was cleaned out and furnished with comfortable chairs hauled in from other parts of the building. A table was set up with chairs placed around it. A coffee maker was purchased by an elderly man who loved to visit and talk about old times. The coffee maker and an assortment of mugs found a home on a small table. Someone placed a donation jar on the table to collect funds for the purchase of coffee. Water for the coffee and tea had to be carried in from the lunchroom. The meeting room was accessed through the office. With the new security system, Sal was able to keep track of who she opened the door for. This resulted in many first name greetings as folks arrived.

Before long, the ladies began bringing plates of baking and a few board games showed up. Watching from the doorway, Jonathon scratched his head and chuckled. To no one in particular he said, "Never would have imagined." He left the rest of his thoughts unspoken.

Sal, standing not far away, smilingly said, "Another thing you might not have imagined is that a couple of romances are budding among the seniors."

This time, Jonathon really was surprised. But after he thought about it for a few moments, he nodded his head. "I have no real comment. I've never lived alone as so many do. I've never been lonely. Have no idea what that feels like." He turned to Sal. Impulsively, he said, "You're single, Sal. Do you ever get lonely?"

The two co-workers had mostly avoided personal issues. The question seemed to just pop out of Jonathon's mouth unplanned. He immediately wondered if he had gone too far.

A sad look flashed across Sal's face before she got control of it. "Not really. I did years ago. But for a brief time, I had a wonderful husband. Once is enough when that once is with the right one."

Jonathon was taken aback and embarrassed. "I apologize, Sal. I've never heard of you being married. Somehow I just supposed...well, I don't know what I supposed."

Sal's sad smile partially returned. "Not to worry, Jonathon.

Very few people know. I don't see the purpose in talking about that part of my life. It was before I moved here.

"Brock was a military man. Army. He intended to make it his life-long career. Well, I guess in one way he did. He was a good man. Good for me, and good for the army, and good for the country. The patrol he went on in some cesspool of a foreign country was supposed to be routine; no real risk. A group of twelve went out. When the media reported the incident, they said four were injured but only one was killed. Doesn't sound like much, does it? Just one. It's the military, after all. Things happen. But when that one is yours, one becomes the biggest number in the world."

Jonathon was scrupulous about not touching female staff or volunteers but he gently laid his hand on Sal's shoulder. "I apologize again, Sal. I just didn't know. That was clumsy of me. I'm so sorry for your loss."

There didn't seem to be anywhere to go from that point so they both turned and walked away. Sal went to her desk and pulled a Kleenex from the bottom desk drawer. On her way to the washroom, Jonathon saw her dabbing at her eyes.

'Sometimes I can really put my foot in it,' the pastor said to himself.

Jonathon sat in his office in a reflective daze, staring at the computer screen without really seeing the words shining from it. It seemed as though God was filling in some blanks in the downtown ministry: food for the homeless; troubled and lonely people phoning in to talk; lonely seniors laughing over board games and old stories; budding romances in the church meeting room; a small somewhat off-the-wall ministry started by a young couple, meeting in the old youth room; a traveling college choir calling and unexpectedly offering a free concert; an arts group picking up the tab for the organ repair; a world-renowned organist visiting. What else might God have in mind?

The delight of Jonathon's pastoral heart, taking precedence over all the rest, was that three couples had been attending from the high-rises the past two weeks. All the work. All the planning. All the prayer. It was all about the salvation of souls; having God do His mighty work in human hearts. Everything else they did was done to nourish that goal. If the church had to do all kinds of peripheral things and jump through strange hoops, that's what they would do if it led to new names being written down in glory.

Jonathon had trouble imagining the apostle Paul wrapping his mind around, or approving, all these different activities. But then, this was a totally changed culture from anything Paul knew. Paul, in the first century, knew nothing of a world where family structure was largely broken; where both spouses were working away from the home; where children were being raised by strangers; where seniors retired to small condos, distant from extended families, facing day after day of feeling useless and having nothing to do; where lives everywhere were being overwhelmed by cynicism. If the church could break into that quagmire of stressed culture and use the opportunities to speak of the love of God, it was all worth it.

Jonathon, as he had done before, tried to imagine the angels rejoicing over a redeemed soul. There was no clear picture; there were too many unknowns. What are angels really like? Do they sing as we understand singing to be? Do they really see all that is going on in the world? Do they have a part in the salvation process? As the Scripture implied, he could only see as if through a glass darkly. Still, picturing angels rejoicing over redeemed souls at Downtown Fellowship was a glorious thought and a glorious sight. "Lord," he prayed quietly, "Let it be."

Jonathon had just turned back to answering some e-mailed correspondence when Sal tapped on the half-open office door. When Jonathon looked her way, she quietly said, "Buzz, from that radio show, is on the line. Do you want me to get rid of him?"

Jonathon hunched his shoulders in resignation. After the last frustrating call from Buzz where he spread the malicious bank-ruptcy rumor, Jonathon had thought long and hard about how he would proceed with the talk show host. Picking up the phone he said, "You're a slow learner, Buzz. I have repeatedly asked you to arrange for a time before you call. This is the last time I'll answer without you doing that. Now, what can I do for you?"

The announcer started in on his familiar patter. "We're on the Can You Believe This Show..."

Jonathon cut him off, "Yes, Buzz, we all know that. Get to the point. You don't seem to be able to understand how busy some people are. I have no time for your foolishness. If you have a question, get it out or I'm gone."

Buzz laughed and said, "My, you're touchy today, Pastor."

"Not touchy. Just very busy."

"OK, Pastor. Here's the thing. I know you run a lunch program for the homeless over there at your church. But now the grapevine has it that your plans are to shut it down. With winter just a few short weeks away and months of cold weather facing these needy folks, don't you think that's a bit heartless? Is that really the reputation you want for your church? Putting the homeless out on the streets, cold and hungry? And that's after accepting taxpayers' dollars for the support of the program. I see some serious problems here, Pastor. I'm sure my listeners would like to hear a clear explanation for those actions."

Jonathon expelled a frustrated breath. "Buzz, you seem to specialize in getting faulty information and spreading foolish rumors. Here's the truth of the matter. We have been doing some research in the interests of efficiency and good service to the homeless. By the way, they are most generally referred to as 'clients'.

"Your spy at city hall must have passed on the news of our inquiry and, as usual with just a small piece of the whole, you ran with the rumor and made up the rest.

"The city spends a lot of taxpayer money on several food

programs. Ours and the Salvation Army's are the only church-run programs. But there are others as well.

"Our church workers, assisted by several volunteers who are not from Downtown Fellowship Center, put in thousands of hours of free labor every year. One-hundred percent of the taxpayers' money goes into food purchases. Not one cent is spent on management or staff. The space for the dining room, the kitchen facilities, the costs of heating, lights, and natural gas for cooking, is all absorbed in the church budget. There is no cost to the public for these items.

"Our account books for this program are provided to the city every year and are open to the public. You could go to city hall and ask to see them.

"By the way, Buzz, let me ask you a question. I'm sure your listeners will be interested in the answer. You live in a building about one block from Downtown Fellowship Center. Just a short walk. Have you ever strolled over and offered to volunteer in the lunch program? You know, serve a meal or wash a dish? Have you ever put in any effort to assist these clients that you claim such interest in or are they merely a convenient tool for causing a stir on your radio program? Tell everyone the truth now, Buzz."

There was silence for a few seconds.

Finally Buzz came back. "I'm not sure how you think you know where I live, Pastor. I'll neither confirm nor deny what you say. And my working in your program is not the issue. The issue is the church taking public money and then shutting down the program. That's what my listeners are interested in."

Jonathon said, "Nice try, Buzz. But no cigar. The difference between you and I is that my research is accurate while yours is questionable at best. Would you like me to give your listeners your full address and your home phone number, plus your cell number? I have them all right here before me. It's all public information, Buzz. Do you remember our first conversation? It was only a few weeks ago. We talked about invasion of privacy and I told you that all this information is publicly available. But, of course, you know that so let's move on.

"The truth, I take it, is that you don't volunteer. OK, let's accept that and again move on. We're not talking about pushing the clients out onto the streets, cold and hungry, as you said. We're trying to find the best way to serve them. I'm sure the taxpayers would be happy to hear that. We'll provide the city managers with all our research once that task is complete. It will then become public information. For now, I'll give your listeners just a hint of what we have found so far. First, there are more lunch services available in the city than there are clients. That's a duplication of services and very inefficient. Second, what the clients appear to need most is breakfast and no one is offering that service. I'm not sure we will either but we're looking into it. In the meantime, we offer lunch as usual.

"So, is there anything else on your mind, Buzz? I have a rather full plate today and I really have to get back to work."

Buzz went into announcer mode, "We've been talking with Pastor Jonathon..."

Jonathon hung up the phone.

When Jonathon walked by Sal's desk a few minutes later, she said, "Why do you let him do that to you? Why get involved? He's little more than a loudmouth."

Jonathon answered, "He's not doing anything to me. I'm using him. Him and his loud mouth. I don't know if he has dozens of listeners, hundreds or thousands. But I do know that we're getting publicity that we could never afford to pay for. I also know that his program thrives on controversy and I have just fed him enough controversy to cause him to call back. When he calls back, you're going to demand that he make an appointment. He's then going to announce to his audience that he will be having me on the show, demanding answers to serious questions. He will name the day and time. His questions are all simplistic nonsense, of course, but people will tune in to hear the controversy carried forward. That's publicity, Sal, and we can use all we can get.

"I'm also going to try to get him to meet face-to-face. Perhaps have his call-in show done in a public venue. I'd like to get to know the man. His show is a gimmick. I'd like to know the man behind the mic."

THE PHONE RANG JUST AFTER LUNCH. SAL PASSED THE CALL along to Jonathon. "It's Terry's secretary on line one. Some kind of an emergency."

Jonathon picked up immediately. "What is it, Bea?"

"It's Terry, Jonathon," came the shaky response. "I found him slumped over his desk. I fear he's had another heart attack. We're waiting for the ambulance now. He's awake and talking, but just barely."

Jonathon's heart caught in his throat. This wasn't Terry's first time around. Jonathon hoped it wouldn't be his last. He took a deep breath. "I assume you've called his wife?" With that confirmed, Jonathon said, "As soon as the medics get there, call me back and tell me what they had to say and which hospital they're taking him to. In the meantime, take charge and keep the office functioning. You might call the foreman on each job site after you know more just so they don't hear something second-hand. But in no case is the work to stop. Tell the crew we'll keep them fully in the loop."

With all that confirmed, Jonathon hung up the phone and went to prayer. "Lord, Terry has had a lifelong struggle with heart issues. You have brought him through crises after crises. I suspect the extra burden he carries because of my absence has contributed to his stress level even though Terry denies this. I also suspect Global's bankruptcy and all that ugly matter entails has been a heavy burden for Terry. I further suspect that our spiritual enemy will do anything he can to disrupt our business, our families and this good ministry You have privileged me to be a part of. Attacking the ministry through the business does not surprise me in the least. You have protected and spared my family for which I give you my eternal thanks. Now I ask You to give the medical people wisdom and Your great love and grace to Terry. Comfort his wife, Blanche, and his family, I pray Lord. And protect Downtown Fellowship Center. The enemy will undoubtedly use this matter to trouble my mind and heart and to disrupt the ministry. We can't allow that to happen and only You can give the strength and protection needed. Extend Your grace this hour and day, Lord. I give you my thanks and worship. Amen."

Jonathon then told Sal about the situation and asked her to clear his calendar for the day knowing that as soon as he heard from Bea he would be heading to the hospital. There was nothing he could do there, of course, but he wanted to be available when Terry woke up.

Jonathon spent a half-hour working on his sermon. At the end of that time, he had no idea what he had written or where he thought the message was going, or even if he was still on his original track. His mind was whirling with thoughts of Terry, Blanche, and their family. Mixed up in all the other emotions running at top speed through his mind and heart was his own interest in the construction business, the Downtown ministry, and the impact of Terry's situation on his own family. His usual 'glass is half-full' attitude was severely challenged.

The construction world is a high energy, high volatility world when everything is going well. To think that a major event like Terry's health would not impact the business would be irresponsible.

When Bea finally called back, he listened to her explanation of events while he hit 'save' on the word processor and shut off the computer. He rose from his desk, shrugged his arms into his jacket, and turned off the office light. "Sal, I'll be at the General. That's where the ambulance is taking Terry. Don't know when I'll be back. I'll call you. In the meantime, would you please call a couple of deacons and have them spread the word. Their prayer support for Terry is critical."

Sal nodded and made a note. "Did you remember to call Janet?"

"I will as soon as I know more."

With nothing further said, he was gone.

JONATHON SPENT A COUPLE OF HOURS AT THE HOSPITAL talking with doctors and trying to comfort Terry's family. The medical people confirmed that Terry was in no immediate danger of death but he also was not going to jump out of bed and get back to work.

"You can expect a long recovery period," the ICU doctor advised the family. "As to working again, that will be in months if not a year or more." That news brought tears to Blanche's eyes and a cold chill to Jonathon's heart. Both were silently thinking 'What am I going to do?'

Terry was under heavy sedation and there was nothing more Jonathon could do for Blanche. He called Janet with the news, then drove to the construction company office before going to each job site. At each stop he brought the crew up to date on Terry's condition and encouraged them to keep going forward as usual.

Isolating Terry from his thoughts until he had more information and more time to think the situation through, he drove back to the church. The work at Downtown Fellowship still had to be his primary task. He stumbled through the remainder of his sermon preparation and put the final touches to the Sunday service, thankful for the others who had proven so dependable at their tasks; Sal, the music team, the ushers, the custodian, the deacons, he knew they would all step up and do what was required.

Several days before Terry's heath issue intruded on their lives, Jonathon had arranged for a 2:00 PM meeting on Thursday with the deacons. Hank Grissom and his wife, the organizers of the lunch program, had been invited to attend the meeting. The interns were prepared to talk at some length about their research into the food for the homeless program. They had also prepared a Power Point presentation showing the various possibilities for the use of the gym. Jonathon had allotted them as much time as they needed for the project. The summer was coming to an end and, with it, the tenure of the interns. This would be their final presentation. Jonathon and Sal had seen the proposal. They applauded the efforts of the young people and were anxious for the leadership team to see it.

The church had always lived on the trailing edge of the digital age. Not finding what he needed at the church, Robert managed to locate one of his college professors. That lady was kind enough to loan him the necessary equipment for projecting the Power Point onto a big screen.

Robert and Darla set up a room with the screen and computer equipment. They placed chairs in a semi-circle like a theater. They had much of the Power Point presentation ready in printed form which they would pass out after the meeting was completed. One of the printed pages listed the helping agencies the interns were able to identify; government as well as private. There was help available from mental health, alcohol and drug addiction treatment centers, veteran's organizations, a group who assisted people with paperwork for personal identi-fication, a volunteer group that helped clients connect with out-of-touch families, and a list of others. There was an abundance of assistance available but few clients sought the help. Jonathon hoped to see some improvement in that area.

The interns had coffee and cookies ready.

"Where did the cookies come from?" asked Jonathon.

Darla, ever sassy, said, "What? You think I'm just another pretty face in the crowd? I made them. And I expect you to like them or at least to say you do."

Jonathon grinned at her. "Very domestic. Thank you."

Jonathon opened the meeting with a brief prayer, specifically asking for wisdom as the board worked towards a decision on the food program. He then said, "What you are going to see is not in any way the primary focus of the church. But it is an effective way to put much-needed help directly before those who most need that help. I think it is fair to say that if the program wasn't already a part of Downtown Fellowship we wouldn't consider starting it at this time. We have other, more pressing issues to deal with. But the fact is that the community sees the lunch program as an integral part of our existence. How we are seen by the community matters a great deal. It would be difficult to get the message of salvation in Christ out to an audience that already had a negative opinion of the church. We must be thoughtful and cautious. As you watch what Robert and Darla have put together, please keep these things in mind."

Jonathon glanced at Darla a couple of times as he spoke, wondering what was going on in her head. It intrigued him that the talk of Christ and salvation no longer caused the young unbeliever to cringe and she bowed her head with the others as he prayed.

Following the Power Point presentation when several questions were asked and answered - and the men were satisfied that they understood the renovations required, the large changes for the volunteers, and all the costs - the interns were thanked and excused.

The men and Mrs. Grissom moved to the table. The coffee pot was passed around for refills while some stood to stretch their legs. They then discussed the presentation with Jonathon taking the lead on the answers. The interns had addressed the physical work only. The philosophy of the why's and how's were left to the pastor and deacons.

The first question from Noble Pearson was, "OK, I understand the need and our desire to continue serving the community, especially these clients. We have been doing the food program for several years. There is, however, a lot of money involved in this proposed change. Not just in the capital costs for the renovations but the ongoing operation will also be costly. Even if we come to grips with those costs, I can't help wondering what any of it does for the rebuilding of the church body. How does it put folks back into those empty pews?"

Jonathon answered, "Truthfully, it probably doesn't. Oh, there may be the odd client who finds his way into the church from time to time but we should probably not expect a great influx. The reason for this initiative is the same as that which moved the board years ago to start the lunch ministry in the first place; it's simply a good thing to do. It's helping some folks who have a clear need. We have the secondary hope that a regular shower and a periodic change of clothing might help these clients feel a bit better about themselves and perhaps make some changes in their way of life. But we are under no illusions. This is a difficult ministry. We are seeing it as a public service to the needy without any emphasis on gain for the church."

Rudy Goetz followed up with, "Tell me again what's planned for the basement. My understanding is that wanting the basement space free is what started this whole thing."

Again, Jonathon answered. "The basement is a large, underused space. Except for the lunch program, the basement has been idle for years. The phone inquiries from the high-rise contacts have exposed several problems that we might be able to put some energy into if that space was better utilized. We've heard of problems that, clearly, we have no hope of solving. Still, we want to do what we can. Plus, some of those problems might be turned into opportunities if we address them correctly. Serving the high-rise tenants is very much what Downtown

Fellowship is about. We live in a skeptical age. People are encouraged from birth to doubt and question. Especially, to doubt and question old cultural, establishment matters including the church. If we can connect with people at their point of need, perhaps we can earn their trust. If we earn their trust, there is a better chance of them listening when we talk about the Lord."

The talk went on for another hour. As the questions wound down, the meeting drew to a close and the men assured the pastor of their support. Jonathon thanked them all and promised to keep them well informed on the matter.

THE CONFESSION AND RECONCILIATION LETTERS WENT OUT
to all the former members and pastors on the last Friday in
August. In total, there were several hundred contact addresses.
When allowance was made for more than one person at many of
the addresses, the total number of recipients was disturbingly
large. Jonathon and the board agreed to make the timing of the
meeting tight to prevent any possible problems from having an
opportunity to foment. There were just three weeks from the
mailing until the meeting. Jonathon, the board, and the church
body had covenanted together to pray and seek God's favor
during those three weeks.

The following Monday afternoon, Sal answered the phone to
hear Buzz Grappler's high-energy voice say, "Buzz Grappler
here; Radio WKS, the Can You Believe This? afternoon show.
Let me speak with Pastor McCann please."

Sal responded, "I'm so sorry, Mr. Grappler. The Pastor is
extremely busy this afternoon. He couldn't possibly be interrupted. Let's make an appointment. I'm sure he'll be happy to
talk with you. I have his appointment book right here. Would
Wednesday at 3:00 PM suit you?"

Sal heard the caller take in a huge breath that sounded like an expression of frustration. "You don't understand, Ma'am. I have a radio audience waiting to hear from Mr. McCann. Please put me through."

Sal was delighted to have Jonathon's approval to say, "No sir, it's you who doesn't understand. The Pastor is very busy doing important work. If I interrupted him for something so frivolous as a radio show, he would be very upset. But I can pencil you in for Wednesday at 3:00."

The caller said, "Alright. Wednesday at 3:00." He then spoke back to his radio audience before he hung up the phone. "There you have it, good listeners," he said sarcastically. "The very important Pastor Jonathon McCann is too busy doing whatever it is he does to answer your questions. But you can rest assured I'll hold his feet to the fire on Wednesday. Be sure to be listening then and tell all your friends to tune in. We'll see what the Pastor has to say for himself."

When Sal told Jonathon about the call and the Wednesday appointment, Jonathon smiled and nodded. "Good work, Sal. Now he'll know that I'm not at his beck and call. He'll also have a larger audience after he talks about the appointment a few more times. It should be a good time."

JONATHON FOUND HIMSELF WISHING HE HAD A GROUP similar to the deacon board to advise him on the construction business. The men on the board - plus a small, select assembly of other men and women - had proven to be the stabilizing factor in the renewal efforts of Downtown Fellowship. With his commitment to the church being his first priority, he was left in a quandary. While Terry was hospitalized, the business was his alone to manage. How could he possibly do both jobs? His small, self-selected board of advisors consisted of his wife, the company accountant and lawyer, and - on occasion - their banker. Although she had always stayed in the background, Terry's wife Blanche would have to be consulted on major decisions.

Jonathon took the day away from church matters to concentrate on the business. His first stop was the office. Bea was fully capable of keeping the office running efficiently so Jonathon simply made the rounds, speaking with each of the staff and assuring them that even during Terry's illness it was business as usual. He asked each of them to give their full support to Bea and received their assurance in return.

Jonathon spent some time with Gregory, the new estimator.

"How is it going? There were two new project bids closing around this time. Did our bids get in?"

Gregory nodded. "The bids are in and one job closes this afternoon. The other is tomorrow. Terry was planning on attending the bid openings. Are you going to do that now?"

"No, you are," answered Jonathon. "Whether we win or lose, say nothing to any of the other contractors. Be friendly but noncommittal. They'll all have heard about Terry. Any serious questions from the owners or architects of the projects you will defer to me."

Jonathon then spoke privately with Bea, thanking her for her steadfast loyalty to Terry and the business. He asked her opinion of his plans for the near future. She stifled some private doubts and finally supported his thought to promote Joe Dulka, the site superintendent on the shut-down shopping center job, to the position of company superintendent, overseeing all the projects.

Joe had been temporarily placed on a school construction job; Jonathon drove to that job and found Joe pouring over the plans with the site foreman. After discussing the progress of the job with the two men, he asked Joe to walk to the car with him. There he presented Joe with the offer to take over Terry's role as company job superintendent with an increase in pay to compensate for the additional responsibility. With some hesitation, Joe accepted the promotion. The two men spent time discussing what had to be done. Jonathon then called the entire school project crew together. When the men had gathered, he brought them up to date on Terry's health and the new position Joe would be filling. He thanked them all for their loyalty to the company and for their good work.

Jonathon visited the other two job sites and repeated what he had done at the school. By the time he completed those visits, the day was well advanced. He called Sal to get an update on church matters and then drove home.

In the privacy of his home office, Jonathon made a call to the company lawyer to inquire about the situation with Global.

Although the lawyer had no concrete news, the indication was that the matter was near settlement as far as the shopping center was concerned. The bankruptcy court was going to isolate that project from the remainder of the Global mess and allow it to proceed. It seemed possible that the crews could be back on the job with new guaranteed financing within the week.

Wednesday afternoon arrived and at 3:00 PM, Sal's phone rang. She barely got the first half of 'hello' out of her mouth when a forceful voice said, "Buzz Grappler, Radio WKS, the Can You Believe This? afternoon show. Let me speak with Pastor McCann please."

Sal answered, "Just a moment please, Mr. Grappler. Jonathon is expecting your call."

Jonathon was standing beside Sal's desk. They had been discussing what to put in the Sunday bulletin when the phone rang. Jonathon grinned at Sal and headed for his office. He picked up his phone and said, "Good afternoon, Buzz. I pray your day is going well."

The answer was, "My days always go well when I can get the truth to pass on to my listeners. I have a couple of questions for you today, Jonathon. My listeners need to know the truth of some matters."

Jonathon wedged himself into the conversation. "I'm always happy to share the truth, Buzz. But before we start, please tell me approximately how many listeners you have on an average day?"

"I'm usually the one asking the questions, Jonathon."

"I understand that and I'm fine with it but you must have some idea how many people we're talking to."

Buzz was silent for just a moment. Finally, "I'll talk with our research people and try to get you an answer for our next radio visit. But right now my listeners would like more detailed information on why you and your church are leaving the homeless and destitute on the street, hungry and cold, with winter just around the corner. Why are you shutting down the lunch program that tax dollars have supported for several years?"

Jonathon couldn't hold back a chuckle. "I have to give you marks for trying again, Buzz. But I've already told your listeners that no such a thing has happened nor do we have concrete plans for the future. I can say that we're doing extensive research into the overall situation in the city. Would you be interested in me sharing that research with you?"

"Anything that is the truth would be welcome, Pastor."

Jonathon said, "Alright, here's what we've found out so far. Some of this I told you a couple of weeks ago." He then went on to tell the radio audience what the interns had found in their city-wide survey. He stressed the problem of food supply and the issues around the donations from the big stores, assuring Buzz and his audience that he recognized the stores generosity. "They're doing a good thing and we are all thankful for it. But the longer-term solution might be found in purchasing the supplies."

He concluded with, "It makes little sense for the lunch providers to have empty seats and wasted food. Clearly our program - or one of the others - is superfluous and a waste. But the need for a breakfast program presents a whole range of issues that we haven't sorted out yet. You have my assurance that we're working on it. I'd be pleased to keep you informed as we go along."

Buzz seemed to be listening but, over the phone, Jonathon had no assurance of that. After a pause, the announcer said, "Let's leave that for now and talk about your construction business that's fighting bankruptcy. And now your managing partner has had a heart attack and is out of the picture. That leaves you with both a business and a church to run. Which one are you going to walk away from? Usually money rules so I suspect you will give up on the church. What do you say about all that?"

"The first thing I would say, Buzz, is that you are malicious and careless with the truth. You know full well that Proctor-McCann is not fighting bankruptcy. One of our clients is facing some serious problems. On the one project we are involved in with that company, everything is under control. Our company has paid all the suppliers and sub-trades fully up to date, and that job is shut down until new financing is in place.

"Our other projects are continuing as normal. Our company is in no financial distress at all. It's true that my partner's heath puts a strain on me and the rest of the business staff but that's being managed by moving a couple of people around. My commitment to the church is for two years, as I've told you before. I'll not be going back on that commitment."

Buzz picked up the conversation by saying, "We'll see about that as time goes along. Bear in mind, Pastor, that neither I nor my listening audience wish you or your company any ill will. We just find it difficult to believe that you can juggle both of these rather large balls at once. I think one, or perhaps both, will fall to the ground." Then abruptly Buzz said, "We'll want to talk again soon."

Jonathon jumped in before the station could go to commercial. "I'm fine with talking again, Buzz, but don't forget to make an appointment. And now I have a suggestion for you and an invitation. I'm inviting your station to set up a remote site at Downtown Fellowship Center and for you to broadcast a couple of your programs from here with an invited, live audience. That way we could talk person-to-person and your audience could put a face to both of our voices. They could even ask live questions from the floor. What do you say to that, Buzz?"

"I say, let me think about it and talk with our production people."

The station went to commercial with nothing more from the announcer.

ON THE FIRST SUNDAY OF SEPTEMBER JONATHON PUBLICLY thanked the interns for a valuable summer's work. Neither were in attendance. Both Robert and Darla had been faithfully attending services with Kyle in the old youth room. While talking about the interns, Jonathon used the opportunity to advise the congregation of the ongoing research into the lunch program for the homeless as well as the other valuable work done by the young people.

Because Jonathon knew how easily people misunderstand what they hear, he put special emphasis on the fact that the leadership was doing serious research only. No decisions would be made without congregational involvement.

For a special thanks and farewell time for the interns, Jonathon invited any who wished to meet on Monday morning.

The next morning, Jonathon, Kyle, Sal, Watson, most of the deacons, plus fifteen church members gathered for coffee and donuts with the interns. Both the young people had to register for school that afternoon. Jonathon presented Robert and Darla with a letter outlining their work experience, thanking them for their hard work and faithful service, and strongly encouraging them in their future pursuits. He also presented each with a check in addition to their agreed remuneration as a further thank you. After a heartfelt round of applause from the gathering, they opened the box of donuts and poured the coffee.

Jonathon couldn't help wondering what thoughts Darla had after her months of exposure to the church and to Christians. He knew she wasn't the same spiritually-unattached young lady they had hired in May but he wasn't sure how far the change went. She hadn't invited personal conversation and he reluctantly respected her privacy. His prayer for her was that it was more than holding the baby that was enticing her to Kyle's services.

On Tuesday morning Jonathon was busy preparing his sermon when Sal called on the intercom. "Jonathon, it's Bea. I think you should take this call."

Jonathon thanked Sal and picked up the phone. "Good morning, Bea. What's happening?"

"Good news on two fronts, Jonathon. First, Terry is much improved this morning. He's out of ICU and in a regular ward. The doctor says if he keeps improving the way he has so far he can go home next week. That's a long way from coming back to work but it's great news anyway.

"The second thing is that our lawyer called. He has written confirmation from both Global's lawyer and their bank that new funding is in place to complete the shopping center. The remainder of Global's world is a tangled mess of lawsuits and creditor claims but everyone seems to have agreed that the shopping center should be completed, although Global is now totally out of that picture. They're urging us to get the project underway just as soon as possible. The bankruptcy court has sent confirmation that this restart has their approval. We'll be reporting to them and they'll authorize the financial distribution. The lawyer just faxed over all the documents.

"I believe everyone involved sees the completion of the shopping center and turning it into a saleable property as one way to recoup some money.

"We also just received a check to cover our last, unpaid draw as well as the builder's liens. The lawyers say it's meant as a good-will gesture to encourage us to treat the project as if it was starting fresh."

Jonathon laughed out loud. "Bea, I could put up with news like that every hour of each day. Especially the news about Terry. And that check will certainly relieve the financial pressure. It's kind of humorous that they would call the paying of legitimate debts a good-will gesture but let's not call them on that. We'll take the situation as it is and let them win the verbal by-play.

"I'd appreciate it if you would call Joe and have him meet me at the office at eight tomorrow morning. Then get a fax out to all the sub-trades advising them of the situation. Ask them to plan on resuming the work on Thursday morning. Then call the men we had to lay off and ask them to plan on working on Thursday also. And be sure to call me anytime you have more good news. Oh, wait, I almost forgot. Be sure to call Blanche and tell her about the project. She can pass that on to Terry. He'll be relieved to hear the news. And thanks for your good work, Bea. I'll be in the office in the morning. If there are details to work out, we can do it then."

"Before you go, Jonathon, there's something else. We just heard this morning. The company has been awarded the contracts on both of those jobs Gregory put together. Now you'll have to try to figure out if we can handle them or pull our bid back. According to the Construction Association rules, we have one week."

Again, Jonathon thanked Bea. His mind was starting to feel like a washing machine on the spin cycle. Matters demanding his attention were threatening to reach the unmanageable level. Closing his mind to business as best he could, he got back to his pastoral duties. 'Do one thing at a time and do it well,' he said to himself.

Jonathon no sooner got back to working on his sermon

when Sal called on the intercom again. "I'm so sorry, Jonathon. I hate to interrupt you again. I have Mark Bannister on line one. You might remember he's the one who was here several Sundays ago. He decided you were just another liberal teacher just like all the other liberals.

"Yes," replied Jonathon, "I remember. It's poor timing but I'll talk to him."

Jonathon took a deep breath, expecting the worst, and picked up the phone. "Good morning, Mr. Bannister. It's good of you to call. What can I do for you?"

The response was not friendly. "What's this foolish letter we received in the mail this morning? On top of all the error you liberals teach, now you want to bury it all under some kind of phony forgiveness and reconciliation nonsense. A kumbaya love-in I think kids used to call it. As if that's enough to cover all the error and liberal teaching that's gone on over the years." As the caller talked, his voice was getting louder, his anger threatening to become uncontrollable. "You need to repent of all your sinful error and start preaching God's good truth. And you need to do it using the only Bible God sanctions and get rid of all those error-filled books you use. Only then can you expect God's forgiveness.

"My wife and I will have nothing at all to do with further error and heresy. I suspect God will judge you all in good time. Don't send us any more of your foolish letters. We washed our hands of this matter years ago."

As Jonathon was formulating a reply, the dial tone sounded; the caller was gone. Jonathon set the phone back in its cradle and thought, 'Lord, have mercy on those who so seriously misunderstand the Scriptures, totally missing the parts about self-righteousness and anger and judging our brothers.'

Jonathon stepped out of his office and walked to Sal's desk. "I knew all wasn't going to be sweetness and light, Sal. Mr. Bannister sounded pretty firm about not wanting any more letters. Although we have no plans for any further correspondence on this matter, it would probably be best to remove their name from the mailing list. Hopefully, we won't have too many more calls like that."

Sal nodded and opened the Word file. She scrolled down to the Bs, highlighted Bannister, and clicked delete. She turned to Jonathon. "Done."

Jonathon put his hands in his pockets and walked slowly up to the sanctuary. As his habit had become in recent weeks, he lifted the key cover on the grand piano. He sat, closed his eyes and played for fifteen minutes, running one song into the next as his fingers found the keys from memory. Playing worship music was the best therapy he had found.

AS COMPETENT AS JOE DULKA HAD PROVEN HIMSELF TO BE on a single construction project, it soon became evident that he was in over his head when overseeing several jobs at once. Jonathon and Terry had both learned the industry through a long, thorough process, beginning with a single small job and progressing on to bigger and multiple projects. Jonathon's respect for his long-time foreman had caused him to misjudge the man's overall ability. Throwing him into the heat of many battles at once had proven to be more than Joe could adapt to.

It was Bea who first sensed that Joe was in trouble, confirming her initial hesitation at Joe's appointment. As the office manager and the first one to receive troubling phone calls from the various job foremen, the alarm bells went off in her mind. After hesitating for two days, hoping that Joe would pull it together, she finally picked up the phone and called Jonathon. Sal put the call through.

"Jonathon, I hate to lay more trouble on you but, judging from the calls I'm receiving from the job sites, I think we have a problem with Joe. I know how highly you and Terry both think of him, and I know he's giving his new position all he's got to give, but I'm not sure he's up to the task. The foremen are already troubled by some of his decisions and with two new jobs coming on stream, well, I think we may need to look in another direction. Added to all of that, no one knows the mall job like Joe does and his time would seem to be fully needed there. I know you put Tony in charge at the mall but my feeling is that it's Joe we need."

Jonathon thanked his office manager and told her he would deal with the matter. That was the easy part. The more difficult part came after he hung up the phone and asked himself exactly how he would handle it.

His solution was to wait until the end of the day and then drive to the mall job. He found Joe in the construction office; the job had resumed a few days earlier. When they were alone, Jonathon said, "I made a mistake, Joe. I managed to lull myself into believing the mall job was close enough to the end that it wouldn't demand all your time. Really, I should have known better. I acted before I had adequately thought it all out. I needed a solution to Terry's absence and I grabbed the first one that came to my mind. On sober reflection, it's obvious that this is your job. No one else can do what you do here. With the Global mess hopefully behind us, we can't chance anything going wrong here. If we let Tony carry on as foreman of our own crew, would you be content to step away from the other projects and mastermind this one? Coordinate with all the trades? Bring it to a conclusion for us? Your extra pay would stay in place."

Joe leaned back in his chair, pushed his hard hat to the back of his head and ran his fingers through the little bit of graying hair that remained. "Those are the sweetest words I've heard in a month of Sundays. It's only been a couple of weeks since I started with the other responsibilities but I knew several days ago that I would either make a mess of something or die of stress and worry." He wiped his gnarled hand through his receding hairline and grinned. "Don't you ever do that to me again. And don't think I don't know what you're doing now either. It's good of you to let me off the hook and lay blame on yourself but, rightly, that's not exactly how it should go. Let's say no more about it and get this mall finished."

Jonathon smiled at his most trusted foreman. "Go home and get some supper and a good night's sleep. We have a mall to build."

Driving away, Jonathon knew he still had company problems to find solutions to. But that was an issue for tomorrow. Right now, he had a family that was waiting supper for him.

The time for the big church meeting was coming close. Several letters, many phone calls and a goodly number of e-mails had arrived at Sal's desk confirming people's interest in putting the past behind them, getting right with God, and reconnecting with old Christian friends. A few notes were somewhat negative but none approached the feelings that Mr. Bannister had laid on Jonathon. A few writers seemed intent on opening old wounds for further discussion. Jonathon and the board were adamant that no such thing would happen.

The deacons had organized a daily prayer vigil, poring over the lists of names of past church attendees. Many tears had been wept in the prayer room as the gathered men and women pled with God for mercy and renewal and oneness.

Jonathon was talking with Sal at her desk when the phone rang. She picked it up and looked at Jonathon as she listened to the caller. Nodding her head as the caller talked, she said, "Just a moment please, Mr. Tanner. Jonathon will be right with you."

Jonathon went to his office and picked up the phone. Before he got a chance to say hello, the caller's excited voice said, "Rev. Isaiah Heffner called me a moment ago. He has accepted our invitation to attend the meeting. I'm both surprised and pleased. He made it clear that he doesn't look forward to coming. He admitted that his wife talked him into it. But none of that matters. What matters is that he will be here. I have arranged for him to stay with us during his visit. This is just one answered prayer among the many prayerful requests we're all making of God on this matter. We'll talk again soon."

Even for someone as matter of fact as Orvis Tanner could be, the call was terse and cut short. Jonathon heard the dial tone with his response still only half-formed. He pulled the phone from his ear and smiled as he laid the receiver back in the cradle. Orvis Tanner had been as excited as Jonathon had ever heard the man. 'Good work, my friend,' he thought. 'And I'd be prepared to believe it's your money that purchased the plane tickets. Oh yes, very good work indeed.'

In his busyness, Jonathon had found himself whispering short-sentence prayers throughout the day. With Mr. Tanner's phone call ended, the pastor leaned back in his chair, closed his eyes and said aloud, 'Thank you Lord for Your faithfulness. Again, I pray for a great outpouring of Your Spirit on our gathering and especially on Rev. Heffner. The man was so deeply hurt. Only Your spirit can heal him.'

It was the Wednesday before the big Saturday church meeting. Jonathon, Sal, and the entire leadership team were totally focused on the coming meetings. Sal had gathered a few folks to set up the gymnasium for the after-meeting social gathering. Tables and chairs were moved from the basement. The tables were spread with white cloths. Centerpieces were set in place. Small vases were arranged, ready for fresh flowers to be purchased at the last minute.

Three hymns were carefully chosen and the words were printed on sheets of colored paper. Only the organ and piano would be used for the song service. The other instruments were put away. The microphone was set up and the sound system tested. Well-known and experienced ushers were selected to be at the doors, welcoming folks as they arrived.

Finally, Noble Pearson, who had taken charge of the sanctuary arrangements, declared that all was ready.

Staff and volunteers all went home on Wednesday evening satisfied that they were as ready as they could be for the big meeting.

After a pleasant and relaxing dinner with the family followed by an early bedtime, Jonathon's home phone rang just before midnight that evening. He was only half awake when he picked up the receiver. He mumbled something that sounded a bit like hello. The frantic voice on the other end of the line almost screamed, "He's gone. Oh my God, Jonathon, he's gone."

Jonathon was coming fully awake by this time. "Sorry, you caught me mostly asleep. Who is this and what did you say?"

"It's Blanche," wailed the voice. "It's Blanche, Jonathon. I'm at the hospital. He's gone. He was doing so well. He was coming home next week. But now he's gone."

Between the screams and the sobs, Jonathon wasn't sure he was getting the message correctly. By this time, Janet was sitting up in bed looking intently at her husband. It finally registered on Jonathon's half-asleep mind that it was Blanche on the other end of the line.

"Blanche? Take a deep breath Blanche and tell me again what happened."

The sobs were louder than ever. "I was sitting right there beside him. We were talking about him coming home. Suddenly he grabbed his chest and groaned. It was another heart attack. Oh my God, Jonathon, he's gone. There was nothing anyone could do. The nurse came immediately but she couldn't do anything to save him. He's gone. My wonderful Terry is gone." The sobbing continued but got more distant until Jonathon heard the phone clatter against something as if Blanche had dropped the receiver.

After calling Blanche's name several times without getting a response, Jonathon put his own phone down. He slowly lifted his face to Janet, barely able to see for the wetness that was forming in his eyes; a wetness partly from the realization of Terry's loss but also from another burden being stacked on top of the stress he was already bearing. With a voice choked with emotion he said, "Terry had another heart attack. He's dead. Throw some clothes on and let's get to the hospital. Blanche will need you."

Jonathon woke his eldest son and told him what had happened. "Your mom and I are going to the hospital. I don't know how long we'll be. You may have to make your own breakfasts and get to school yourselves." The young man just nodded numbly and laid back down, wide awake, his eyes staring at his father.

The midnight traffic was light so the trip to the hospital was brief. Still, it seemed like an eternity to Jonathon and Janet. The two of them sat in stunned silence, each struggling with their own thoughts. As Jonathon maneuvered the car into a parking space and reached for the door handle, Janet touched his shoulder. He leaned back towards her and their eyes met. Jonathon laid his head against the headrest and wrapped Janet's hand between his own. He tried to speak but all that came was a stifled sob. Another glance at Janet confirmed that her cheeks were wet with tears. The bucket seats and the center console separated them but still Janet managed to lay her head onto Jonathon's shoulder. They sat that way, in silence, for several moments.

Finally, Jonathon said, "We have to do this."

Janet quietly said, "I know. But we need to be strong for Blanche. Terry has been strong in the business so that you could minister at Downtown Fellowship. Now it's our turn." She sat quietly for another moment before saying, "You know, of course, that this is another challenge from the enemy. The evil one will attack anything to prevent God's work from going forward. What was it Joseph said when he finally confronted his brothers in Egypt?"

Jonathon's voice was so quiet Janet could barely hear it, "You meant it for evil but God meant it for good."

Janet lifted her head from Jonathon's shoulder and patted him twice on the arm. "Let's go do some good." She meant it in the human sense. It was too soon to hope to see what good God would bring from Terry's death.

There were few words possible when Jonathon and Janet

entered the quiet and dimly-lit visitors' room. The hospital chaplain was sitting with Blanche. Jonathon was tempted to ask what happened but then he realized the inadequacy of the question. The details may matter later but not right at that moment.

Blanche had risen when Janet reached for her and the two women wrapped themselves in a long, silent hug before Janet eased Blanche back onto the couch. The chaplain unobtrusively slipped away. The two women were quietly talking. Jonathon took the opportunity to walk out to the nursing station. The chaplain was waiting for him there.

"I thought you might come along. Do you want to see your friend before they move him?"

Jonathon just nodded, afraid that if he tried to speak he would burst into tears.

The chaplain led Jonathon to the second door down the hall and eased it open. He held it while Jonathon hesitantly stepped through the opening into the dimly-lit room.

With tentative steps, Jonathon moved towards the bed. All the monitors and other equipment had been removed. Terry's face had been washed and his hair combed. The staff had done the best they could with the man they had worked so hard to save but there was no way to make a dead man look alive.

The bed was neatly made with the starched white sheet pulled up. All that was visible of Jonathon's friend and business partner was his still face, gray in death.

The chaplain stood quietly inside the door after he silently eased it closed. He stood, as he had so often before, casting his eyes to the floor to provide as much privacy as possible to the mourner. There was an unbreakable hospital rule against family members being alone with the recently-deceased. The caring man had done this far too often. It was the part of his job he enjoyed the least.

Jonathon stood immobile and unbelieving. His every emotion was to cry out to God, railing against the unfairness of this good man having lived and struggled for years with an unhealthy heart when so many robust men were less deserving. As other thoughts and emotions jumbled and tumbled in his stressed mind, leading him towards anger and bitterness, he seemed to hear a very quiet voice crying to be heard. Jonathon's first reaction was 'not now'. He immediately felt guilty for the rebuff but still, for another short while, he allowed his emotions to run rampant. Finally, with a great expelling of a breath he hadn't realized he was holding, he gently laid his hand on Terry's forehead and raised his own eyes to the ceiling. He spoke no words as he surrendered his emotions.

The chaplain lifted his head as he heard Jonathon release the held breath. He was in time to see the grieving man's shoulders sag as if in resignation. After Jonathon lifted his hand away from Terry's brow, the chaplain stepped over to him. He placed his hand lightly on Jonathon's shoulder. "We should go. The staff have patients waiting for this bed."

Without a word, the two men turned and left the room. As they passed the nurses' station, the chaplain guided Jonathon towards the desk. He gave Jonathon a business card with his name and phone number on it. "I'm needed in the children's ward if there's nothing more I can do for you here." He turned his face to the nurse on duty. "Angie here knows how to locate me if you or your friend need me."

Angie nodded at the two men and turned back to her computer.

Still not speaking, Jonathon stood and watched as the chaplain stepped towards the elevator. Just as he was about to push the elevator call button, the doors opened and five people stepped out. Jonathon was relieved to see Blanche's parents escorting Terry and Blanche's three teenage children; two daughters and a son. A look of unbelief and pain was universal across the five faces.

Blanche's father saw Jonathon and stepped toward him. Jonathon said nothing. He simply held his arm out, pointing the way to the visitors' room. The older man nodded and led the little family down the corridor. In less than a minute, Janet stepped out and joined her husband. Jonathon turned to Angie and asked, "Is there somewhere to get a cup of coffee this late at night?"

The nurse answered, "Chaplain's office, main floor."

Jonathon walked to the visitors' room door and beckoned Blanche's father. "We'll stay a while in case we're needed. We'll be at the chaplain's office on the main floor. I'm told there's a coffee pot available there."

AFTER THE LONGEST NIGHT OF THEIR LIVES, JONATHON AND Janet drove home. The house was empty, the kids having gone to school. Dirty dishes in the sink were evidence that they had not left hungry.

Janet had called her employer earlier and arranged for the day off. The exhausted woman immediately went back to bed.

Jonathon's call to the construction office was one of the most difficult he had ever made. Bea immediately broke down in tears upon hearing the news. Jonathon gave her time to pull herself together before saying, "Bea, if you could please call each of the job foremen, give them the news and ask them to keep the men working, I would appreciate it. There is no possibility that we can shut down any of the jobs, even for one day. After you make those calls, send the office staff home for the day, lock up the office and go home yourself. Perhaps you could put a new message on the phone answering system. We'll need everyone back at work tomorrow."

Jonathon then had a shower and dressed for work. He was as exhausted, physically and emotionally, as he had ever been but, with the big church meeting only a couple of days away, he couldn't bring himself to stay home.

When he arrived at the church office, Sal took one look at him, saw the strain on his face, and asked, "What's going on? You look like you haven't slept in a week."

"Very perceptive, Sal. It hasn't been a week, but Janet and I were up most of the night. Terry passed away around midnight. We've been at the hospital since then."

Sal didn't ask any unnecessary questions, simply saying, "Jonathon, I'm so sorry. What can I do to help?"

"There's nothing any of us can do at this time. Terry and Blanche both have parents and siblings in the area. The family has it under control. But thanks for the offer."

In his office with the door closed, Jonathon sat at his desk and bowed his head in prayer. Strangely, he could think of no words to express his thoughts and grief. Believing and having taught that sometimes the most meaningful prayers are broken-hearted silence before God, and knowing that God is a discerner of the thoughts and intents of the heart, he was content with his own silence.

Sal, in the meantime, made a couple of calls informing the deacons of Terry's death and the added strain on Jonathon. Within minutes, an impromptu prayer support plan was put in place.

Jonathon picked up the phone and called his parents' home. His mother answered. The news was shared as briefly as possible. Again, the details could wait. Mrs. McCann said, "We'll be praying for you and everyone involved. Do you wish to speak with your father?"

"No. There's nothing else to say at this point. We'll talk soon."

After an hour of ineffectively pushing paper from one side of his desk to the other, Jonathon put on his coat and went for a walk. Sal watched him leave, wondering what else anyone could do to relieve the pain in the man's heart. She didn't know where the pastor was heading on his walk but she had an idea where he might end up. She called Kyle.

Jonathon - hands in pockets, shoulders hunched, with his

eyes cast downward to the sidewalk in front of him - walked east down Third Street until he was in an area he wasn't familiar with. He had been seeing and feeling nothing except grief. He barely noticed that a chill fall wind was threatening rain. The downtown streets had become a swirl of dirt and discarded paper and refuse, all caught in the gusting wind. When a sudden blast blew dust into his face, he stopped and turned away, pulling up his collar to protect himself while he waited for the wind to subside. The squall seemed to wrap itself around him as if it were blowing from all directions at once. The thought entered his mind: 'Just like my feelings and my thoughts; all over the place and doing no good at all, accomplishing nothing'. He circled the block and headed back west.

His aimless walk eventually led him to the little coffee shop he had found the first week of his ministry. He had used the small cafe for meetings several times over the months. Not really needing more coffee but finally tiring of the wind and dust, he walked into the familiar shop seeking shelter. He simply nodded at the man behind the counter and took a seat in the corner booth, the one that offered the most privacy.

When a cup of coffee was placed before him, he glanced up and thanked the server with a silent nod of his head. In another minute, the server was back, placing a just-out-of-the-oven muffin on the table. The loud conversation from another booth blocked out Jonathon's quiet 'thank you' although he hadn't ordered the baked treat.

Jonathon ignored the food. A strong man in many ways, Jonathon had dug deep to show that strength to Terry's family during the hospital visit. Janet was a strong woman as well, but still Jonathon had held his emotions in check while the two of them had ministered to Blanche. It belatedly occurred to him to be thankful that Janet felt free to weep with the distressed widow.

As the thoughts of Terry's death and all that it meant flashed through his troubled mind, Jonathon was suddenly overwhelmed with sadness bordering on despair. The loss of a friend, the impact on the business, the unspeakable loss to Blanche and the family, the further complication of his life; so much happening, so much to deal with.

He wasn't sure when the tears began spilling down his cheeks. He couldn't remember ever weeping in public. In fact, he hadn't consciously wept in years. He didn't purposely bury his face in his big hands either but somehow it had just happened.

His quivering lips caught him by surprise.

His shaking shoulders should have been a warning that the inner sobbing was about to become audible.

The folks in the other booth had left. He was alone in the little shop except for the server and that man had the wisdom to allow his one customer his privacy.

The distressed pastor sat for several minutes with his face buried in his hands. As the sobbing stopped, he wiped his still-closed eyes with the heel of his hand. The emotional meltdown had left him feeling empty. 'You're going to have to fill this empty, hurting void, Lord. I fear my strength is gone.'

Jonathon was startled when he finally opened his eyes to see Kyle sitting opposite him. The young man had kept his silence as he slid into the booth. Neither man spoke. Jonathon took the paper napkin the server had placed beside the muffin and wiped his eyes again and then his nose. He ran his fingers through his hair and adjusted his tie. He cleared his throat and looked at the cup of coffee before him. Just as he was about to take a sip of the now-cold drink, the server arrived with two steaming cups, placing one before each man. He picked up Jonathon's cold cup and quietly walked away.

Jonathon took a sip of the hot drink, looked at Kyle, and quietly said, "You find me at my weakest."

Kyle, wise beyond his years, answered, "I don't believe that. You're one of the strongest men I've ever met, spiritually and in every other way. To grieve for a friend lost is not weakness."

The two pastors sat in companionable silence for some time,

neither knowing where to take the conversation but also not uncomfortable with the silence.

Kyle finally spoke quietly as was his nature, "My father always believed that if we kept the first things first, God would deal with the rest at the correct time. I'm sure I don't fully understand your loss but what I do understand is that you have the biggest church meeting you are ever likely to lead coming up in just a couple of days. I don't know the details of the meeting and they are none of my business. But the little bit I do know tells me that you have to leave everything else to the Lord until the meeting is past. You are needed. No one else can do what you do. And it's no disrespect to the deceased to move that issue forward a few days. It'll all be there when you get to it."

Jonathon studied the young man for an uncomfortable length of time. Kyle started to fidget, thinking he might have offended the older pastor. When Jonathon finally spoke, he looked Kyle directly in the eyes and said, "You will go far, Kyle. Your heart and mind are open to the Spirit of God. You keep it that way and God will do great things through you. Thank you for coming to rescue me. Now I'd best get back to work."

As Kyle slid out of the booth, he chuckled a bit and said, "Rescue. I hardly think so."

AS BUSY AS HE WAS PREPARING FOR THE MEETING ON Saturday evening, Jonathon still took time on Friday to visit all the construction jobs currently in progress. The men would need encouragement and assurance that the business would carry on even with the loss of Terry. Questions regarding the future operations of Proctor-McCann, Jonathon deferred to a future date. "After the dust settles down," he told each man.

Upon his return to the construction office, Bea mentioned the two new contracts that were due to break ground in the next couple of weeks. "I just don't know, Bea. It's hard to even give it much thought with all that's going on. Remind me again on Monday. Perhaps you and I can take a bit of time to look at our options."

Blanche called and asked Jonathon to bring a short eulogy to the memorial service being planned for the following week. Terry and Blanche's own pastor would be preaching the service. "I'm honored," he told the grieving widow.

The loss of Terry gave Jonathon and Janet the opportunity for a meaningful family discussion on death, dying and the need to be prepared for eternity. The kids, seeming to understand the sadness enveloping their parents, had been quieter than normal during the meal. Their spaghetti-sauce laden plates were stacked on the counter. Jonathon had scooped a bowl of ice cream for each of them. The kids had smothered their ice cream with chocolate syrup, cleaning up their bowls in record time.

It was common at this point in their meal routine for the kids to scatter in three directions but with all that had happened there seemed to be almost a melancholy spreading itself over the little family. Janet took the initiative to open the conversation. Looking around the table, she said, "I'm sure we don't have to explain to you how big a thing it is to lose Terry. It's a huge matter in the business but it's much bigger to Terry's family. They will need our love and support to get through this sad time. We are all comforted a little bit to know that Terry loved Jesus and that he really wasn't afraid to die. Still, we know he wanted to live. He had a family to raise and a business he had worked hard for. But God had other plans.

"We pray for a long, healthy and happy life for each of you and for the families you will have in the future," Janet said, "but we never know. God may have plans that don't match with our wishes."

Grady, the eldest son, very quietly said, "Pete was hit by a truck while he was riding his bike. He was only twelve. I didn't know him really well but still... It pretty much shook up our school."

Jonathon, not wishing the time to become morbid, said, "As sad as that is, Grady - and I well remember the incident - and as sad as Terry's death is, there is no doubt that Terry was totally depending on Jesus to care for him and his family. I hope Pete was too. God chose to care for Terry by taking him Home where he will never again have heart problems. Even in our sadness we have that to be thankful for."

After a short silent pause, Janet said, "Each of us has given our hearts to Jesus as well. Now it's important that we keep that commitment for our lifetimes. Your father and I will always support you in prayer to that end."

"Grandpa and Grandma pray for us, too," offered ten-year-old Babs.

Somehow that happy thought brought light laughter to the gathering. Jonathon reached over and ruffled her hair just a bit. "Of course they do, Punkin. Of course they do."

SATURDAY MORNING, THE DAY OF THE BIG MEETING, THE church sanctuary was eerily quiet. After a restless night wrestling with a jumble of thoughts and with little sleep, Jonathon rose early, showered and dressed, and made his way to the church. He knew of no work that needed doing. He just wanted to be there. His parents were to pick up Janet and the kids later in the afternoon. They would drive into town together. The plan was to have an early dinner downtown before the meeting.

He made his way through the office area and up the few stairs to the sanctuary. As usual, he stood for a short while studying the colored patterns as the morning sunshine gloried its way through the stained-glass windows. 'I'm not at all sure why I'm so struck by these windows, Lord. But struck I am and have been since my youth. Thank you for showing me a bit of Your majesty every time the sun falls on that beautiful artwork.'

The pastor walked over to the grand piano and lifted the key cover. Hanna had left the music for the three hymns that had been chosen for the meeting on the top of the instrument. Although she would be playing the organ for the meeting, she had been practicing on the piano, experimenting with rhythm and tempo.

Jonathon placed the sheets before him on the piano. He started to play, slowly and softly at first. Finally, closing his eyes and playing from memory, he sang, joining the wonderful words of praise and worship to the magnificent melody penned years before by the gifted composers. As he played and sang, he picked up both the tempo and the volume. He played for one-half hour and then closed the key cover.

Feeling his nerves becoming jittery thinking about what this day might bring, the pastor climbed the stairs to the main platform, making his way to the grand old wooden pulpit. He had never preached from this dais. But he frequently imagined the day when the sanctuary would have enough worshipers in attendance to justify its use.

Jonathon was usually more comfortable before God when he knelt in prayer. However, without thinking about it, he folded his hands on the top of the pulpit, leaned slightly against the carved oak, and closed his eyes. He said nothing for a long time as his mind pictured the evening meeting. It was the heartfelt desire for Jonathon and so many others that God would allow His Holy Spirit to enter the sanctuary that evening, visiting upon the gathered believers repentance, forgiveness, acceptance of each other, and true oneness in Christ.

An hour later, he was still in prayer, reciting many of the names he remembered from the lists prepared by the research team. While he had no knowledge of individual or personal actions, he didn't really think it mattered. The overall issue, the one that needed to be dealt with decisively, was the matter of disagreement within the Christian body. The disagreements - powered by ego and pride and gossip, and now hidden by the passage of time - had been allowed to separate the family of God. A few dominant people had been outspoken and others started choosing sides. No one Jonathon had talked with could remember any major issue from those days and, from the perspective of lapsed time, it all looked petty. Still, the results were a broken and scattered church family and a dying downtown church.

Interestingly enough, the few times where clear sin was involved, the church leadership had handled the matter with dispatch and there was little disruption within the body.

Jonathon found himself weeping as he symbolically held his hand on the list of names. 'This is becoming a habit,' he said to himself as he wiped his eyes with the back of his hand.

He concluded his prayer time with, 'God, we are asking you to deal decisively with our pride, our spiritual arrogance, our lack of love, our refusal to give ourselves totally to Your will. And if you could deal with the gossip habit at the same time, what a blessing that would be. Heal us Father, we pray, and build within us a sense of true family, true togetherness. Do this for Your own sake and glory, Lord, and for our betterment.'

As the pastor was strolling through the sanctuary, silently praying again as he touched each pew he passed and imagining who might be sitting there in just a few hours, his cell phone rang. He answered to hear, "Mort Jenner here, Pastor. I had originally intended to drive up, leaving early this morning, but decided to fly at the last minute. We're loading now. I arrive at your airport at 11:30 this morning. Do you suppose you could find someone who can save me a taxi fare by picking me up? It would be much appreciated."

"I'll be there myself. I look forward to meeting you."

It was a long drive to the airport. Jonathon left early enough to stop for coffee along the way and was standing at the arrivals door when Pastor Jenner stepped through that portal. The two men shook hands in a warm greeting. "I have only this carry-on bag so we can get underway as soon as you wish."

After a couple of ice-breaking comments between the two pastors, each giving the other permission to use first names, Mort Jenner said, "I never take in food before preaching but I could use a bite of something now, if your schedule allows for that time."

Jonathon simply nodded in agreement and headed to a well-known family restaurant. Seated comfortably in the homey cafe, the two men were soon discussing the day and what lay before them.

"You have assigned a major undertaking to yourself, Jonathon."

"I didn't really assign it to myself. I'm sure you know Orvis Tanner, he of the silver tongue and the determination of the most outgoing mountain climber."

Mort Jenner chuckled and said, "Oh yes, I know Orvis alright. In fact, we've talked several times since I agreed to be here tonight."

Jonathon thought, 'I'd love to have heard those conversations'. Instead he said, "I sat as a young boy under his teaching. We've remained in occasional contact ever since. He saw the need at Downtown Fellowship and invited me for lunch. And here I am. I have no regrets as far as taking on the ministry goes."

Jonathon hesitated for a moment. Finally, he continued, "I'm not a trained or experienced pastor. I took a two-year leave from my business to answer the Lord's call to Downtown Fellowship. Hopefully, by the end of the two years the church will find a qualified man to take over and I can return to the business. But my business partner passed away a few days ago and I have no idea how to solve the issues surrounding that loss. I've tried to push it all into next week. What faces us today and tomorrow are enough for my mind to deal with."

Mort Jenner was a long time answering, all the while carefully scrutinizing Jonathon. Finally, he said, "We could talk about your business loss but I doubt I would have anything of value to add. Just know I am sorry to hear that news and I will add your burden to my prayer list. As to tonight, have you come to believe that your people are ready to be challenged and to respond gracefully?"

Jonathon chose his words carefully. "First, I know what you mean when you say 'my people' but I have only been on staff for a few months. I believe the leadership is on my side and many of the others, both with my ministry and with tonight's effort. There are some who are still weighing the evidence while they watch me very closely. All in all, it would be premature to call them 'my people'. Still, for the sake of discussion, we could consider them as such. I truly believe that the existing body of attendees at Downtown Fellowship wishes to come together and to have old rifts healed and put behind them. They are, overall, a doctrinally strong people. They understand the need to be disciplined by the scriptures. They're eager for change and will be welcoming of your ministry and message, just as long as it leads to healing and hope for the future.

"After researching the attendance files for years past, we've invited several hundred people to tonight's meeting. We've had responses from, perhaps, one hundred or so. Most of those will be here tonight. I'm sure there will be many others also. A good many local pastors have asked if they can intrude into what is essentially a private meeting. They've been told they'll be welcome and I wouldn't be too surprised to see a number of lay visitors from area churches as well. Hopefully all those who come will be eager for change and reconciliation.

"Some of the former pastors will be here. There's been a great deal of prayer focused on this weekend, not just at Downtown Fellowship but at many other congregations. We've been praying for great things to happen."

Mort Jenner stared out the window for a moment or two, finally turning to Jonathon. "Good, good. We'll move forward and leave the results to God."

Jonathon drove Pastor Jenner to a hotel two blocks from the church. "There's a room reserved in your name, and paid for. The meeting this evening is at 6:00 PM. Your time is your own until then. I'll be at the church all afternoon. Come over any time you wish."

The two new friends shook hands and went their separate ways.

The afternoon dragged on slowly for Jonathon until about 4:00 PM when a crew arrived to set up the coffee and snacks that would be served later. He joined the group and did what he could to help.

At 5:00 PM, the ushers arrived. They unlocked the big front doors and blocked them open. They put a sign outside the doors advising that the meeting was private, not open to the public. Noble Pearson had his usher team prepped and ready for when folks arrived. He had cautioned them to be friendly but not overwhelming in their greetings. Many of the visitors would be bringing suspicions and old hurts with them. They would need time to settle in and feel comfortable.

Watson, the custodian, made a thorough circuit of the sanctuary and then moved through the hallways to the gymnasium. When he was satisfied that the building was ready to receive visitors, he stationed himself at the side door to welcome folks who had found parking spaces on the back streets.

Mort Jenner arrived shortly after five. Noble escorted him to Jonathon's office. There the two pastors spent one-half hour in prayer. They were having a casual visit, watching the clock and waiting for the meeting time, when a frantic sound-tech burst into the room. "There you are. I've looked everywhere for you, Pastor Jenner. You said you wanted to be free to walk around the sanctuary so we have to get you wired up." He clipped on a lapel mic and passed the transmitter to the pastor. "Hook that onto your belt and click the switch when you're going to speak. Run the wire inside your jacket if you wish." The harried man left with no further instructions.

As 6:00 PM drew closer, Jonathon was a bundle of nerves. It seemed like everything in the church's future was resting on this meeting. He and the leadership had done what they could;

anything left undone at this stage would remain undone. Just as he was about to suggest they move to the sanctuary, Hanna placed her hands on the keys of the pipe organ and the first notes of 'Holy, Holy, Holy' reverberated through the building. Jonathon chuckled a bit and said, "I guess that's our cue." Holding his hand towards the door, he said, "Shall we?"

THE TWO PASTORS CLIMBED THE FEW STAIRS TO THE sanctuary level, stepped through the doorway and stopped in amazement. They looked at each other and then took a second look at the sanctuary. Mort Jenner smiled at the expression on Jonathon's face. The place was packed. The ushers were having difficulty finding places for the late arrivals. The balcony had been opened and it was quickly filling up. Still, there were many small groups of old friends gathered along the rear and sides of the sanctuary, shaking hands and hugging their greetings. The ushers were encouraging them to find seats but it was clear the old friends were reluctant to part. Jonathon was sure there would be other groups who were avoiding each other. But a great many people had been praying earnestly that that situation would be corrected before the evening was through.

Pastor Jenner put his hand on Jonathon's shoulder and urged him forward. Jonathon walked as a man in a trance. One of the ushers stepped forward and quietly said, "We've saved two spaces for you on the front row. Janet is already there. The former pastors and their wives are on the other front pew. Follow me."

Hanna had time to play two more hymns before the six

o'clock starting time rolled around. Promptly at 6:00, Tom Bradshaw climbed to the platform and walked to the big oak pulpit. He adjusted the mic to his comfort level, smiled, and said, "Wow. If ever there was a sight for sore eyes, this is it. Welcome to each of you. You are so very welcome. We're looking for a special touch from God this evening and we're going to get right to it.

"We thought it appropriate to begin by singing praises to our wonderful Savior. For those of you who don't have a hymn book available there are colored sheets of paper in the pew racks with the songs printed out. You will also see at the bottom of those sheets that there will be a fellowship time in the gymnasium following our service here. Please join us for a snack and a visit. Now, let's sing."

Hanna struck the chords for 'To God be the Glory' and Tom lifted the crowd to its feet with a gesture of his hands. The first few bars of the song were tentatively sung as the crowd felt its way into the mood of the gathering, perhaps still a bit suspicious of the motivation of the leaders. But it wasn't long before the singing was in earnest. By the second verse, the sounds of twelve-hundred people singing brought tears to Tom's eyes. By the third verse, he had ceased conducting while Hanna took the lead with her inspired playing. Tom simply stood there with both arms raised over his head and his eyes closed, singing in earnest worship of his Lord. Many in the congregation joined him with raised hands. Others stopped singing as their throats closed with emotion and tears poured down their cheeks. For most, it had been a long time since they had stood with these old friends, singing their long-loved favorite hymns. Having Hanna playing the organ after all the years of its silence added a dimension that was difficult to explain.

The loosing of suspicion and pent-up emotions became almost a living vibration in the old building. Clearly, many had come with open hearts and expectations of God's blessing. With souls prepared for a touch of grace and a willingness to allow God to work in their lives, it took only a few minutes for those open hearts to respond. Those who were contrary to that position didn't make their feelings known openly.

Hanna's playing was outstanding. She found a way to project the joy of her heart, along with the musical freedom that Jonathon had brought into the fellowship, through the big old organ. The singers rose to the occasion. She finished the first hymn and rolled right into 'I Stand Amazed in the Presence'.

As the voices raised the praises of the people to the Lord and the meaning of the words came home to so many, Jonathon could not have expressed his overwhelming emotion. He found himself repeating, 'Thank you, Lord. Thank you, Lord'. He realized he was saying it aloud when Janet looped her arm around his and sent a radiant smile his way.

The plan had been to sing just the two hymns. As if Tom was reading Jonathon's mind, when the hymn ended, he said, "We just have to sing one more. Hanna played 'Holy, Holy, Holy' as we were filing into the sanctuary this evening. Now I feel we must put our voices to that wonderful hymn that has been sung so many times in this old sanctuary. Hanna, please."

Most of the people sang from memory, many putting in the harmony parts that were so missed in the newer songs. As the last verse started, Hanna quit playing and raised her arms in worship. The acapella voices carried the song to the end. Hanna then closed off the singing with a drawn-out amen on the beautifully rebuilt organ.

It was as if the people would be content to sing the evening away, such was the vocal enthusiasm. But Tom stopped the music after the three hymns, indicated that folks should take their seats, and quietly stepped off the platform.

During the singing of the last song, Jonathon had leaned over to Pastor Jenner. "I was to do a welcome but we're ready to hear the Word."

Mort Jenner studied Jonathon for a moment and then nodded his assent. His walk and his approach to the pulpit demonstrating rare humility, the man of God opened his Bible and quietly but firmly said, "Hear the Word of the Lord."

Speaking slowly and carefully he read:

†Rather, speaking the truth in love, we are to grow up in every way into him who is the head, into Christ, from whom the whole body, joined and held together by every joint with which it is equipped, when each part is working properly, makes the body grow so that it builds itself up in love.

After a short pause and after looking over the sanctuary, he continued,

THAT THERE MAY BE no division in the body, but that the members may have the same care for one another. If one member suffers, all suffer together; if one member is honored, all rejoice together.

WHEN HE WAS FINISHED READING, he placed his Bible on the pulpit, stepped back two paces, and studied the audience. From corner to corner and from the front oak pew to the last row of the balcony, he seemed to look into each set of eyes as if he was able to read the very intent of each soul.

Finally, he spoke; even with the quietness of his voice, somehow the words found authority and sureness, "Those are not private verses. They are not from some esoteric book that you would only find in an exclusive seminary. They are not locked away in some private collection of ancient quotes. They are not mysterious and they are not at all difficult to understand.

"Those words come from Ephesians 4:15-16 and 1 Corinthians 12:25-26. They are not exclusive to my Bible. I would bet my life that you can find them in your own Bibles or the Bibles in the book rack in front of you.

"Those verses and many others bearing the same message are an important part of the Word of God as it applies to His blood-bought family, His church. Every word written in those verses applies to you and me."

He took another long pause, giving the audience time to mull over those thoughts. He continued, "We are here together this evening to face up to some wrongs from the past. Some wrongs that have caused division among God's people. We are not going to address every possible issue from every age in the past. We are still flesh-and-blood human beings and we seem to be able to find more than enough mischief to get ourselves into. No, we are not going to address those multiple issues at all.

"We intend to address only one issue; that of disagreements among the family of God. If the clock would stop moving, we could spend a lot of time talking about what the Scripture has to say about the tongue and the dangers of not controlling it. My, what a world of hurt has been caused by loose, unruly tongues. But the clock is not going to stop moving so we will restrict ourselves to solutions rather than causes.

"We are not here to confront anyone or to attempt to lay blame. We are not going to try to sort anything out. We can't bring back a word spoken and we're not going to try. Nor are we trying to unscramble an egg. We're simply going to face our own failures and name them for what they really are: sin. And those that are willing to humble themselves before God are going to confess those sins. And at the same time, those who have not already done so are going to forgive those who have sinned against them so that the full unity of the body might be restored.

"It's as if we were to draw a red line across our lives and say all that preceded this no longer exists. From this time forward, I am a new person and this is a new time.

"We are going to do those things in the quietness of our own minds and hearts without intruding on the thoughts or prayers of others. We need only confess to God. No human needs to hear your private confession.

"I caution you that what others are doing is none of my business, or yours. For most of us, our own sins provide ample burden for us to carry and deal with. In all of Scripture, God never once directed His people to sort out the actions of others. We are responsible only for ourselves. But make no mistake about it, we are responsible for our own actions and we will give an account before God for those actions.

"Where there has been division in the Body of Christ there is sin. We can make all the excuses in the world but, when we are done with excuses, we will still be faced with the truth that our actions were sin before a holy God."

He took a further long pause.

"Most of you don't know me. My name is Mort Jenner. I pastor a church in another city. I am not here this evening because of who I am. I bring no special giftedness with me. Rather, I am here because of who I am not. I am not of this particular fellowship or any other fellowship in this city. I am not of this city. I do not know any of you on a personal basis. I met Pastor McCann this morning for the first time. I am here primarily because I am neutral. I bring no prejudices with me. I know no details of your past nor do I wish to know.

"It's your future that we wish to talk about. A future that is brighter than a prairie sunrise if we will but surrender to the will and correction of God, our Savior."

Looking over his audience, the pastor could see that many were fully in tune with the message but not all. There was a sprinkling of crossed arms, scowls and solemn faces. He prayed a very brief, silent prayer for those stern saints.

Pastor Jenner went on to show from other Scriptures what God's view of sin is. He emphasized the very sinfulness of sin and showed how the Scriptures leave no room for excuses. He then went on to talk about the church, showing again - even though everyone there already knew - that the church is people. God's redeemed people. God's much-loved family.

He spoke, quoting from memory, *"Teacher, which is the greatest commandment in the Law?"*

Jesus replied, 'Love the Lord your God with all your heart and with all your soul and with all your mind. This is the first and greatest commandment. And the second is like it: 'Love your neighbor as yourself.' All the Law and the Prophets hang on these two commandments."

"You will easily locate those verses in your own Bible in Matthew 22: vs. 36 – 40."

Pastor Jenner stepped back up to the pulpit. He slid his Bible out of the way and leaned his elbows on the old oak book rest as if he were about to talk confidentially to a few friends. Smiling at the group, he said, "I might just as well fess up here and now that we have gone through this process in the church I pastor. We chuckle from time to time about the Baptist telegraph that seems to be able to transfer information faster than the Internet. So some of you will have heard about our experiences. I also admit to writing a small volume on this subject that has found only a few sales.

"I am in no position to guarantee that your experience will parallel our experience but I will tell you in glad joy that confessing our sins and mending fences between believers changed us. Those actions turned our church right around. Where we were a struggling, somewhat discouraged people, we were given new life and a new determination to do better; to walk upright before a Holy God. Another amazing thing happened; God started sending us new people. It was almost as if He thought, 'Alright, now I can trust them with the hearts of more of my people.' We saw over two hundred people come to saving faith in the next year.

"But before that happened we had to admit to ourselves that we had a problem. We were working hard and going through all the motions, but the filling and the power of God's Holy Spirit seemed to be somehow lacking. Knowing we had to do something, we pulled a few folks together and charged them with prayerfully examining the history of the church with a view to identifying factors that might have contributed to the cooling off of the Holy Spirit's blessing on our fellowship. It took them almost no time at all. It was as if the answer jumped right out at them. It seemed it was just a matter of days before they presented a report to the board. The entire report focused on the interactions between people that ended with hurt feelings and lost friendships. A broken Christian body.

"But that little committee went further in their boldness than just identifying our problem. They named the problem as sin. And that put a whole new perspective on the past.

"I'm saddened to admit how petty some of those matters, those sins that divided us, had been.

"I won't share confidences here but please know that there was considerable embarrassment within the quietness of people's hearts when folks started owning up to their own actions. I had many people telling me after the meetings how glad they were that they were able to keep those things private."

Walking slowly to the stairs, Pastor Jenner stepped down to the floor level. Coming within touching distance of the people in the first row, he said, "The God we worship is a God of love. We all know that. We preach that good news constantly. We also all know that God desires that His people be a people of love. We give lip service to that truth."

There was another long pause as the pastor stepped over to the center of the sanctuary. He slowly walked up the center aisle, making eye contact with each person as he passed and gently touching a few shoulders along the way.

"Everyone in this room understands full well that lip service just doesn't get the job done. If your spouse was fighting and bickering with you constantly and yet claiming to love you, you would have a legitimate question. It's no different in God's family. When we claim to love one another, there had better be some evidence to support that claim."

He continued talking as he walked towards the end of the aisle. When he stepped under the balcony, his wireless mic cut out. He smiled at the frantic look from the tech manning the sound booth. Seeming to be in no hurry, he took the silence as the opportunity to walk to the outside aisle. Back in range of the remote pick-up, he continued.

"People who love one another don't argue over little things. Further, people who love but still disagree over little things don't allow those little things to become big things. To continue in that vein, when their little issues have sinfully become big issues, people who love don't break fellowship. The Scripture gives clear instructions on how to resolve disputes among Christians."

Pastor Jenner continued slowly down the outside aisle, touching a shoulder here and there, still talking quietly but firmly. "When fellowship in the Christian family is broken, we can safely name that as sin. Sin before our Holy God."

Arriving at the front of the sanctuary again, the speaker stood and looked over the congregation. "Now, the big question for this evening is not has sin happened in this matter. That question was answered long ago. No, the question for this evening is, are we prepared to face up to that sin and make confession to God?"

He picked up his pace just a bit as he strolled towards the center aisle. When he arrived in front of Jonathon and Janet, he stopped. Placing one hand on each of their heads, he said, *"Blessed are the peacemakers for they shall be called sons of God."*

Strolling back up the center aisle but this time facing the other section of the pews, he quoted Scripture from memory, "In Psalm 23 David tells us that God restores our souls. Don't we all need soul restoration from time to time? And then, again in Psalms 51:12, we read, *'Restore to me the joy of Your salvation, and uphold me with a willing spirit.'* Don't you often find yourself longing for the joy of your salvation? I do. But I and so many others have discovered that if we are to approach God, hoping to have Him fill us with His joy, we must approach Him with clean hands and hearts."

Again, he stopped talking while he crossed under the balcony to the other side aisle, waiting to get back into range for the wireless pickup. Turning down the outside aisle, he said, *"Finally, brothers, rejoice. Aim for restoration, comfort one another, agree with one another, live in peace, and the God of love and peace will be with you.'* That's 2 Cor.13:11."

Mort Jenner turned to cross the front of the room again. Coming to the row of former pastors he stopped. He carefully looked at each man, trying to read their thoughts. Again he slowly looked over the gathered people. "Sitting before you are some of the men who have served as your pastors in previous years. Beside them are their wives. Now I'm going to let out a secret just in case some of you have misunderstood. In spite of their heart's true desire to faithfully serve you and our loving God, these men are not perfect. They have all made mistakes just as you and I have all made mistakes. And just as your actions sometimes hurt others, so it is with these men. But I can attest to the truth that when you are the one in charge - that is, giving leadership - your actions and the actions of others towards you become magnified, sometimes magnified beyond all reason. Thankfully, the joys are also magnified. But sometimes the hurts we do to one another hurt so bad that the joys are pushed into the background and are barely recognized. Collectively, you will have to own up to the reality that some of your actions fell directly on the shoulders of these servants as their actions fell on your shoulders."

Rev. Isaiah Heffner had hunched himself almost into a fetal position if such a thing could be done while sitting on an oak pew. His sobs were audible and heart-wrenching. His wife, tears streaming down her cheeks, was tenderly rubbing his shoulders and back. Orvis Tanner, sitting beside him, was gently cradling the back of his head in one of his big hands. Mort Jenner stopped before the grieving man and, for the first time since rising to the pulpit and with his hands lying on Pastor Heffner's head, he prayed, "Lord, God, You are the healer of the nations. You are the healer of the human heart and soul. Together we ask You in all humility to reach into this man's most inner-being and bring Your eternal light to his troubled soul. Do it for his and his wife's betterment, Lord, and for Your glory."

Pastor Jenner stepped back onto the platform and walked to the pulpit. He picked up his Bible and read: *"Love is patient and kind; love does not envy or boast; it is not arrogant or rude. It does not insist on its own way. It is not irritable or resentful; it does not rejoice at wrongdoing, but rejoices with the truth. Love bears all things, believes all things, hopes all things, endures all things. Love never ends."*

"That's the message of God to you this evening. You know the right thing to do. You knew before you came here. Now it only remains for you to do serious business with God. For you who claim Christ as your Savior, you have the privilege of laying your sins at the foot of His cross and walking away clean.

"For you who may feel that your confession has already been made to God, I commend you for that. But be careful. In I Corinthians, the apostle Paul says he knows of nothing standing against himself but then he reminds us that it is God alone who does the final judging.

"The organist is going to play softly while we do private business with our loving Savior. I beg of you, don't hold onto old hurts. Let them go. Don't hold onto old resentments. Let them go. Don't hold onto secret sins. Confess them, and let them go.

"Sitting, kneeling, standing; it doesn't matter. But don't waste this opportunity to get into full fellowship with our Lord and with each other."

Pastor Jenner then prayed God's empowerment over the actions of His people and the room went silent except for a few sobs, a few deep breaths, and some shuffling of feet.

JONATHON AND JANET, THEIR FINGERS FIRMLY ENTWINED, bowed their heads and prayed, asking God to search their hearts and to make plain to them any unseen sin. They then again asked earnestly for the Holy Spirit of God to take full charge of the meeting and to do His rescuing work among the saints.

They both stood and turned to the audience.

There was a continuous murmur of voices rising from the pews as many hundreds of men and women poured out their lives before God. A few were standing, many were kneeling. The big oak doors opened and a number of people left. Jonathon couldn't help but wonder about them.

As Jonathon was glancing over the crowd of worshipers, his eye fell on a face that was somehow familiar but no name came immediately to mind. The man was standing aside as if he somehow didn't belong. As Jonathon watched, the stranger took out a pocket-sized, coil-backed book and started jotting down notes. He stared over the sanctuary, seeming to pick out individual people, and then made more notes. He walked down the side aisle and repeated his actions. Jonathon watched this process until he finally made a connection. 'Buzz Grappler', Jonathon said to himself. 'I should have put it together sooner.

He looks exactly like the photo I found on the Internet, old leather jacket and all. Well, now, that's interesting.' Jonathon smiled, thinking of the next conversation with the radio talk-show host. The thought crossed the pastor's mind that he should explain to Buzz that the meeting was private and ask him to leave. A cooler second thought was, 'Let him stay and think what he will. Who knows, God may use this experience in unexpected ways'.

Janet was swept up into a small group of ladies who had gathered around a weeping woman. Janet knew none of them. "I'm so sorry, I'm so sorry," the penitent kept repeating. Her knees seemed to weaken and she staggered just a little bit. Janet took her by the arm and gently led her to the front pew where she took a seat. As a spontaneous action, the ladies laid hands on the weeping woman and an elderly lady that Janet had never seen before started to pray. 'Lord, You have heard Mable's words and You read her heart. We few gathered around her lay our hands on her in support and not in judgment for we each have enough sin of our own to worry about. Forgive her we pray Lord and confirm in her heart that she is fully forgiven. Comfort her as only you can and give new life to Mable and each of us gathered here. Accept our thanks, praise and adoration, we pray Lord.'

As friends of Mable's took seats on each side of her, Janet slipped away. She made her way towards the row of former pastors. Four pastors, along with Orvis Tanner, were on their knees praying with Rev. Isaiah Heffner. Mrs. Heffner was left alone on the oak pew. Janet walked to her and asked, "May I join you?"

The older lady picked up her Bible and hymn book and held them on her lap, making room for Janet. "Please, sit. You're Mrs. McCann, I believe."

Janet took a seat and answered, "Yes. I am." After a short pause, Janet turned sideways and looked Mrs. Heffner directly in the eyes. "I only know bits and pieces of the past, and have very little interest in the details. I am far more interested in the future. However, may I presume that you did not escape unscathed during your ministry here?"

Her answer was slow in coming. "On a personal basis, I escaped totally unscathed. No ill will was directed my way that I was ever aware of. No, whatever hurts I experienced were all secondhand. But don't ever underestimate the damage second-hand hurts can cause. It was extremely difficult to watch my husband suffer, knowing there was nothing I could do. In short, three couples - led by the women, I might as well admit - took it upon themselves to force Isaiah out of the church. They took such a strong dislike to him that they put great pressure on the denominational office to remove my husband's credentials from him. They weren't successful in that but they might as well have been. By the time we finally decided to leave, Isaiah was a broken man. He never preached or ministered again."

Janet said nothing for there was really nothing to say. Finally, Mrs. Heffner spoke again, "Do you know the strange part? Each of those couples left the church right after we moved away. You'd have thought they would be happy after we were gone. I have no idea what became of them. I doubt they are here this evening though."

Janet wasn't sure when she had started holding the other woman's hand. The two pastors' wives sat there in silence for a short time. She was pretty sure that what Mrs. Heffner had told her was a much-shortened version of the events. Janet finally asked the logical question, "Where were the leaders while that was taking place? Did no one come to your rescue?"

Mrs. Heffner lifted her eyes to Janet. "Friends and Christian brothers and sisters. It makes it all very difficult. Several deacons were close personal friends with a couple of the antago-nists. I'm sure everyone just hoped it would all settle down and go away. It didn't, of course. Isaiah had no real choice but to resign. In their favor I must say that, a short time after we left, the deacon board and each deacon personally sent a conciliatory letter to Isaiah apologizing and asking for his forgiveness. He was quick to forgive but the damage was already done. Isaiah has grappled ever since with the concept of the love of God. It was all he could do to get up in the morning and go to his simple job. Ministry was the furthest thing from his mind. And then the guilt set in. He had firmly believed God had called him and prepared him for the ministry. Now he was clerking in the city tax office just to pay the bills." She took on a despairing look and hunched her shoulders. "Now it's years too late."

Janet wrapped the woman's hand in both of hers. "I'm so sorry. Life can be cruel sometimes. We will continue to pray for healing for both of you. May I pray with you now?"

The two women prayed and when they looked back up, there was another woman standing a few feet away. Mrs. Heffner took a deep, shocked breath, her hands flying to her mouth. The other woman said, "I know, I know, Trudy. I didn't think I'd have the courage to face you."

Trudy Heffner couldn't hold back the tears. Through a choking sob she managed to blurt out, "Helga?"

Janet couldn't find a graceful way to rise and walk away so she continued sitting there.

Helga had taken a firm grip on herself. She knew if she didn't, she would never get through this time. "Trudy, I have wept many and many a bitter tear over my treatment of you good people. You were better pastors than I ever deserved. It took me years to get some control of my tongue and my bitterness. Those two sad failings cost me my marriage. I should have contacted you long ago but I just didn't get it done. I can't really explain that. I can't repair the damage I did either but I desperately need your forgiveness. I was wrong. My husband was wrong and the others were as well. What we did was of the enemy. There is no other way to explain it. Please forgive me."

Trudy Heffner still held her hands over her mouth, the tears coursing down her cheeks. "I never once thought we would see you. But, but, but, yes, of course. Forgiveness is not in doubt."

Trudy was getting a grip on herself. She turned her mind to the woman's actions that had hurt her husband so badly. "The one you need to say these things to is kneeling there on the floor."

"Of course, you are correct."

With that she placed a hand on the shoulders of two of the men praying with Pastor Heffner. Urging them to make room, she lowered herself into a kneeling position. She reached her hand out and touched Pastor Heffner's face. He opened his eyes and looked at her. There was no sign of recognition. Haltingly, she said, "Pastor, it's Helga."

The pastor's eyes focused and his mouth twitched a bit but no sound came.

"Please forgive me, Pastor. I treated you and Trudy abominably. I am the cause of so much heartache. You are a good man and a good pastor and I was wrong. So totally wrong. Pastor, I must know that you will forgive me sometime if not now."

Pastor Heffner had trouble speaking, "Yes, of course, yes. Think no more about it. I'm happy you came and I wish you well. You must speak with Trudy."

"I have done that pastor. Thank you."

She made a move to rise. Two of the pastors assisted her. As she stepped away, Orvis Tanner took a step with her. "That was not easy for either of you but both of you honored God in those actions. Thank you." Helga only nodded.

Janet moved on to stand beside Jonathon's parents. The three of them stood off to the side watching as the church prayed and wept. The kids had moved into the gymnasium to search out the snacks.

Jonathon made his way to the back of the sanctuary where he found Noble Pearson in earnest conversation with Mark and Greta Bannister. After the last phone conversation, the Bannisters were the last couple he expected to see at the meeting. And yet, as he watched the two men in sober conversation, he couldn't help but notice that Mark Bannister's lower lip was trembling and his eyes seemed to be misting. Perhaps he was softening. He could see by the body language that Noble was trying to reason with the other couple. But it was not to be. Finally, Mark Bannister shook his head, straightened his back, took his wife by the arm, and with a stern face headed for the door. Noble stood with his arm gesturing, accompanying his final words, but the door opened and closed and the Bannisters were gone. Noble dropped his arm and his head and stood silently with his eyes closed.

A few people sought out Jonathon. He chatted with some and prayed with others. He took a position at the back where he could see the doors without seeming to have that purpose. He smiled to himself when Buzz Grappler strolled past, making a point of not seeing him. He was sorely tempted to speak to the radio man but finally resisted that temptation. Buzz pushed the big oak door open and was gone without having said a word to anyone. Jonathon thought, 'I'd love to get a glimpse at the notebook of his'.

Pastor Jenner approached. "It's a good day, my brother. I'd have to say that the prayers of the leadership are being answered. I'm not sure how you will follow up on all of this but I suspect there's a plan in place."

Jonathon said, "It's a difficult question when our desire is to rebuild our church body without emptying other church bodies. We have decided to do nothing specific to entice former members back into our fold. Of course, they're welcome, but our real goal is towards the unsaved. I'm sure you took note of all the residential buildings just outside our door. When Orvis Tanner first approached me, his hook was those buildings and the many folks that call them home. My memory might not recall the exact words but when he spoke of the church he said something like, "We must bring the old girl back to life. She has a ministry to lost and hurting souls that is not yet completed. And God has placed those hurting souls right at her doorstep. We have but to set the banquet table and invite the folks in for a feast of soul-nourishment that will change their lives for eternity."

He smiled at his new friend. "What are you going to do with a man like that, and with a vision like that?"

Mort Jenner laughed out loud, shaking his head. "I've know that old arm-twister for decades. You can either run for the hills or you can try to catch his dream. There is no middle ground. I think you've done just right. What I think you may consider doing though is getting more news out to as many churches as possible and ask for continuing prayer support. Then keep on doing what you're doing."

The two men stood in companionable silence for a few minutes watching the interactions of the people. Many folks had moved to the gymnasium. Perhaps two hundred or so had left the building. Most of them either nodded at Jonathon or said a quick thank you. Jonathon figured they would rather get home than have coffee and more visiting.

A COUPLE OF USHERS WERE LEFT TO LOCK UP AFTER everyone had left the sanctuary. Jonathon and Janet decided to follow the people as they moved into the fellowship time. They could hear the rumble of many voices far down the hallways leading to the gymnasium. There was the odd loud voice exclaiming greetings to old friends. A bit of laughter broke out over the general clatter of dishes and visiting voices.

Kyle stood at the doorway of the gymnasium. Jonathon saw him and stepped over to ask, "Were you at the meeting, Kyle? I didn't see you in the crowd."

"I was there. Natalie opted out. The baby wasn't feeling quite right so we canceled the sitter. Sometimes a baby just needs its mom."

Janet said, "I'll see you fellas later," and moved off into the crowd. Jonathon turned back to Kyle. "Any thoughts?"

"You broke the mold tonight, my friend. Nothing can ever be the same. I understand Pastor Jenner has overseen something similar at his own church but, for this city and for this time, you have broken the mold. The leadership and the people honored God this evening. God will honor the church in return. The enemy won't be happy but that's good."

Again, Jonathon was impressed with the thoughts and maturity of the young man. "Well, I pray you're correct on that. We'll see in the next few weeks just what the results will be."

Kyle gestured towards the food and drink preparation area. "Busy place and a lot of work. It's too bad so many had to miss the meeting to get all this prep work done."

Jonathon replied, "Our people didn't miss anything of the meeting. These are all volunteers from a couple of other churches. We asked for their help and the response was overwhelming. We're very grateful."

The visiting and the greeting of old friends went on for so long that the leaders were tempted to turn off some lights as an indication that the day was about over. Jonathon and Pastor Jenner were in demand non-stop. The former pastors hardly had time to sip a cup of coffee such was the crush of people wishing to shake their hands and visit. Even Pastor Heffner had a steady stream of greeters although it was obvious that he was wilting with exhaustion as the evening wore on.

As the evening progressed, Jonathon thought he recognized a slight lightening of spirit in the much-hurt former pastor. Orvis Tanner, taking a protective stance, was seldom very far from Pastor Heffner.

Jonathon and the leadership were aware that not every past problem would be solved during the long, tiring evening. But a good many old issues were dealt with and they hoped the seeds planted would bear good fruit in the future.

As they were about to leave the meeting, Millard Crown and his wife sought out Jonathon. The two men shook hands warmly. Jonathon said, "Mr. and Mrs. Crown, I saw you in the meeting but didn't have the opportunity to greet you personally. How good of you to come."

"Not at all, Jonathon," answered Mr. Crown. "It was our privilege to be here. You have probably figured out that we've been running from the church for some years. I hope we have not been running from the Lord at the same time. There is much to think about for us in the coming days. We should have lunch soon and include the ladies this time."

"I would treasure that opportunity," responded Jonathon. "You pick a time and we'll do our best to accommodate."

Millard Crown's face took on a serious expression. "This isn't the time to talk business so I won't, except to say how very sorry we were to hear about Terry. He was a well-respected man in the construction industry. I know you'll miss him greatly as will his family, of course. But the industry will miss him also. He was one of the good ones."

"I appreciate you saying that. I'll pass those words on to his wife and family."

Jonathon and Janet arrived home at nearly midnight after visiting and praying and laughing with more people than they ever imagined possible. The kids had driven home with Jonathon's parents. Janet checked their bedrooms.

"They're all asleep," she whispered to Jonathon. "And that's what I'm going to be doing in the next three minutes. I don't know when I've ever been so tired."

Jonathon gave her a hug. "Thanks for all the help this evening. I don't think you ever stopped. You get yourself to bed. I'm too wound up to sleep. I'm just going to sit on the couch and recap the evening a bit. I'll be up shortly."

Janet found him on the couch in the morning. He was still in his suit. His shoes lay on the floor beside the couch. He was stretched out with one arm over his eyes as if to block the morning sun. She shook him awake. Startled, Jonathon pushed to a sitting position and looked around as if to ask where he was. Janet smiled and said, "You remember that old joke about the man who didn't want to get up and go to church but he had to because he was the pastor?"

MORT JENNER MET THE CHALLENGE OF THE SUNDAY morning service with wit, charm, and urgency. He took the packed house from gales of laughter as he recounted examples of the foibles of human nature to serious contemplation as he talked of God's original plan for humanity. He talked of the shortness of time, whether that time was compared to the age of the believer or the prophetic signs of the times. He emphasized that the recognition of that shortness of time should fill us with an urgency to get right with God and with each other. He lamented the many wasted years and the tragedy of lost fellowship when the saints don't get along.

"And the worst of it is that we bring dishonor to our loving Lord." He took a long look over the congregation. "It is yet to be seen what God will do through people who are surrendered to His will and who are determined to make themselves useful and available in His work."

The service ended on a high note with Tom Bradshaw leading singing while Hanna played the grand piano. They had started the service with the pipe organ but closed it with the newly-formed small orchestra that included Jonathon on the keyboard, William Preston on his guitar, Madison Palmer playing his clarinet, and - for the first time - Madison's very nervous wife Tilly keeping the beat on drums.

Again, people wanted to visit after service. Tilly was thronged with people gushing over her skills on the drums. The ushers didn't get the last door closed and locked until early afternoon. No one was rushed to leave. Knowing that most of the people attending would be back at their own churches the next weekend, the leadership had no desire to bring the informal portion of the meeting to a close.

Jonathon had kept his eye on the four people at the back of the sanctuary. They seemed to be waiting to see him. Finally, he broke free and headed their way. He smiled at Carl whom he hardly recognized; he no longer looked like the despairing, young homeless man who had walked into the church many weeks before. The two men shared a warm handshake although Carl still exhibited an expressionless stare. He couldn't hold eye contact for more than a second or two. Jonathon was tempted to give the man a hug but restrained himself, fearing a negative reaction.

"Carl, how good to see you. I'm so glad you're here." He turned to the other man and shook his hand also. "Col. Garneau, welcome to you as well. And who might these ladies be?"

Phillip Garneau answered, "Pastor McCann, I'd like you to meet Carl's wife, Allison, and my wife Lena. And please call me Phillip. The colonel thing is well retired."

Jonathon shook each woman's hand in turn and said, "This has been a great morning for me but meeting you folks like this is the icing on the cake. And, please, call me Jonathon. My wife is around here somewhere but I don't see her right now."

Phillip Garneau said, "We won't take up your time. I really just wanted you to meet the ladies. Plus, we're going for lunch and thought there might be an outside chance that you could join us."

Jonathon's face showed his disappointment. "We would love to have a meal and a visit with you but it can't happen today.

We'll arrange it for soon though. Today I have to drive our guest speaker to the airport. That's going to be our only opportunity to debrief." With a smile, he said, "Can I borrow that military term or do I need to send in a requisition in triplicate and wait for permission?"

Phillip laughed out loud. "Permission granted, Jonathon. And I'll call you to arrange a further lunch meeting."

"That would be great, Phillip." With that, he turned to Carl and Allison. "Carl, you're looking great. And Allison, I hope we will be seeing more of you and get to know you."

The pastor desperately wanted to ask how things were progressing with Carl and the military and the PTSD but caution kept the question unasked. Allison spoke into the awkward silence. The attractive young lady appeared strained, but gracious. "It's good to meet you too, Pastor. I'm very much out of place here this morning but Carl wanted to come so I agreed. It seems I knew nothing at all about what was going on. Until Phillip came into Carl's life, I knew nothing about PTSD. Of course, I had heard the term but it didn't connect in my mind. So, obviously, I had no understanding of what was happening to my husband or to our lives. I don't rightly know how I could have been so blind.

"And I certainly know nothing about church. I've never been inside a church before except a couple of times when I was very young. My grandfather took me with him when we were visiting one summer when I was maybe five or six."

Allison was looking at Jonathon so intently he felt she was waiting for him to respond.

Hesitantly, he said, "None of us really knew anything about PTSD either, Allison. It was when one of our young interns was visiting privately with Carl that the light came on for him. And then Sal, our secretary, thought of Phillip. You know the rest."

Allison nodded. "Well, we're thankful for all of that. But just so you understand a bit more, the two children and I are living with my grandparents. We're a long way from the 'happy family' thing yet. Phillip found a room for Carl close by. Phillip has been very generous with his time. Lena, too. But there's a long way to go for Carl and for me, too. I hate the military with every ounce of my being. I hate what it did to my loving husband and to our children and me. I'm afraid hate and distrust are my primary emotions these past few months. Except for the children, of course. And my grandparents. Together they shine a bit of hope on my life."

Although Allison hesitated, she seemed to want to say more. The others all gave her time to gather her thoughts. Finally, she said, "I find it very strange to hear the joyful singing here this morning when I have no joy at all in my own heart. And to listen to a message of hope from a man who is talking about a God I don't even believe in. It's like my head is full of static with all the conflicting thoughts and emotions."

This time, she seemed to be finished talking. Jonathon quietly said, "Believe it or not, Allison, I understand those kinds of conflicting emotions although my questions lie in other directions."

Turning, he said, "Phillip, we must make that social date real soon. Can I leave that with you?"

Phillip confirmed his agreement just as Janet and Mort Jenner joined the group. The hall was nearly empty and the ushers were picking up the few things that had been dropped or left behind.

Janet, walking up behind Jonathon, put her hand on his shoulder. With a smile, she said, "My dear, if we don't leave right away, Pastor Jenner will miss his plane. Can I tear you away after you introduce Mort and I to these folks?"

The interruption afforded the perfect ending to the conversation. Jonathon made the introductions. With Janet's input, the lunch date was changed to a dinner date. "I work full-time and couldn't get away for lunch. But I'd love to join you all for dinner."

It was all agreed and the two parties went their separate ways.

Jonathon and Janet drove Mort Jenner to the airport. The debriefing didn't really amount to much so the drive was mostly silent. There was either little to say or so much that none of them knew where to start.

Jonathon lifted the other pastor's small suitcase to the sidewalk. As the two men shook hands, Jonathon said, "I'm afraid words fail me my friend. You'll have to settle for a simple thank you for now. But you know there's much more meant by it. Thank you and God bless."

"It's always my pleasure to speak the Word, brother. I promise that you and the work will be high on my prayer list. Please keep in touch."

Janet gave him a hug and a smile and they parted.

Again, it was silent in the car as they drove towards home. It was as if the two people were awash in fatigue.

The many trials yet facing the church, the decisions yet to be made, the death of Terry, the future of the business; all these were rambling through Jonathon's mind. Still, he drove in silence.

Finally, Janet said, "I saw you head-to-head with Orvis Tanner. What has he to say today?"

"He said much. But summed up, what he meant was the Lord might save the old girl yet."

Jonathon, with a wistful look on his face and a lopsided grin, took a quick glance at his wife. "And he might. He just very well might."

A LOOK AT MAC'S WAY

RAISED IN POVERTY IN MISSOURI, MAC IS DETERMINED TO FIND A better life for himself and the girl who is still a vague vision in his mind. Work on the Santa Fe Trail, and on a Mississippi River boat give him a start, but the years of Civil War leave him broke and footloose in South Texas. There he discovers more cattle running loose than he ever knew existed. Teaming up with two ex-Federal soldiers, he sets out to gather his wealth, one head at a time.

While gathering and driving Longhorns, Mac and his friends meet an interesting collection of characters, including Margo. Mac and Margo and the crew learn about Longhorns, and life, from hard experience before they eventually head west. Outlaws and harrowing river crossings are just two of the challenges they face along their way.

AVAILABLE NOW FROM REG QUIST AND CKN CHRISTIAN PUBLISHING

ABOUT THE AUTHOR

REG QUIST'S pioneer heritage includes sod shacks, prairie fires, home births, and children's graves under the prairie sod, all working together in the lives of people creating their own space in a new land.

Out of that early generation came farmers, ranchers, business men and women, builders, military graves in faraway lands, Sunday Schools that grew to become churches, plus story tellers, musicians, and much more.

Hard work and self-reliance were the hallmark of those previous great generations, attributes that were absorbed by the following generation.

Quist's career choice took him into the construction world. From heavy industrial work, to construction camps in the remote northern bush, the author emulated his grandfathers, who were both builders, as well as pioneer farmers and ranchers.

Quist's heart was never far from the land. The family photo albums testify to how often he found himself sitting on a horse, both as a child and into later life, when he and his wife owned their own small farm, complete with kids and horses.

Respect for the pioneers, working alongside skilled, tough workmen, and learning from them, marrying his high school sweetheart and welcoming children into the world, purchasing land for the family to grow on, and riding horses with the kids, all melded together to influence Quist's life and writing. Over, and under, and wrapped around his life is Quist's Christian heritage. This too, shows itself in his writing.

Quist's writing career was late in pushing itself forward, remaining a hobby while family and career took precedence. Only in early retirement, was there time for more serious writing.

Quist's writing interests lie in many genres including children's work, short lifestyle stories, cowboy poetry, western novels, plus Christian articles and novels.

Woven through every story is the thought that, even though he was not there himself in that pioneer time, he knew some that were. They are remembered with great respect.